# STEAL *the* DRAGON

## PATRICIA BRIGGS

ACE BOOKS, NEW YORK

THE BERKLEY PUBLISHING GROUP
Published by the Penguin Group
Penguin Group (USA) Inc.
375 Hudson Street, New York, New York 10014, USA

Penguin Group (Canada), 90 Eglinton Avenue East, Suite 700, Toronto, Ontario M4P 2Y3, Canada
(a division of Pearson Penguin Canada Inc.)
Penguin Books Ltd., 80 Strand, London WC2R 0RL, England
Penguin Group Ireland, 25 St. Stephen's Green, Dublin 2, Ireland (a division of Penguin Books Ltd.)
Penguin Group (Australia), 250 Camberwell Road, Camberwell, Victoria 3124, Australia
(a division of Pearson Australia Group Pty. Ltd.)
Penguin Books India Pvt. Ltd., 11 Community Centre, Panchsheel Park, New Delhi—110 017, India
Penguin Group (NZ), 67 Apollo Drive, Rosedale, North Shore 0632, New Zealand
(a division of Pearson New Zealand Ltd.)
Penguin Books (South Africa) (Pty.) Ltd., 24 Sturdee Avenue, Rosebank, Johannesburg 2196,
South Africa

Penguin Books Ltd., Registered Offices: 80 Strand, London WC2R 0RL, England

This is a work of fiction. Names, characters, places, and incidents either are the product of the author's imagination or are used fictitiously, and any resemblance to actual persons, living or dead, business establishments, events, or locales is entirely coincidental. The publisher does not have any control over and does not assume any responsibility for author or third-party websites or their content.

STEAL THE DRAGON

An Ace Book / published by arrangement with Hurog, Inc.

PRINTING HISTORY
Ace mass-market edition / November 1995

Copyright © 1995 by Hurog, Inc.
Cover art by Gene Mollica.
Cover design by Annette Fiore DeFex.

ISBN: 978-0-441-00273-3

ACE
Ace Books are published by The Berkley Publishing Group,
a division of Penguin Group (USA) Inc.,
375 Hudson Street, New York, New York 10014.
ACE and the "A" design are trademarks belonging to Penguin Group (USA) Inc.

PRINTED IN THE UNITED STATES OF AMERICA

16   15   14   13   12   11   10   9

With appreciation to the following people:

Michael, husband and (self-appointed) editor in chief.

Laura Anne Gilman, editor (professional), who asked for a *major* change—thank you, thank you, thank you!

Mark and Kristi Dimke, for their friendship, patience, and printer—in that order.

Bob and Jolene Briggs, for their love and support...and for putting up with my horse.

*This story would never have been told without them.*

# STEAL *the*
# DRAGON

# ONE

She stretched her arms wide, hands open, holding the pose for an instant before bursting into furious motion. Each placement of foot and angle of wrist was choreographed, thoughtless, perfect. Her body flowed from one movement to the next, graceful, seductive, submissive in turn.

The beat of the drum was a familiar companion: its rhythm consumed her. Her heart kept time with the deep bass tones; the lighter beats of the small instruments were the quick movements of her hands and feet. The dance slowed, and her movements became languid, erotic.

She reveled in the euphoria that accompanied her dance, the pain of straining her muscles for the perfection of her art only adding to the exhilaration. Sweat blinded her, but she didn't need her eyes to see—the floor was sanded and flat and she knew where the music would take her.

The beating drum accelerated again, built to a crescendo, then abruptly it ended. The brief silence pounded at her ears as she collapsed facedown on the floor, fighting for breath. The clapping of a single pair of hands replaced the fading memory of the drumbeat.

"Very nice, Little One," said the Master's hated voice.

RIALLA SAT BOLT UPRIGHT IN HER BED. HER BEDCLOTHES were saturated with the sweat of a dance long past. Automatically her hands went to her neck, but the slave collar had been gone for a long time, and the scar on her face still replaced the hated tattoo.

Trembling, she bowed her head and ran her hands through her hair. She threw the covers back and got out of bed, though the dawn was hours away.

IN THE MAZE THAT WAS THE OLDEST BUILDING IN SIANIM, Ren, better known as the Spymaster of Sianim, settled himself in his chair and looked out the open window at nothing in particular.

The chair had been made for his predecessor, who had been a much larger man. Ren's slight, balding and graying person looked a little absurd sitting in it, like a child playing at grown-up, but no one in the mercenary city-state of Sianim would have called the Spymaster absurd: he held more power in his hands than many kings.

Turning his chair away from the window, he propped his feet on top of his crowded desk, ignoring the resultant thump as a pile of papers fell to the floor. He rested his chin on his hands and waited patiently for the arrival of one he had summoned.

At last there was a soft tap on the door.

"Who?" he barked.

"Rialla of the horses, as ordered, sir." The voice that answered him was soft and shy. Ren's mouth tightened in annoyance. If she was as meek as she sounded, he might as well send her back home.

Ah, well—it wasn't the woman's fault that his informant had misled him. Even if she wouldn't serve his purpose, he could use whatever information she could provide.

Schooling his voice into a more welcoming tone, Ren called out, "Come in, Rialla of the horses. I've been expecting you."

The door opened with a sigh and squeaked a protest when the horse trainer shut it behind her. She was taller than he was, but so slender that she appeared fragile. Her red hair was pulled tightly back in a short braid that barely reached her shoulders. He got a quick glimpse of emerald-green eyes before she dropped her gaze to the floor.

She waited silently for him to speak, her arms held loosely at her side and her face expressionless. He noted absently that she would have been beautiful if it weren't for the scar that covered most of one cheek.

He greeted her in kind tones. "Trainer."

The green eyes briefly met his. "Spymaster." There was a slightly mocking note that someone who was less observant would not have caught. Ren was so fascinated by the inconsistency between the demure mien and that subtle disrespect that he let the silence stretch uncomfortably long.

When he didn't reply, she shrugged and turned her back to him to examine a nearby bookcase. The illusion of fragility was shattered with her movement. She moved with the grace of a trained athlete, and sinewy muscle corded her arm as she reached to pull a book out of its shelf.

The Spymaster watched her with a tingle of pleasure. This just might work. Experimentally he held his silence. She turned a page and seemed to become engrossed in the book.

Finally, Ren laughed softly, pushed his chair away from his desk and said with a smile, "Aren't you the least bit curious about why I called you here today?"

She replaced the book and turned back to him. "Yes." This time her voice was as meek as it had been at first.

"I spoke with Laeth, I believe he is a friend of yours, who informed me that you speak native-quality Darranian.'' He turned the statement into a question with an inquiring look.

She shrugged indifferently, but her left hand came up to finger the scar that marred her face and her gaze shifted back to the floor.

Darranian slaves were all elaborately tattooed on the left side of their faces for identification. In Darran, slaves could not be freed; the tattoo marked them for life.

Ren decided to change tactics. "Do you know who Lord Karsten is?" he asked bluntly.

"You mean other than Laeth's brother?" she asked, but continued in indifferent tones without waiting for a reply, "He is one of the Darranian lords pushing to ally the kingdoms of Reth and Darran. I understand that the proposed alliance involves the marriage of King Myr of Reth to the king of Darran's older sister."

Ren nodded his head in agreement. "Lord Karsten is the most influential member of the regency council. With his support the new alliance is a virtual certainty."

The light mockery eased back into Rialla's voice as she spoke for the first time without being prompted. "Sianim wants to prevent the alliance? Maybe an accident for Lord Karsten?"

"Of course not!" replied Ren in a shocked tone, widening his eyes improbably to show his innocent dismay at her suggestion. "My dear young woman, Sianim *never* interferes with the politics of any government. We are mercenaries, and merely hire ourselves out to the highest bidder."

He knew when the corner of her mouth turned up in a reluctant smile that she caught the satire with which he spouted their official dogma.

"So," she said, "tell me. Why is it that Sianim doesn't intend to hinder the alliance? The feud between Darran and Reth has diverted a steady stream of gold into our coffers over the past century or so."

Ren looked at her with the same pleasure with which a schoolmaster might regard a pupil asking a thoughtful question. He rubbed his hands together with satisfaction and began to talk.

"The Great Swamp has long been a barrier between the East and our West." He gestured to her impatiently. "Sit down, girl. This will take a while. Now then . . . the only trading currently done with the East is through the Ynstrahn sailing fleets that dare thread the shoals and reefs in the Southern Sea.

"Once there was a road through the Swamp. The magic of the Archmage held back the Uriah, wights and other nasty swamp dwellers. But as the seasons changed so did the Archmage, and other matters became more important. The road was overrun and swallowed by the Swamp."

He paused and sipped water from a glass that sat on the corner of his desk.

"I have heard that there was once such a road," commented Rialla, "but what does that have to do with Darran? The Swamp is nowhere near there." She had cleared off a place for herself on a worn tapestry chair, and sat on the very edge of the seat, though her hands were open and relaxed in her lap.

"Have patience and I'll tell you. Now," Ren fell back into a storyteller's voice, "when I came into office, I noticed that we lacked information on anything on the other side of the Swamp. An oversight, of course, which I have corrected.

"For some time I have been monitoring the expansion of an Eastern empire called Cybelle. A decade ago it was a small country and very poor, then its ruler died leaving no legitimate heirs. When the ensuing fight for power was over, the man on the throne was a religious fanatic who called himself 'the Voice of Altis.' I have tried for ten years to find information on his background, but he seems to have appeared from nowhere.

"This man professes to believe, as do his followers, that the ancient god Altis appeared to him and revealed that it was Cybelle's destiny to rule from the Eastern Sea to the Western, from the far Northlands to the Southern Sea. In the relatively short time that 'the Voice' has been in power, he has managed to take over most of the countries between the Eastern Sea and the Great Swamp.''

Ren glanced at Rialla to make sure that she was still listening before he continued. "Long ago, after the Wizard Wars, the people of the East rose up in anger against anyone who practiced magic, much as we in the West did. In the East, however, there was no refuge. Without countries like Reth or Southwood to shelter them, the mages disappeared into stories told to frighten children.

"The religious revival is spreading even faster than the rule of Cybelle; the last few countries to join the empire have not even put up a fight. I am informed that the Voice of Altis performs miracles. Altis has given him the power to make light where there was only darkness, to make a building burst into flame with a wave of his hand. He can kill with a word. Sound familiar?''

Rialla looked up at his question. "A trained mage has set himself on the throne of Cybelle." Her voice had lost all traces of timidity or mockery and was merely thoughtful.

Ren nodded and smiled with the growing conviction that she would turn out to be an adequate tool for his purposes. "He plans to continue through the Great Swamp by clearing the ancient path through it. My sources say he can do it.''

The Spymaster's smile dropped from his face and he sat forward intently on his chair. "Sianim, for all its military fame, is just a small city-state; alone against Cybelle we'd stand no chance at all. The Western nations need to face the Easterners as allies if we are to have a chance to stand against them. I have been working to patch old hostilities for the last few years. The most difficult conflict to smooth has been the persistent fighting between Darran and Reth.''

"So what do you need me for? There are other people

who speak Darranian," said Rialla quietly, obviously not stricken with any sudden urge to be of assistance.

"Lord Karsten is the driving force behind the Rethian alliance. There are people who don't want Darran to be tied to Reth; the last outbreak of war is still fresh in the minds of those on both sides who lost kin. The antagonism is in no way helped by Reth's traditional link with magic; as you well know, Darranians view sorcery as something twisted and defiled. Karsten's influence is such that he is capable of overriding the objections of his peers in the council—if he survives to do so."

Ren cleared his throat before continuing, watching the woman narrowly to gauge her response. "Last week an assassin's arrow killed the horse that Lord Karsten was riding. Karsten was lucky, but I want to know who was behind the attempt so I can have them stopped.

"Lord Karsten is sponsoring a week-long celebration of his birthday at his country estate, Westhold. Because of the attempt on his brother's life, Laeth has agreed to attend the celebration to see what he can find out."

Ren leaned forward intently. "But I need something more. My dear mother used to say, 'An unguarded tongue will bring down the stoutest walls.' Around Lord Karsten's brother every word will be weighed, measured and carefully doled out.

"What I need is someone no one notices—a part of the furnishings of the keep. Unfortunately the furniture can't tell me what it hears—but a slave can." Ren watched Rialla closely for her reaction, but not so much as a twitch gave away her thoughts.

She stared silently at the floor for a moment, then lifted her eyes to meet his. "I would do a great deal for Sianim; but not this. Paint a tattoo on someone else and I will teach them to be a slave, but I will leave Sianim before I go back to Darran." Her voice was cold and hard, the voice of someone with the courage to cut the skin from the side of her face and cauterize the resultant wound.

Ren sat back undismayed: he still had a carrot to dangle

in front of her. "To make the alliance more acceptable to Rethians, Lord Karsten has proposed several changes in Darranian law. Marriages with outsiders will be legal; this is required, of course, to permit the marriage between the princess and King Myr. Trade taxes will be lowered or possibly eliminated." He paused and softened his tone to attract her attention. "The third change is the elimination of slavery within Darranian borders. This was deemed necessary because Reth views slavery as an abomination used only by the most barbaric of people."

He couldn't see if she had gone for his bait yet, so he rambled on to give her time to think. "In a strange way, the last change is the one that the Darranians find most objectionable. Slavery is not integral to their economy; slaves are merely luxuries that only a few can afford, but they are integral to Darranian culture. Most of the nobles of the council own several, and are loath to part with them. You, I am sure, have a greater understanding of this than I."

The former slave bowed her head for a moment and then looked back at the Spymaster. Ren had been waiting for a reaction and he finally got one. "Do you know what you ask of me, Spymaster?"

"Yes," he answered. "With your help, it may be possible to eliminate slavery in Darran. Laeth told me that you would be interested in such a mission."

The tension left her body as suddenly as it had come. In a weary voice Rialla said, "Tell me the essentials and give me some time to think it over."

Ren leaned back in his chair, satisfied that his strategy was working. "Most of the powerful nobles in the kingdom will be at Westhold with their entourages. Obviously, they aren't likely to discuss their newest attempt on Lord Karsten's life. I want you to determine who supports the alliance, who resists it and—most importantly—why. Don't worry if your information seems trivial; I assure you that the most innocent facts are capable of illumination when combined with intuition and intelligence."

Rialla rubbed the scar on her cheek, as if to relieve some persistent ache, and asked, "You are sure that Laeth agreed to this? For all that he has chosen to live in Sianim, he is Darranian. For him to agree to spy, or escort a spy to his brother's home is the worst sort of betrayal."

Ren nodded, "He agreed because of the threat to Lord Karsten."

"When would we leave?" Rialla asked neutrally.

"Five days."

She nodded and got to her feet. "I'll give you my answer tomorrow morning." The door shut quietly behind her as she left.

FEELING NUMB, RIALLA MADE HER WAY THROUGH THE busy streets to the stables where the war horses, a source of income for Sianim second only to its mercenary services and training, were kept. She slipped under the ancient stone archway that lead into the stables, and allowed the familiar smells and the sounds of the horses moving quietly in their stalls to calm her. It was lunchtime and she had the place to herself.

Ignoring the friendly muzzles that were extended to her over the stall doors, she found a bench that wasn't too cluttered with bits of mending or grooming tools and huddled on it, drawing her legs up beside her and leaning wearily against the wall.

The gray stone was cool against her cheek. She closed her eyes and contemplated what she'd been asked to do. Even the idea of going back to Darran was enough to raise a cold sweat. Darran had stolen her family, her heritage and a part of herself. In return she'd been given the scars she carried, inside and out.

Perhaps it would have been different for someone born into a more restrictive society, where women had little control over their destiny. Rialla had been born to one of the wandering Trader clans that traveled throughout the South; primarily through Southwood, Ynstrah and the little principalities that made up the Anthran Alliance. In the

Trader clans, women were people of power. The women controlled a clan's finances and determined where the clan would travel the next season.

Rialla had learned how to train horses from her father. The horses he trained were widely sought after, for he'd had a fine touch with animals. Often he staged exhibitions in which he would take some vicious beast and turn it into a usable animal. He brought prestige to their small clan, so that Rialla's clan rarely had to worry about money, and were free to travel where many other clans were forbidden.

Rialla had been born an empath, able to perceive the feelings and sometimes thoughts of the people and animals around her. It was a rare talent, but not unheard of among her people, and it was valued highly by a people who lived on the whims of others. Almost as soon as her ability was recognized, her father had her working with the horses, using her empathy to enhance his training and teaching her to control her gift at the same time.

Because of her value to the Traders, the women's council and her father contracted an advantageous marriage for her with a wealthier clan. It had been at the betrothal festival that the outlander had come among them.

There was nothing unusual about his presence because everyone was welcome at festivals, even nonclansmen. The only reason that Rialla noticed him at all was that he was one of the few people she'd met that she couldn't use her empathy to read. She had felt his eyes on her as she danced for her betrothed. She couldn't recall the boy's face now, though she remembered thinking him handsome.

After the festival the Trade clans split up to travel again, with the understanding that they would meet at the same place in exactly one year for the marriage, as was customary.

Two nights later the slavers attacked Rialla's clan, killing the men and the old people—and taking the younger women and children as slaves. It was the outlander who led the slavers. She could still feel the first touch of his hand on her face. It was the first time she'd been able to read him with her talent: her first taste of a Darranian slave trainer.

Rialla shuddered heavily against the cold granite of the stable wall, ignoring the tears that ran down her cheek. If she hoped to function as a Darranian slave, she would have to cope with the past.

After all these years the slave trainer's face wasn't clear in her memory—a slave didn't look at a person's face often—but his voice haunted her nightmares.

On the third day of her captivity, Rialla, huddled in the small group of women and children that were the remnants of her clan, watched as a rider entered the camp. He was greeted warmly by her captor. She couldn't understand the language they spoke to each other, but the rider's name was familiar: Geoffrey ae'Magi, the Archmage.

Rialla heard later that the Archmage was killed shortly after this visit; she had no sorrow for his death.

One by one the children and women had been taken to the tent where the slave trainer stayed; only Rialla and two others were spared. She didn't *see* what the ae'Magi and the slaver did to the remaining captives, but she heard their screams and felt their anguish in empathic detail. The horror of her knowledge ravaged her mind until it closed down to protect itself, leaving her with only a shadow of her former gift. What little empathic ability remained after the Archmage's visit was so erratic it was all but useless.

For a slave, though, it was probably just as well.

FOR TWO YEARS RIALLA WAS TRAINED AS A DANCER, and she was rewarded with the tattoo at the end. Dancers were popular in Darran and she was good, very good. She was treated well and allowed more freedom than most slaves, who were intended for brothels or worse, but she was still a slave.

For five years she danced as her master bade. Finally,

there came a day when the opportunity to escape presented itself and she ran.

She killed a man when she escaped. Even the slight remnants of her empathy had been enough to make her cry out with the pain of his death. Nevertheless, with shaking hands she searched the dead man and took his knife and what little money he had. She stole a horse from the stables and fled.

She escaped over the border to Reth, where she used the knife, heated in her camp fire until it glowed, to rid herself of the hateful tattoo.

At the next town she traded her horse for an unbroken gelding and a handful of coins. Eventually, she made her way to Sianim, where her skill with horses earned her a home. The mercenary city-state had offered her refuge, but now it offered even more.

She had been given the opportunity to take something from the slavers, if she had the courage to do it.

Safe in the stables of Sianim, Rialla let her hand rub the scar on her cheek. If she agreed to return to Reth, she would have to let them tattoo her again, over the scar. The scar would brand her as an escaped slave; as such she would be watched even closer than most. Something could go wrong and she would be forced to remain a slave; a second escape would be virtually impossible.

The whisper of sound alerted her that she was no longer alone. She wiped her cheeks, but knew it would be obvious she'd been crying. Drawing a deep breath she turned to see who had joined her.

The man who stood in the dim light of the stable was of average height. He had dark hair, darker eyes and skin that was tanned by many days out in the sun. His build was slight, but he moved with the trained grace of a warrior.

Rialla raised her chin in an unconscious gesture of defiance that was not lost on the man watching her. "Laeth."

He nodded a greeting and leaned against a stall partition across from the bench where she sat, leaving the width of the aisle between them.

It was virtually unheard of for a Darranian lord to train at Sianim. Though the schools of warcraft at Sianim were famous, Darranians kept to themselves. When Laeth had come to Sianim for training two years ago, Rialla had avoided him until they were assigned the same instructor for hand-to-hand combat.

The instructor didn't speak Darranian, and Laeth only knew what little of the Common tongue he'd picked up since he came. Darranians, being an insular people, had little use for learning languages other than their own.

She watched him struggle for several days before moving next to him and interpreting. It had been a combination of the way that he'd persisted, laughing at himself and trying again, and her refusal to let herself be manipulated into hating all Darranians for what a few had done that made her help him.

He had turned to her, ignoring the betraying scar on her cheek, and thanked her in a quiet voice. The friendship that followed was a surprise to Rialla and, she thought, to him also. She taught him Common in the evenings and he told her a little about himself.

The younger son of a powerful Darranian lord, he'd amused himself scandalizing his family for most of his life. Then he'd discovered a shy little maid called Marri, whom he'd met at a party given at a local estate. Her family hadn't approved of her marriage to a black sheep, even of so exalted a family, so he'd settled down and persuaded his father to give him a small manor that he worked for a year, preparing it for his intended bride. When he received an invitation to his older brother Karsten's wedding, he decided that the time had come to inform his family that he'd found the girl he intended to marry.

When he returned home for the wedding, his family welcomed him and his brother introduced Laeth to his new bride—Marri. Karsten had decided to marry a local girl.

Laeth had smiled politely at his love's unhappy face, understanding that a Darranian girl of good family could not refuse a marriage arranged by her parents. He'd even congratulated his brother. The next morning Laeth told his parents that he'd received notice of trouble at his little farm that required his immediate presence. He would have to leave before the wedding.

His family never knew why he returned to his outrageous behavior, his journey to Sianim only the most flagrant act of disgrace. Since his brother's wedding, the only time he'd returned to Darran was to attend his father's funeral.

ONE OF THE HORSES BUTTED LAETH IMPATIENTLY AND he scratched its nose. "Are you going to come, Rialla?" he asked softly.

"Yes," she replied. "The Spymaster allowed me little choice."

"I wasn't sure that I should give Ren your name, but knowing him I thought that he probably knew that you spoke Darranian anyway."

She nodded and curved her lips without humor. "I know several people who can speak Darranian better than I can, and I imagine that he does too. What he needed was someone who could be a Darranian slave. I'm sure that the devious weasel knew everything about me long before he talked to you."

"You're probably right," replied Laeth, visibly relaxing at Rialla's easy tone. "He does have that reputation." He looked around at the quiet stable and then said, "I'll treat you to lunch."

Rialla shot him a skeptical look, "At the Lost Pig?"

"They don't pay mercenaries like they used to. Besides, it's not that bad," said Laeth. "Yesterday they only had two people get sick."

Rialla obediently groaned at the old joke and held her

hands up in mock surrender. "All right, all right. But this time I'm not going to rescue you from the waitress."

Laeth widened his eyes. "Haven't you heard? Letty's decided to try for the tall blonds."

"Who's she after now?" inquired Rialla, getting up off her bench and following Laeth out the door.

"Afgar, you know, the lieutenant in the Fifty-seventh."

Rialla thought a moment and came to a halt. "Not the big Southwood man, the one who used to be a tanner?" she asked incredulously.

Laeth nodded, tugging her forward with a light grip on her upper arm. "The one that hides in the corners when a woman comes by. He's so dedicated to avoiding women that I don't think the two women in his troop have ever seen him. Last night I thought that he was going to choke to death when Letty rubbed up against him. If I weren't so busy being thankful that it's not me anymore, I'd feel sorry for him."

"Ha," snorted Rialla. "You enjoyed it almost as much as she did. You didn't run away so fast she didn't catch you a time or two."

He sent her a meek look and said, "What can I say? I'm only a man. Besides, she's got great"—Rialla raised her eyebrows warningly—"teeth."

Rialla laughed and shook her head as they came within sight of the Lost Pig.

The bottom half of the bar was built from old stone blocks set one on top of the other; the top half was made of wooden planks of various sizes and ages. Rialla had heard that fifty or so years ago the Seventy-first troop of a hundred and six men, drunk on victory and alcohol, lifted the wooden half off the stone and set it in the middle of the road on a lark.

They replaced the top after extracting a bargain from the owner. The wooden half was now held down securely by thick rusted chains on all four corners of the building, and the Seventy-first still got their drinks for half what other people were charged.

Being the source of food and drink nearest to the stables and to the training ground that serviced a number of troops, the Lost Pig was usually busy. Rialla and Laeth were waved at by several acquaintances as they squeezed through in an attempt to find an empty table.

As Rialla slipped too near one of the tables, she felt a hand pat her on the hip. Without stopping to see who it was, she grabbed his wrist and caught the leg of his chair with her foot, sweeping the wooden legs forward as she pushed him back. The man and his chair made a satisfying commotion that rose over the general din that filled the tavern.

More than a little drunk, the man started up with a growl, but Laeth caught his shoulder under the pretext of helping him up. Helpfully, Laeth dusted off the man's coat and generally distracted him, until the drunk's initial hostility subsided into bewilderment at all the attention.

When it became obvious that the stranger was no longer a threat, Laeth said congenially, "She doesn't like it when men touch her without an invitation. You're lucky that she's in a good mood or she'd have just cut your hand off—that's what she did to the last man who tried it."

A friend of Laeth's leaned over from a nearby table and said sadly, "Poor Jard was never the same."

"Remember what she did to Lothar?" added another man, shaking his head.

"Took us three days to find all the pieces so that we could bury him," commented one of Laeth's fellow lieutenants, a stocky, bald man with a friendly face. He leaned closer and said softly, "But then, Lothar tried to kiss her."

Rialla was still laughing when they found a small table that was unoccupied. "Did you see his face? That poor man. If I'd known what you were going to start, I'd have let him get away with it."

Laeth grinned cheerfully. "It'll teach him to keep his

hands to himself. Speaking of which, did you know that one of the greenies in my troop fancies you?"

"You mean the young Rethian who hides behind the fence and scares the horses I'm working with? The one who offers to take me to dinner every night and has been leaving flowers outside my door? About your height, sandy hair and brown eyes? No, I hadn't noticed him at all," she replied.

Laeth laughed at her disgruntled expression. "I'm sorry, I didn't know that he was getting to be such a problem. I'll do something about it this afternoon."

"No," gasped Rialla in pseudo-horror. "Not the strange disease that causes impotence with merely a touch. There are still several members of your troop who cross the street when they see me."

"No," agreed Laeth, "I used that one the last time. I'll have to think up something new. It's your fault, you know; you could gain a few pounds, or do something about your hair."

"I'll dye it gray tomorrow, or better yet, I'll shave it off," offered Rialla with a thread of seriousness in her voice. The scar didn't seem to harm her looks as far as the mercenaries were concerned. She'd far rather have been plain, so she wouldn't attract so much unwanted attention.

Before Laeth could reply, the barmaid, Letty, appeared from the crowded room. How she knew who had ordered and who hadn't in the mass of people in the bar was a mystery that Rialla had never solved.

"What's good, love?" asked Laeth.

"Afgar," sighed Letty, expanding her sizable chest.

"To eat," clarified Rialla, then added hastily, "for us. Food."

"Oh." Letty's full lips briefly formed a half-pout for Laeth's benefit, but she said, cheerfully enough, "The bread is fresh and Cook just pulled a honey ham out of the oven. The beef is a bit overdone and dry."

"Sandwiches then. Two ham?" Laeth looked at Rialla and she nodded. "And two mugs of watered ale as well."

When they were alone, Laeth said, "Ren called me in this morning. He wanted me to see if I could talk you into going."

Rialla shook her head. "He did a good enough job of that himself."

"Why are *you* going?" asked Laeth semi-humorously. "I'm going to protect Karsten, but all that I have to face is seeing Marri as his wife, and a possible death sentence if anyone discovers that I am spying for Sianim. You have to go back to being a slave."

"Ren says that Karsten intends to outlaw slavery in Darran," replied Rialla. "He heavily implied that my presence would help, though come to think of it, I'm not really certain how."

"You're risking a lot for slaves that you don't even know, Ria," commented Laeth.

She tossed him a wry smile and fingered her scar. "I'm not doing it for them. Most of them are probably quite comfortable being slaves; in Darran it's not much worse than being a wife most places, maybe even better. I'm doing it for revenge. The slavers who live in Darran stole something from me, and I'll never get it back. It's my turn to help steal something from them—from him."

Letty brought their food and accepted several coppers and a kiss from Laeth before she left.

"Aren't you worried?" asked Laeth quietly, fingering a slice of fresh bread.

Rialla swallowed her bite and sipped from her glass before answering. "About being a slave?" She shrugged. "I wouldn't go with anyone else, if that's what you mean. I know that I can trust you not to leave me there. For someone not used to it, owning a slave is a heady thing; and I am a dancer—more valuable than most. I could bring you more gold than most people will see in a life-time." As she spoke, Rialla could feel her face stiffen into its accustomed mask. Her voice went flat, losing the animation that characterized it.

"I won't do that," said Laeth softly.

She smiled at him, dropping her slave face. "I know that. Why do you think I wouldn't go with anyone else? You've owned both slaves and estates, and chose to relinquish them. Even if I didn't know you, I'd rather go with you than a Southwoodsman who has never thought about owning a slave in his life."

Laeth bowed his head in acknowledgment of the compliment of her trust. They ate without speaking for a time, the silence comfortable between two old friends.

"When you talked to Ren, did he say what he was going to do about the tattoo?" Rialla touched her cheek lightly.

Laeth nodded and finished swallowing before saying, "He has a magician who can disguise your scar and replace the old tattoo with an illusion. Ren wants the tattoo to be the same as it was originally, in case someone recognizes you. Couldn't it be used to trace your previous owner?"

She shook her head. "I've been gone for seven years; after five, a slave doesn't need to be returned to the original owner. Though I understand that it's considered proper to do so anyway. As long as Lord Karsten doesn't make a habit of inviting slave trainers to his birthday parties, I won't have to worry."

"No," he answered, relaxing, "a nobleman would no more invite a slave trainer to a formal occasion than he would invite a swineherd."

"So I thought," agreed Rialla.

"Ren also wanted me to tell you that if something happens, he'll get you out of Darran by fair means or foul; so you don't have to worry about getting stuck as a slave," added Laeth.

Rialla shot him a nasty grin. "After all these years of training in Sianim, I don't think that I'll have to worry much about someone keeping me as a slave." Saying it made her feel as if it were true, and some of her tension loosened.

Laeth returned her smile with one as wicked, as he posed the favorite question of one of the combat instructors, "How many ways are there to kill a person with a knife?"

"It doesn't matter, it only takes one to do the job," returned Rialla.

They finished their sandwiches in mutual good humor and left just as a new wave of mercenaries pushed through the door. Laeth stopped her just outside with a hand on her shoulder.

"I've got some things that I have to get taken care of before we go. Ren told you that we leave in five days?"

She nodded.

"I'll see to the supplies for the trip, if you can make sure the horses are ready."

"I'll find a couple," answered Rialla. "I'd better find a dancing costume or two as well."

"If you can't find one, you might try Midge's girls. I suspect that one or two of them might have something that would work."

"I thought you said you didn't pay for it," she teased.

Laeth grinned. "I didn't."

Rialla flashed him a smile. "I just bet you didn't. I'd best go see who I can find to take over my horses while I'm gone."

"Go to it," he said. "I'll talk to you tomorrow."

THE EARLY MORNING SUN BARELY LIT THE SKY WHEN Rialla saddled a horse and took it out. She wasn't the only one working horses, but the other riders were using different arenas.

Her stallion's feet thump-thumped rhythmically on the packed sawdust of the enclosure, but his attention was on the mare that was being ridden over the jumps on the other side of the fence. He gathered himself in preparation to dump his rider as he had thrown so many others—and got tapped warningly with the short crop his current rider used.

Reminded that he had to obey this upstart who sat on his back, he continued on the path she chose, with his ears plastered as flat as he could get them. Rialla laughed at the plodding canter that replaced the stallion's normally buoyant gait.

He really didn't need the workout. She'd found trainers for all the horses she'd been working on. Rialla had taken the stallion out for a last ride rather than wait around for Laeth and worry about things that she couldn't change— like the gold, black and green tattoo that graced her scarless face once more.

Taking advantage of her momentary distraction, the red-bay stallion threw himself sideways in a move that had tossed more than one of his former owners. Rialla sat it easily. With a disgusted snort the big horse flipped his tail and settled back into his canter, insulted that she hadn't even noticed what he'd done.

Rialla put the horse through his paces until he quit playing and she was tired enough that she forgot about what she had agreed to do to herself. The memory lapse didn't last long. When she took the horse in to give it a much-deserved rubdown, Laeth was waiting for her in the stables.

"Are you ready to go?"

Rialla nodded and handed the horse off to one of the grooms. "Let me change my clothes and grab my stuff and I'll meet you back here."

In her room she slid over her head the simple gray slave's tunic that she would wear for the journey. She looked at herself in the flat piece of polished copper that she kept on her wall as a mirror, and she couldn't see the person that she'd worked so hard to become.

She saw instead a white-faced slave with a slave's tattoo on her left cheek; an unfamiliar plain gold earring dangled from her left ear, projecting the illusion—though she could feel the scar with her fingertips. A faint whip scar marred the deep tan on one of her arms: the slave trainer had beaten the servant responsible for marring so valuable a property. Swallowing, she raised a hand in a grave salute. "Good luck, slave."

She picked up the small bag that held her dancing costumes, stepped out of the room and closed the door.

# TWO

Like a plague of locusts, the ravenous tide of war had fed upon the small Darranian village of Tallonwood, leaving destruction in its wake. Several once-fertile fields lay barren, the salt from the mines that were the region's greatest source of wealth turning the rich earth into sterile soil that drifted in the winds, a silent testament to the centuries-old feud between Darran and its neighbor Reth.

As the closest village to Westhold (so named because it lay to the west of the salt mine), one of the principal holds in east Darran and Lord Karsten's family estate, Tallonwood had been overrun on numerous occasions. The once-prosperous village was poor now, even by Darranian standards. After Darran had lost its most recent war with Reth, even the richest of the villagers had trouble putting food on the table. Last winter, which was mild by all accounts, two of the elders and three infants had died from lack of food.

Lord Karsten, who ruled Westhold and several surrounding villages, including Tallonwood, was one of the few Darranian lords who had not revoked the ancient laws that made it punishable by death for peasants to hunt in the forests. He worried that the animal populations might be decimated as they were elsewhere in Darran; peasants were less valuable to his recreational pursuits. His overseer saw that his wishes were followed.

One of the few buildings in decent repair in the village belonged to Tris, a healer of rare talent. His reputation had spread beyond the village, and the nobles from the hold sought him out for the healing of their gout, indigestion and boils, for which services he charged them royally.

Without Tris, Tallonwood would have suffered far worse than it had this past winter. Using the gold and jewels he charged the nobles, he bought grain from the hold's stores and cattle to slaughter.

When the hold's reserves were too lean to allow the hold castellan to sell any more, Tris risked the wrath of Lord Karsten and hunted the forest animals himself. He maintained that years of sneaking around catching herbs unaware lent him stealth that served him well against both the forest animals and the two-legged beasts that the overseer hired to keep the peasants from helping themselves.

In the front room of his two-room cottage, Tris wiped down the counter that kept his customers' children out of the various pots and jars that he stored on the shelves. The rag that he used was not as stained as his powerful hands, which were presently an interesting shade of lilac. He'd found a patch of avendar on his walk this morning, an herb useful for making burn salve and dark purple dye.

To his immense surprise, the healer had found contentment in the little village. He was even fond of the neat little cottage that stood on the other side of a small hill from Tallonwood. The location allowed him the illusion of privacy and the convenience of being upstream from the village waste.

Tris looked up, rubbing his beard, as the door chimes announced the entrance of the headman's mother, Trenna.

Old and crippled as she was, she carried herself with an air that made even the lord treat her with respect. If she'd been born in another place, she would have been trained as a mage. In Darran she was the village wisewoman, advising the elders on such things as which goat would give more milk and which should be butchered, or when the first snow would fall.

If Tris knew that her accuracy was due to something other than observation and experience, then she knew that there was more than herbs in Tris's recipes. The magic that they used was different, but it was magic just the same.

It had been Trenna, searching for an elusive plant, who found Tris where his own people had left him: bound and waiting to die. Her magic sometimes expressed itself in the rare ability to see into future possibilities. That gift allowed her to discern his nature and see hope for her village. She offered him a bargain.

If she freed him, he would serve her village for a year as healer. The conditions would be difficult. Her people were hostile to magic, so he would have to hide his nature—at the same time helping them to the best of his abilities.

Tris had been waiting patiently for death. Even if he could have escaped, his rash act of kindness would have exiled him from his people forever. Dying did not seem so harsh—until he'd been offered a chance at a life. He agreed to her terms.

The bonds that held him were designed to resist magic, but not the simple steel knife that Trenna used when hunting plants for her potions. After she healed his wounds with her crude herb lore (Tris had difficulty working the healing magic on himself), Trenna told the village elders that he was a relative, a healer who had grown tired of his travels and had come to stay there.

The elders accepted her story. Trenna was getting too frail to carry out the duties of healer, and there was no one skilled enough to take her place. They accepted Tris

gratefully; in their desperation they were willing to overlook his foreignness.

Tris wasn't sure Trenna understood what he was, but
she knew that he would cause no harm to the people of
Tallonwood, and that was all that mattered to her. His
year was long over, but he remained in Tallonwood. He
had nowhere else to go.

"Lady." He greeted Trenna in his peculiarly accented
Darranian. He took the swollen hand that she extended
over the counter and kissed it gently in true courtier style.

"Sir," she smiled up at his gentle flirting; he was taller
than any man in the village, and she was a small woman.
"How are you this fine spring morning?"

"Remarkably well. I just got back from wandering in
the woods and I discovered another patch of thyme; the
old one was getting picked over. Can I mix a powder for
your rheumatism? I found some tharmud root last week
that should make this batch more potent."

"If you please," she answered. When he turned to his
work, she flexed her hands carefully. They were notice-
ably less swollen than they had been before he'd touched
her.

Tris was usually careful that the villagers saw nothing
that they wouldn't expect to see. For Trenna, though, he
could be as theatrical as he liked—she enjoyed it almost
as much as he did. So his ingredients were mixed with
flashes of light and strange noises, and the end result had
an eerie green glow when he put it into the leather bag.

"Now," he said handing it to her, "remember to take
this in the morning and at night. You can take one other
dose during the day if you must. If you need it more often
than that, come back and see me. Steep the powder in hot
water for as long as you can hold your breath before you
drink it."

She smiled at him, giving him a glimpse of the beauty
she had once been, and started to take the bag. When their
hands touched, she let the pouch fall unheeded to the floor

and clutched him with a strength that belied her swollen joints. He felt the pulse of her magic under his fingers.

Her body hummed with tension as she spoke in a strained voice. "Two come from Sianim . . . a man and . . . the dancer. You must aid them stem the tide of the cat god . . . Beware the creatures *he* calls from the Swamp." She swallowed and gasped for air, like a fish on land. Sweat glistened on her forehead and she shifted her urgent grip to his forearms, her tongue twisting around a few phrases of his native language.

The magic released her, and she shook as if she'd been out in a blizzard. Before she could fall, Tris rolled across the counter, heedless of the small planter he sent tumbling to the floor, caught her and gently lowered her to the padded oak bench that spanned the far wall. He sat next to her and kept his arm around her until she quit shaking.

"Sorry," she said when she could.

He shook his head in exasperation. "Lady, I thank you for your advice—you have nothing to apologize for. Do you remember what you said?"

She shook her head. "No. Sometimes I can remember—or at least see pictures, but . . . I saw a flash of red and green gems . . . No, I think they were eyes." She shook her head again. "That's all. I hope that it will do you some good."

Again he took her hand and kissed it, "That, Lady, is best left for time to tell us. May I see you home?"

She smiled and stood up slowly, but steadily enough. "No. For some reason I am feeling much better now. If you could retrieve my powder for me, I will pay you and go."

Tris gave her the powder but shook his head when she offered him a bit of copper. "No. Send your grandson over if you'd like. There's a corner of the roof that needs rethatching before the next rain. He's grown to be quite a craftsman under Edgar's tutelage." She and he both knew that he'd pay her grandson when he came, but after a moment she nodded and left.

Tris watched her leave, and with a soft voice he repeated the phrases that Trenna had spoken in his own language: the first lines of the bonding ceremony. He had been alone for so long . . . Was there to be an end to it?

After a moment of stillness, he found a broom and began to remove the remnants of the planter from his floor, gently picking up the plants and setting them aside for repotting.

THE DINING HALL IN LORD KARSTEN'S HOLD WAS LARGE enough to seat six hundred people, but only one of the six ancient, rough-hewn tables was being used. This room showed the improvements that Lord Karsten was making throughout Westhold.

Several of the heavy timbers that supported the ceiling were obviously new. A circular fireplace complete with chimney dominated the center of the room, replacing the more common fire pit. The crude openings high in the outer wall, necessary with a fire pit, had been filled with colored glass visible from outside the keep.

Rialla stood quietly behind and just slightly to the left of where Laeth sat, her eyes focused on the floor, like any proper slave. She'd had surprisingly little difficulty adjusting to being a slave again; it helped tremendously to know that she was just pretending. Once she took on the role, her nervousness faded until she almost enjoyed herself. She was comfortable enough that she was beginning to suffer from the most chronic condition of slavery—boredom.

Darran was as she remembered it, though she'd never dealt with nobility in their own element before. The place she'd spent most of her time as a slave was a private club where all the young, rich men went to sow their wild oats, away from proper company.

Rialla snorted softly to herself. Darranians did even that in a very civilized manner; they had a customary procedure for breaking society's edicts.

She and Laeth had been at Westhold for over a week,

and Rialla had learned nothing about the political situation here that Ren probably didn't already know. If it weren't for the entertainment she found in watching the properly trained Darranian nobles deal with Laeth, she would have been *really* bored.

He was well connected, and no one wanted to offend him; on the other hand, his complete disregard for propriety could not be ignored. Noblemen just did not become mercenaries; and if they did, they should have the good sense to be defensive about it.

Laeth was more than happy to scandalize his listeners with stories that Rialla suspected he made up on the spot. Second Division General Tyborn *had* carried the head of a fallen enemy to Sianim, but he didn't hang it over his dining table—at least Rialla had never seen it there.

Laeth took care to insure Rialla knew who was who— greeting people by their full names. She in turn made a great effort to remember people's identities and what faction they were with. The latter had been simple up to this point, since most of the people who were invited for the full week of festivities were staunch supporters of Lord Karsten.

At the thought of Laeth's brother, Rialla suppressed a smile. Who would have conceived a wildman like Laeth could have a brother like Lord Karsten?

They looked alike enough, though to Rialla most Darranians had that tendency. They even had a few of the same characteristics. Lord Karsten was eloquent and intelligent, if even more bound by the rules of society than most Darranians—something that Rialla would have sworn was impossible. He was so charming it would have been difficult not to like him, if one weren't a slave or peasant. He was unfailingly courteous to even the most menial of servants, but Karsten was unconcerned, not unaware, that his overseer was an animal who abused servants, peasants and slaves alike.

He talked of change and the importance of reforms, working for them with the dedication of a zealot. The

revisions that Lord Karsten had made in Darran law
would do a tremendous amount of good for the peasants
and middle-class citizens of Darran; but his own serfs
were starving.

All in all, Rialla preferred his younger brother, who saw
with clearer vision, and was much less bound by society's
strictures.

Laeth had slipped back into his role as prodigal son,
and rubbed shoulders with Darranian nobility as comfortably as he did with the mercenaries of Sianim. Even
seated beside his brother's wife, Marri, he didn't lose the
easy charm. Only Rialla knew from the whispered conversations she had with Laeth at night that his feelings for
Marri hadn't changed.

There were over a hundred people in the dining hall.
Laeth had told Rialla that by the next evening that number
would triple, and over five hundred people would attend
the ball two nights hence. The day after that, she and
Laeth would return to Sianim. For all the drama and high
emotion that had started this trip, it was beginning to look
as though they might return to Sianim without incident—
or information.

When Laeth finished his meal and waved Rialla back
from the table, she assumed a position near a window
where the wind would give her a little fresh air.

She was the only slave in the room. It was unusual and
vulgar to bring one's slave to a public function, but Laeth
shrugged it off and said that he had only recently purchased her and wanted to keep an eye on her for a while.
Since it was obvious that she was expensive (the tattoo
proclaimed her a highly trained dancer as well as indicating who trained her), no one made a fuss.

Laeth was talking with a small group of people con-
sisting of Lord Karsten, the sharp-eyed, fox-faced Lord
Jarroh, who was Karsten's constant companion, and Lady
Marri, who clutched her husband's arm tightly and stood
with her gaze fixed determinedly on the floor. Rialla wondered absently about the topic of conversation. Laeth's

face held the sardonic smile he adopted to hide his feelings. Karsten appeared to be pale under his deeply tanned skin.

As Rialla watched with growing speculation, sweat gathered on Karsten's forehead and trickled down his temple. He said something and bowed to excuse himself. He gave his wife's shoulder a dismissing pat, and put her clinging hand on Lord Jarroh's arm.

As Karsten turned to go, he collapsed suddenly—falling to his knees. Laeth was there only a moment before Lord Jarroh, who was hampered by Marri's grip. Laeth managed to get a shoulder under his brother's arm and half carried him to a heavily stuffed sofa.

Her erratic empathy chose that moment to flare briefly to life, and Rialla cringed at the pain Karsten was suffering, though the sofa was close enough that she could tell not a sound crossed his lips. He merely gripped Laeth's hand and closed his eyes.

With Laeth kneeling at the head of the sofa, Marri had little choice but to pull up a padded bench and sit near the foot.

With an imperious gesture, Lord Jarroh summoned a waiter carrying a tray full of empty glasses. His cool voice was decisive enough to carry over the growing chaos in the room.

"Send a groom and an extra horse to the healer in the village. Tell him it's urgent, Lord Karsten is ill." His voice had a bite that sent the waiter running out, heedless of the few glasses that fell from his tray to the floor and shattered.

Lord Jarroh's eye fell on Rialla and he summoned her to him as well. "Go to the kitchens and have one of the maids bring up clean cloths, hot and cold water. Find a house servant and tell him to bring blankets." If she hadn't seen the muscle jump in the side of his face, Rialla would have thought Lord Jarroh as unaffected as he looked.

Rialla ran off to follow Lord Jarroh's orders with as

much speed as the waiter had shown. Lord Jarroh's name
had the same magic as his voice: all Rialla did was mention who sent her and the house and kitchen servants
scrambled to obey. She was on her way back to the dining
hall when she noticed a stranger in servant's garb slip out
of the room.

It wouldn't have caught her attention, since Lord Jarroh
had been in the process of emptying the room of unnecessary onlookers when she left, except she didn't recognize the man's face. Rialla thought she knew all the
indoor servants in Westhold, at least by sight. This was
one she'd never seen, but he strolled down the hall as if
he'd been born here.

Rialla glanced casually around to make sure that no one
was in the hall, and then started after him. In the broad
corridors of the main floor of the keep it was difficult to
follow without being seen, but the servant didn't seem to
notice her. He sauntered casually to an ornate brass-and-
wood door that led outside and left the keep.

He walked around the side of the building to the stable
yard where the hold livestock was kept. Rialla hesitated;
there were not many reasons that a slave would be wandering through the stable. She was bound to be questioned, and she wasn't sure that it was worth calling
attention to herself. Before she made a decision, the servant returned from the stable mounted on a well-bred
courser he must have had saddled and waiting.

Rialla watched him ride at a nonchalant trot to the outer
gates. As he passed through, another horse bolted into the
courtyard, lathered and blown. To Rialla's surprise its
rider pulled it to a skidding halt next to where she stood,
just outside the ostentatious door.

She had little chance for anything other than a brief
glimpse of the man's bearded face and the impression that
he was big. He swung down, shoved the reins at her and
yanked the saddlebags off his mount.

''Take him to the stables and see that he's cared for,''

he ordered shortly. Without waiting for a reply, he ran to the door she'd just left.

She rubbed the sweating gelding's head soothingly to calm him. He was a sturdy enough animal, in good shape—but of no particular breeding; not a horse a noble would ride.

His rider hadn't been wearing nobleman's clothes either, for all the confidence in his command. Rialla concluded that he must be the healer that Lord Jarroh had sent for; there would have just been enough time for a messenger to make it to the village and back.

The horse butted her impatiently with his head, and she began walking him toward the stable. Even though the man she'd followed was long gone, she could ask about him in the stables; there was just something about the way the servant had been so casual in the midst of the confusion of Lord Karsten's collapse that made her curious about him.

The stables were dark and cool and smelled like horses and fresh straw—none of the foul odors that would hint of slovenliness. Rialla felt herself relax in the familiar atmosphere.

The horse she was leading whinnied piercingly at the scent of the unfamiliar animals. A stable boy appeared from a nearby stall. He tossed Rialla a friendly smile and reached for the reins, saying, "The healer's beastie, eh? Here now, I'll cool him out a bit and find an empty corner to stick him in."

Rialla handed the horse over to him and then asked, "Did you see the man that just came in here and took out a liver-chestnut mare?" A proper slave would never attempt conversation with anyone other than another slave, but the groom seemed cordial enough.

The boy glanced around, probably to see if anyone was watching—a stable boy was hired to work, not to chatter with slaves. Satisfied that everyone else was busy, he said, "That was the Lord Winterseine's man, Tamas. He's here a lot. If I were you, I'd try and avoid him if you can."

"Winterseine or Tamas?" Rialla asked.

"Tamas. Winterseine's all right. Tamas, though, is awful quick with a whip or a fist." The boy looked at her meaningfully. "He likes it rough, makes him feel powerful. Stay out of his way unless you like it that way too." Without further delay he led the horse down the aisle to begin cooling it off.

Thoughtfully, Rialla returned to the castle and sneaked back into the room where she'd left Laeth—or at least she tried to sneak back in. Laeth met her at the door and said in furious tones that the whole room could hear, "Where have you been, girl? It couldn't have taken you so long to carry out Lord Jarroh's orders."

Rialla took in the room at a glance. Her fragmented talent caught the suspicion that was in the air, directed at Laeth. She bowed her head humbly and said in clear tones that would carry, "Master, this morning you told me to see if I could find the pin you were missing. When someone mentioned a groom, I remembered that you were wearing it yesterday afternoon when you went hunting, but I didn't see you wear it to dinner. I thought that maybe when you were in the stall with the servant girl . . ." She cowered nervously, as if realizing that she shouldn't have said anything about that.

Someone laughed and made an obscene comment; sleeping with servants was commonplace, but not to be talked about in public. Laeth backhanded her forcefully on her face, knocking her to the ground. It looked more impressive than it was. Laeth's blow was no worse than many a strike they'd exchanged on the practice floor at Sianim. Like any good slave, Rialla cowered and whimpered; all slaves learn quickly that if it looks as if the blow hurt, it isn't as likely to be repeated.

To Rialla's astonishment, a large, gentle hand touched her shoulder and the healer helped her to her feet. "She was near the stables and took my horse when I arrived. You shouldn't give orders unless you want them followed, my lord."

Rialla barely restrained a gasp at the healer's tones. No commoner talked to a noble in that tone of voice—not if he wanted to live to face the morning.

Mercenary or not, Laeth's upbringing as a Darranian noble caused his eyes to flash with outrage. The healer didn't give Laeth a chance to reply before turning to Lord Jarroh. "I have managed to counteract the poison in Lord Karsten's system. He'll be weak, but should be well enough in an hour or so. I'll leave my bill with the clerk as usual." He swept out of the room with as much presence as any of the nobles.

Deliberately Laeth reacted to his frustrated anger as most of his peers would have under the circumstance. He knocked Rialla to the ground again, hitting her open-handed on her cheek with a blow that was more flash than substance.

"Wait for me in my room," he snarled.

Rialla scurried gratefully out, and holding a hand to her face, she headed to the bedroom while Laeth complained loudly about poorly trained slaves.

As she turned the first corner of the hallway, Rialla was stopped by a hand on her arm. Startled, she looked up to see the healer. Before she could draw away, he touched her untattooed cheek with his hand. Raising an eyebrow, he tilted her head so he could see the side of her face clearly in the torchlight.

"There is no mark where he hit you." His comment was in a mild tone, but firmly spoken. Clearly he would have answers before he left her alone.

Rialla looked around frantically and saw with relief that there was no one in the vicinity. She grabbed his sleeve and pulled him into the nearest room. From the glimpse she had while the door was open, it seemed to be an unused study in the midst of remodeling. There were no windows to allow light in, and it was as dark as a cave in the small room after she pulled the door closed. Rialla made a frustrated sound.

"Hold on," she said, falling out of character. "I'll find

a flint . . ." There was a crash as she fell over an object left in the middle of the floor and cracked her head on something hard.

"Perhaps I might be of some assistance." A light flared as the healer spoke, a candle flickering in his hand. His voice was carefully void of humor, but there was something in his face that hinted at it, and Rialla glared balefully at him from her position on the floor before she remembered that she was supposed to be a slave.

It was the first time that she'd had a chance to look closely at him, and she realized what had troubled her before: the healer was no more Darranian than she was. It wasn't just that he was taller and bigger boned, but his coloring was wrong. His hair was almost blond, though the short-trimmed beard was darker. His eyes were hazel, but they weren't as green as hers; his had flecks of light blue that seemed to come and go in the candlelight.

Ignoring her glare, the healer said, "Now, you will please explain to me how you got hit hard enough to knock you to the ground without even so much as a red mark on your face."

Rialla jumped lithely to her feet, with the grace of the dancer she was, and dusted herself off to gain some time to think. Finally she said, "Lord Laeth needs to keep up appearances, but he doesn't want to damage me. The blow was a warning more than a punishment. He disciplines me in other ways." It was the best that she could come up with on short notice, and it wasn't very good.

"That was Lord Laeth," the healer's voice took on an odd tone, "visiting from Sianim?"

Wary of the interest in his voice, Rialla nodded.

The healer raised an eyebrow and reached out unexpectedly to touch her face, muttering a few words under his breath as he did so. He jerked his hand away, as if from something hot, and an intense expression that she couldn't interpret crossed his face.

"Who would have thought it?" he said obscurely, and smiled. "I thought that Sianim frowned on slavery."

Rialla felt as if she'd missed half of the conversation, and groped for an answer. "My master told them I was his servant and they pretended to believe him." It was the explanation that she and Laeth had chosen, but it sounded threadbare to her ears.

He shook his head, but shrugged. "It doesn't matter, I suppose, what your story is. My name is Tris. When you need me, anyone in Tallonwood can tell you where to find me." With that odd statement he blew out the candle and left the room.

Rialla stared stupidly after him. Healers, she supposed, ought to be a bit eccentric, but this one seemed to push it to an extreme.

Cautiously Rialla opened the door and checked the hall. Seeing no one, she continued up the stairs to the suite of rooms that she shared with Laeth.

IT WAS LATE WHEN LAETH RETURNED TO HIS ROOMS. HE was pale and seemed shaken by the attempt on his brother's life.

Without a word, Rialla helped him take off the formal, close-fitting dining jacket. She hung it up and silently offered him a cup of warmed brandy, then perched on a fragile table, ignoring the knickknacks that sat on either side of her, and waited for him to speak.

Just as he opened his mouth, the door shook with a series of impassioned knocks. Rialla slipped back off the table and stood near a wall looking discreet, like a good slave—not that the woman who entered when Laeth opened the door had any interest in Rialla.

"Laeth, you must leave. They think that you were the one who attempted to kill Karsten. They say that you'd have the most to gain from his death." Marri was very much a Darranian lady. She reminded Rialla of a frantic butterfly: beautiful and useless.

Laeth looked at Marri, and not even Rialla could read his face. He shook his head slowly. "There are many people that stand to gain by Karsten's death, lady. He is

threatening to unite Darran with a country full of abom-
inations. The Eastern miners are worried that he's going
to cede mining territory back to Reth; the slavers are worried because he's threatening their livelihood. Indeed, unless someone saw you come in here, there is no reason to
believe that my motive for killing my brother is stronger
than anyone else's."

Marri shook her head at him with apparent exasperation, her dark eyes flashing with anger. "Plague it, Laeth.
Don't give me that lordly sneer, it doesn't suit you. No
one saw me come here."

Laeth bowed his head and said politely, "Accept my
apologies, madam. Pray feel free to leave if my sneer
offends you."

Marri closed her eyes and took a deep breath. There
were white lines of anger along her aristocratic cheek-
bones. "Will you listen to me, you mule?" Rialla bit back
a smile, and decided that she might like Marri after all.

"Do you think I'd risk coming here if I weren't certain
you were in danger?" continued Marri sharply. "Don't
be any stupider than you must. There is someone here
who is deliberately setting you up to be Karsten's murderer—there is no reason suspicion of you would be that
strong otherwise."

Her voice softened. "Karsten knows that someone is
trying to kill him, and we have taken every precaution
against his assassination. You are not needed here. He
may think that you are here for his birthday, but I know
you better. Nothing less than the attempt on his life last
month would have induced you to return."

Laeth raised an eyebrow and sauntered back to his bed,
where he sat down and began to tug off his boots. "Every
precaution? It didn't seem to help him much tonight, did
it?"

"Neither did you!" she replied hotly. Rialla noticed a
hint of moisture in her eyes. "I *can't* stand worrying
about both of you."

"Tears, Marri?" asked Laeth in a biting voice.

"Yes, plague take you." Marri wiped her eyes quickly. "I'm sorry for what happened before, but it wasn't solely my fault. You left me for a year without any word of how to reach you. My parents were in debt and losing the manor, and your brother proposed marriage to me. I have a younger brother and three younger sisters; do you think I should have let them be reduced to poverty when I could stop it? You hadn't even made a firm offer to me, let alone my parents. Should I have told them not to accept Karsten's offer because his brother had flirted with me?"

Midway through her speech Laeth had lost his cold manner. Instead he clenched his fists and stared at the floor. When he spoke, it was in a voice very close to a whisper. "It was more than flirtation, Marri."

Her anger left her abruptly, and there was only sadness in her face. "I know that, but how could I have explained it to my father? I'm not sure that I believed it all the time myself. When you left, you didn't tell me where you were going or what you were going to do."

"You knew that I'd be back."

"Did I?" she questioned, and then sighed. "I suppose that I did, but you didn't say so."

She paced the room, ignoring Rialla's presence. After a while Marri said, "I really do care for him, you know. The chances that he'll survive until the princess marries King Myr are not very good. He explained it to me, as if I were a child, and then patted me on the head and said that you'd look after me." She bowed her head and clenched her arms around her midriff. "Gods," she said bleakly.

It was too much for Laeth. Without his temper to protect him, he couldn't resist her misery. He left the bed and, with one boot on, strode to Marri and wrapped his arms around her. "Nothing is going to happen to me, and I'll do my best to see that nothing happens to Karsten either. You'll have to be satisfied with that."

Laeth hugged her and rested his chin on the top of her head, staring blindly at a wall. Marri leaned against him a moment and then whispered, "I'd better go, before my maid starts to worry. She wouldn't say anything, but it's better not to tempt fate."

Laeth allowed her to draw away and then said, "I'm sorry, Marri. I'm sorry that I didn't talk to your father. I'm sorry that you're worried." He slanted a faint grin at her and lightened his tone. "I'm even sorry that I'm a stupid mule. Karsten is a good man, even if he is my brother."

He took Marri's arm in a formal hold and escorted her to the door. "Thank you for your warning, lady. I'll keep it in mind. If you find out who started the rumor that I'm behind the assassination attempt, I would like to know his name—but send a servant with a message."

He put a hand on the door to open it, and Rialla casually attempted to use the remnants of her talent to scan for someone lurking in the hall. She suspected that even if there were someone there, she wouldn't be able to tell—so she was astounded when she found something.

"Laeth, stop," she hissed urgently, abandoning her post against the wall to sprint to the door and hold it shut. "There's someone out there. Wait." Taking a deep breath, she pressed her forehead against the smooth wood of the door. The person outside the room was in a consuming rage; only the force of his emotions allowed her contact at all. Sweating, she tried to find out more.

The anger she felt was directed at . . . the cat. The miserable, sharp-toed, speedy tabby who'd left with the tasty scrap of meat he was saving for a snack . . . Rialla could feel the flush of embarrassment that crept up her fair skin. It was one of the castle dogs. The hunting dogs were allowed full run of the keep—one of Karsten's little eccentricities.

Animal thoughts had always been easier to pick up than human ones—their thoughts were simpler and more tightly connected to their emotions. She could pick up their thoughts almost as easily as she could touch their emotions.

She was just about to turn and try to explain why she'd stopped Marri from going out when she caught the last edge of a thought . . . a whisper of resentment at the leash that kept him from the cat. She tried again, without success, to touch the person on the other side of the door, but only the dog came in clear.

Her head was starting to ache with the effort of stretching the old scars that limited her empathy, but she ignored it. Unable to reach the person, she touched the animal a different way. Clearly audible on the other side of the door, the guard dog began barking.

Laeth narrowed his eyes at her, but waving Marri out of sight of the door, he called out in a loud voice, "Girl! Go see what is wrong with that plaguing dog, and shut it up!" He strode to the bed and sat down on it, beginning to struggle with the remaining close-fitting, knee-high boot.

"Yes, Master," Rialla replied demurely and yanked at the ties that held her hair up. She bit her lips to make them look kissed and opened the ties at the top of her tunic.

She cracked the door and slipped out, but not before she gave the man outside a clear view of Laeth tugging at his boot. She didn't recognize the man holding the dog, but that wasn't surprising. He wore the uniform of the guards—they kept mostly to the grounds and away from the keep; she only knew the indoor servants.

He took a good look at her and lost a few more inches of leather to the straining dog. She bit her bottom lip and leaned back against the door with all the sultriness a dance-trained slave was capable of displaying.

"What's wrong with him?" she asked in a husky voice.

The man's mouth opened, but nothing came out.

Laeth's voice carried clearly through the door. "Shut that beast up now!"

Rialla gave a squeak of fright and ran to the dog, crooning, "Shh, puppy, that's a good boy."

That pulled the guard's attention from the shadows of

her cleavage. "Don't. He's a trained guard dog . . . He'll kill you." He said the last in a small voice as the dog rolled over in ecstasy onto the slave's lap while she rubbed his belly.

She turned her big emerald eyes at the guard and said inanely, "I've always had a way with dogs. Do you think that he'll start barking again, if I quit petting him? My master has an awful temper: if he hears the dog bark again, he's liable to kill it." She watched the guard closely and whispered, "And probably you as well."

Everyone knew that Laeth had spent the last two years training in Sianim. Rumor had it, truthfully enough, that Laeth's temper was even more impressive than his outrageousness.

The big guard swallowed and grabbed the dog's collar. As he did so, Rialla touched his hand briefly for a minute and caught a stray thought: . . . *couldn't use the coppers I'll get for this job if I were a corpse* . . .

He'd been paid to spy, but on whom? Rialla watched as the guard tugged the dog down the hall and around the corner. Once she could have read him as easily as she could close her eyes. She hit the floor in frustration and jumped to her feet.

Opening the door to Laeth's chambers, Rialla said, "All clear."

Marri slipped out and gave Rialla a penetrating look before leaving in the opposite direction the guard had taken. Rialla stepped into the room and closed the door gently behind her.

"All right, Ria, just how did you know someone was there?" Laeth was lying on top of the colorful tick on the bed with his hands behind his head and his legs crossed.

Rialla leaned against the door and said, "Would you believe that I heard them?"

"After the dog started barking, yes. But I doubt you could hear them walking from the opposite side of that door," replied Laeth shortly.

"Hmm," said Rialla in a frivolous tone, tapping her chin in thought. "How about . . ."

"The truth," said Laeth firmly.

"You won't like it, and probably won't believe it either," commented Rialla, wandering back over to the little table she'd sat on before and fiddling with a hideous purple glass vase.

"Ria." He sounded impatient.

She put the vase back. "Don't say I didn't warn you. I am an empath. Sort of anyway."

"A what?" asked Laeth incredulously.

"An empath. You know, 'I know what you feel . . . I know your thoughts.'" Her voice took on a sonorous and slightly sinister tone, but she easily dropped it again as she continued, "Like the mindspeakers in the traveling fairs."

He sat up and said with obvious disbelief, "You can read people's minds?"

"Well, I used to be able to, but not much anymore." She picked up a crude figurine and continued, "Animals are easier. I can pick up emotions pretty clearly if they're strong ones, and occasionally the thoughts that go with them. Marri thinks that you're as handsome as ever." She nodded at his start of surprise.

"You read Marri?" This time there was a strong thread of anger in his tone.

"Nothing that anyone couldn't have seen in her face if they were looking." Her voice was noncommittal and she set the figurine next to the vase. She wanted to back away from his anger; somehow it was harder to resist her conditioning while wearing the garb of a slave.

"Plague it, Rialla, that's worse than eavesdropping. You violated her privacy!" He stood up, and she could see his outrage tightening the muscles of his arms. She could feel her heartbeat pick up as he closed in on her.

She could either fight back or cower. The latter was smarter, but if she cowered she might as well be the slave whose guise she wore.

"You Darranians and your overdeveloped sense of propriety," she said with a quiet bitterness that stopped him short. "I know all about the rules by which you live your lives. Take the aristocratic, immaculate Lord Jarroh, your brother's best friend and staunchest ally. He frequented the little bar where I danced. He never spilled a drop of the single glass of white wine he drank. One must never be excessive when imbibing alcohol. He always tipped the waiter—just the proper amount. Then he went upstairs and beat the little slave girl he kept there. Sometimes he used a whip, sometimes he used his fist. Crippled as I am, I still felt her pain every time, including the last time—when he killed her." She smiled at him humorlessly. "His slave had seen twelve summers when she died."

She could see that the anger had left him, but now that she had started she couldn't stop. "The slave trainer responsible for my capture took twenty-three other people from my clan at the same time. Twenty of them he tortured and killed. I felt each of their deaths too. Thanks to that I can't simply turn my abilities off and on as I used to: I hear what I hear." She raised her brows and continued with bitter mockery, "I *am* sorry if that offends your Darranian sense of decorum."

Laeth's face was curiously blank. He reached out and touched her cheek with one hand. It wasn't until then that she realized that she was crying or that she'd backed away from him despite her determination not to do so. The door was solid against her back.

"Sorry," he said in a soft voice. "I didn't mean to frighten you." He went back to the bed and lay on it, closing his eyes. In the same soft voice he said, "What was a guard doing patrolling the corridor when he should be out on the walls?"

She closed her eyes too, and pressed harder against the door. Her voice when she spoke was quietly controlled. "Sometimes if I have physical contact with a person, I can pick up a few scattered thoughts. I think someone bribed him to come here, but I couldn't tell who he was supposed to be watching. It could be you, or Marri, or any of the fifteen other people in this wing of the keep.

"If it was Marri he was watching," she continued after a moment's pause, "he probably followed her from her rooms. He'd know that she came in—but not that she came out before you had time to do anything. If he was sent to watch you, he may or may not have been here to see Marri come. If he was watching someone else, we don't have any worries."

"You said that you couldn't tell who he was looking for. Could you tell who paid him?" Laeth's voice was still excessively gentle, so she knew that her face wasn't as blank as she wanted it to be, and she redoubled her efforts.

"No," she answered. The metal of the doorknob was cold against her hand. "I could tell it was someone that the guard was not afraid of, and that this wasn't the first time he'd asked the guard to do this kind of work. The guard wasn't worried about leaving his post, so it was someone with enough authority to stop any punishments. It wasn't your brother, because he wouldn't have had to bribe the guard at all. You'd know who would best fit such a description."

"Lord Jarroh?" he suggested, doubtfully.

Rialla opened her eyes and shook her head. "No. All the servants are terrified of him and I'm sure that the guards would be too. Besides, that's not his style. He would never hire someone to spy; it's not something that a proper noble would do."

"The only other person besides Lord Jarroh, my brother and myself with the authority to halt a punishment would be my uncle, Lord Winterseine. But he's not here yet."

"How about the overseer?" asked Rialla.

Laeth shook his head. "Dram's orders wouldn't be questioned. He'd never have to bribe a guard to patrol the corridors of the keep rather than the walls. Not to mention that the guard would be terrified of him."

Rialla nodded and then said, "Lord Winterseine's servant Tamas was here this evening."

Laeth nodded. "I saw him and asked around. He came with Uncle's luggage as he always does. Were you chasing after him this evening? I wondered where you were. He probably left to tell Uncle about the poisoning attempt."

"Couldn't he have arranged for a guard to watch someone for your uncle?" suggested Rialla.

"He could have," replied Laeth, "but I just can't see my uncle doing something as improper as spying; he's worse than Karsten when it comes to decorous behavior."

"It is possible that the guard was sent to protect someone rather than spy on them," Rialla commented. "I don't suppose talking about it all night will help us. I think I will sleep in the slaves' quarters; sometimes they have information no one else has."

Before he had a chance to protest, Rialla slipped through the door and into the darkened hallway.

THE SLAVES' QUARTERS WERE IN THE BASEMENT, NEXT to the wine cellar. Rialla supposed that they had originally been put there so as not to use space in the valuable ground floor, while allowing the slaves to attend their owners quickly. Whatever the reason, the result was that the quarters were more comfortable than the rest of the castle. Underground there were no chilly drafts in the winter, and in the summer when the rest of the castle was baking, the quarters were cool enough to need the single blanket that lay neatly at the foot of all the bunks.

In Darran, slaves were used for pleasure rather than work, so most were female. The few male slaves primarily worked in pleasure houses where a wealthy Darranian would be preserved from the social stigmatism of homosexuality. Women in Darran did not own slaves. With little need to separate male and female, the slave quarters at Westhold consisted of a single, large room.

Rialla didn't really expect to find out anything in the

quarters, but she wasn't ready to relax and sleep either. It might have been a touch from her talent or just instinct, but something caused her to hesitate before she entered.

". . . sleep here. You will stay here until I come for you in the morning. Do you understand?"

The man's voice was gentle and quiet. There was nothing in it to account for the sudden cramping of Rialla's stomach or the shaking of her hands.

She turned frantically to the locked door of the wine cellar. Traders teach their children how to pick locks and pockets as soon as the tots are tall enough to reach a doorknob. The wine cellar lock had never been intended to keep out anyone but the servants, and it gave her little trouble.

Rialla closed the door of the cellar quietly behind her. She huddled against the wood in the darkness and heard the man's hard-soled boots click across the stone floor. He paused briefly before the wine cellar door, as if he'd heard it open. But he continued up the stairs without investigating further.

Rialla folded her arms around her knees and listened to the pounding of her heart in her ears. What was her former owner doing in Lord Karsten's hold? As Laeth had put it, Karsten would be as likely to invite a swineherd as a slave trainer to his celebration.

She'd spent seven years as his slave, but most of that time was spent in the little bar in Kentar, the capital city of Darran. The rest had been in a small estate in the south. Uneasily, she remembered little hints that he might have been more than a simple slave trainer: the servants who called him "lord," and the ambience of age and respectability at the estate where she was trained.

If he was highly connected, it would be possible for him to take part in polite society, as long as his occupation as a slave trainer could be kept quiet. Laeth, she knew, had never had any interest in the slave trade. It was feasible that Laeth knew her former owner, but didn't know he was a slave trainer.

Rialla knew that she ought to go back to Laeth's room and warn him that the slave trainer was in the castle, but . . . in the dark, beer-scented room she was safe. She curled into a tighter ball in the corner of the room and rested her cheek against the side of a wooden barrel, letting the rough wood dig into her tattooed skin.

She despised the cowardice that had been beaten into her, but that didn't keep her from shaking with bone-deep tremors. If her father could see her, he would be ashamed. She'd worked so hard to shed the habits of a slave, and all it took to bring them back was Laeth's anger or her old master's voice.

She swore silently and dug her nails into her palms, reminding herself that he would be unlikely to visit the quarters again this night. With a shuddering sigh, she came to her feet, wiping the tears from her face with the sides of her hands. Like most of the Traders she had good night vision, but in the underground cellar the darkness was absolute. It took her a moment to find the latch on the door.

Taking a deep breath, she exited the wine cellar, locked it, and walked with outward calm to the slave quarters. If one of the slaves noticed that she'd been crying, they wouldn't comment upon it—such was a slave's lot. Quietly she let herself into the large room.

A few scattered torches lit the large room, allowing Rialla to see that only twenty of the bunks were occupied. That meant the rest of the slaves were either working, or sleeping in their owner's rooms. There was no one awake, so Rialla strode quietly to a pair of unoccupied bunks away from the door.

She climbed to the top bunk and stretched out on it: only a new slave would take the vulnerable bottom bunk. Among slaves, status was very important. Occasionally fights broke out in the quarters when one slave tried to establish dominance. The top bunk offered some protection against unwanted aggression.

Rialla had started to close her eyes when she heard a

slight noise from the bottom bunk next to her. She leaned over the edge of her bed and looked at the girl lying there.

As a Trader, and later as a horse trainer in Sianim, she'd seen every color that a person could come in—from her own pale ivory to the deep bronze of the Ynstrah people—but this slave's skin was closer to black. Fine dark hair that might be brown or red in daylight cloaked her shoulders in waves of curls. Her face was buried in the thin mattress and her body shook as she cried.

Rialla reached a hand to the girl, but caught herself in time. She was doing the best that she could to end slavery in Darran, but she couldn't do anything for this other slave now.

RIALLA DREAMED THAT NIGHT OF A FOREIGN LAND IN-habited by people who looked like the strange slave girl. They spoke a language that she had never heard before, but understood in a way that her empathic abilities had once allowed her. It was a nightmarish dream with fev-erlike images that randomly appeared and disappeared without warning.

She awoke in a cold sweat with a screaming pain in her chest. Leaping quickly off the bunk, she took a step toward the strange girl's bed, but it was too late.

From somewhere the other slave had found an eating knife that she'd used to stab herself in the chest. Rialla gasped harshly with the pain of the slave's wound, feeling as if something had torn through the barrier that had blocked her abilities for more than a decade. The dull knife's work had been made even more painful because the girl didn't know where to stab herself. Still, her am-ateurish attempt worked after a fashion. Even as Rialla watched, the girl took a last breath and smiled.

Rialla looked at the body of the girl that she now knew almost as intimately as she knew herself. The young slave had been an empath strong enough to project her fears past Rialla's mental scars and into her dreams.

Rialla knew the slave's name and that she was fifteen

summers old. She knew that somewhere in a foreign land the girl's family thought that she was serving the gods—a position of highest honor. They had let her go with sadness, but she had gone gladly as the servant of Altis had requested.

Rialla could feel the echoes of the girl's horror and disgust when she found out what her duties were going to be. She could tell without looking that the girl's back would be covered with fresh whip marks and that the inside of her thighs were bruised badly enough that it would show even on her dark skin.

Rialla tightened her jaw and carefully stepped around the blood that was pooling on the floor. A slave avoided attracting unpleasant attention. By the time the body was discovered, there would be no slave left in the quarters and none would admit sleeping there last night—but only the knowledge that the slave trainer would probably be sleeping allowed Rialla to start up the stairs that led to the main part of the keep.

She entered Laeth's sleeping chamber quietly, without waking him. She sat on the hard-sprung sofa near the bed and stared into the darkness, waiting for the dawn.

# THREE

"I thought that you were going to sleep in the slaves' quarters last night." Laeth spoke softly, but Rialla jumped anyway.

She hadn't been thinking, just staring into the shadows in the corner of the room; Laeth's voice, like the early morning light streaming through the windows, took her by surprise. She must have been sitting there for longer than she realized.

Laeth managed to sit up, but he closed his eyes again as he rubbed his face to bring himself awake. He was not at his best in the morning.

Rialla felt her lips quirk in an involuntary smile at the familiar sight. Answering his question rid her of the smile soon enough. "I did sleep in the quarters, at least part of the night."

He cast her a sharp look that belied his sluggishness and asked, "What happened?"

"There was a new slave in the compound last night: an Easterner. This morning she killed herself with an eating knife. I thought that it would be better if I weren't there when her body is discovered—no sense in attracting attention.'' Rialla fingered the now-familiar needlepoint pattern on the back of the sofa.

She could feel Laeth's steady gaze, as he waited patiently for her to continue. She kept her gaze on her hands and added briefly, "Especially as her owner is the man who owned me before I ran."

Laeth drew in a breath of surprise. "The slave trainer? You're certain?"

Rialla nodded, without looking up. "I didn't see him, but I heard his voice. It's not something I am likely to mistake, but I checked her tattoo. She too bore his mark."

"Well, then," said Laeth with satisfaction, "I suppose I need to think of several obnoxious ways of refusing to return his slave."

Rialla looked at him then, and shot him a grin. "I wasn't worried that you were going to turn me over to him."

"No?" he said, his tone serious. "Then what are you worrying about?"

Rialla shrugged. "I'm not." At his snort she smiled faintly. "I suppose I am. I wasn't prepared to meet him again . . . and the girl's death was particularly unpleasant. An eating knife is not the way that I would choose." Rialla looked down again and swallowed. At least the Easterner had found the courage to make the choice.

Rialla remembered staring at a sharp little dagger that someone had left carelessly sitting on an eating bench. It wouldn't have made much of a weapon, but she remembered considering using it to take her own life—she'd been too much of a coward. The only other time she'd come close to suicide was just after she'd escaped, when she discovered she feared freedom more than slavery.

"Rialla." Laeth's tone was gentle, and she knew that it wasn't the first time that he'd called her name. "What was your owner's name?"

"Isslic, but I don't know his family name—slave trainers don't often use their full names."

Laeth nodded. "Especially if he's well enough born to

receive an invitation here. Isslic's a common name; I can think of three or four men who answer to it.''

"If it is his real name at all,'' added Rialla with a shrug. "I did notice something that might be worth mentioning to Ren, although it's mostly speculation.''

"What is it?''

"My former owner liked to travel to find the slaves he trained. He preferred to take them himself rather than wait until an untrained slave came to auction. He contended that most of them had already acquired too many bad habits by that time.'' Rialla could feel her face relaxing until there was no more emotion in it than in her voice. "So if he had, say, a slave from Southwood, he probably went to Southwood to get her.''

"Turn around, so I can get out of bed,'' ordered Laeth briskly.

"Modesty?'' she teased, feeling herself begin to relax for the first time since she'd heard her old master's voice in the cellar.

"I thought to protect your sensibilities. If you want to see me unclothed, by all means watch,'' he retorted, "but I can't think without my boots on.''

Rialla laughed and faced the wall while he dressed.

"So what you're saying,'' said Laeth finally, "is that if the girl you saw was from the East then the slave trainer went to the East to get her.''

Rialla nodded. "Yes.'' She paused and looked at Laeth, who was now fully dressed. "Did Ren tell you about what is happening in the East? That he thinks the leader of the Easterners is a magic user trained in the West?''

Laeth nodded.

"Though my master was a Darranian, he was also a trained mage.'' Briefly Rialla recalled the screams of her slain kinfolks. "I am no judge of such matters, but I was told that he'd trained with the last Archmage—certainly an indication that he had some ability. The slave who killed herself was from the East. She thought that she was going to serve the Voice of Altis.''

Rialla rose to her feet. Pacing restlessly around the room, she continued with the story that she had pieced together from the fragments of her dreams while she'd waited for Laeth to wake up. "She knew that such service would include concubinage, but she didn't realize that it would entail slavery in a foreign land. She believed that the man who enslaved her was the Voice of Altis."

Laeth sat on the sofa that Rialla had abandoned, relaxing bonelessly on the hard cushioned seat. "You think that the man who used to own you is the Voice of Altis?"

Rialla shrugged. "I don't know. I wouldn't have thought that he had the charisma for demagoguery. He was not the sort of man who could sway a crowd. Though his personal servants were obedient, I don't think that any of them were particularly loyal to him."

"Magic?" questioned Laeth.

Rialla shrugged. "You know as much as I do. I've heard rumors that the last ae'Magi had such a spell, but you know how that is. There are rumors about magicians and their spells all the time. What I *know* is that the slave was convinced that her master was the Voice of Altis."

Laeth gave her a thoughtful look and then said, "You must have had quite a long conversation with this Eastern slave."

"Actually," Rialla replied, with a tired smile, "she practically forced it down my throat while I was sleeping. She was an empath, too—maybe stronger than I was."

"I thought that empaths were supposed to be rare," complained Laeth, throwing one hand across his brow in the best tradition of court theater.

Rialla gave him a sympathetic look. "We are. She's the first one I've ever met." She walked to the shuttered windows, saying, "What surprised me most, I think, is that she died still believing the man who enslaved her was the Voice of Altis. I would think that an empath as strong as she was could have told that he was lying."

"Is it significant that you and this Easterner are both empaths?" asked Laeth seriously.

Rialla thought about his question before answering slowly, "I don't think so. I'm not sure that my master ever knew I was an empath. I tried to keep it hidden at first—then I lost most of my ability soon after he acquired me."

She drew a deep breath and switched to the point that she had been aiming at. "Laeth, if he is the Voice of Altis, he has good reason to want to stop an alliance between Darran and Reth. He could do that by killing your brother."

Laeth nodded. "I know. But it sounds as if he just arrived last night, after the attempt on Karsten."

"If he's got the kind of connections that would get him invited here, he could have the influence necessary to arrange an attempt on Karsten." Recalling the poisoning attempt brought another memory to the surface; Rialla snapped her fingers. "I forgot to ask you last night, what do you know about Tris, the local healer?"

"You mean besides the fact that he likes the Darranian aristocracy about as much as you do?" Laeth grinned at her but continued more soberly, "He showed up here sometime after I left. I never met him before last night, but I have heard a lot about him. If you believe even half of what he is credited with, he has the gods' own power over death. After the way he managed to keep Karsten alive, I might almost believe it."

"He stopped me and offered to help us," said Rialla.

"You didn't tell him about what we're doing here?" asked Laeth incredulously.

She gave him an insulted look. "Of course not. He was waiting near the stairs to see how hard you hit me—at least I think that was what he was doing. When he saw that you hadn't done any damage at all, he got curious and started to ask questions. I told him who you were; he told me to ask him for help if we need it. I thought that you must know him for your name to spark such a response."

Laeth frowned, then shook his head. "No. He didn't

strike me as familiar when I saw him last night; I have a good memory for faces. He's supposed to be a relative of one of the villagers, but he certainly doesn't look Darranian."

Rialla thought about her impression of the man. "I think he might be a mage as well. He acted rather oddly, as if he were working a spell."

"First empaths and now mages," grumbled Laeth, without any true distress. He rubbed a thoughtful hand through his hair. "Where do you think that he fits into all of this?"

She tilted her head in consideration. "I don't know, who can understand mages—or healers either for that matter? He wasn't faking his concern when he was checking my face for bruises. I can't see him poisoning Lord Karsten and then saving him at the last minute, unless he's trying to get something from Karsten. If that were the case, wouldn't he have been more courteous when he was here?" She sighed. "I doubt he is working against us, but I can't fathom why he would be supporting us—even if he knew what we're doing here.

"Uh, Rialla, sweetheart," interjected Laeth mildly, with a twinkle in his eye. "Have you looked in a mirror recently?"

Rialla snorted at him, much in the manner of her beloved horses. "He offered his help when he found out who you were. It had nothing to do with me."

She opened the window shutters and said, "I'd better get down to the kitchens and bring up breakfast before it's all gone."

She ducked into the small closet that served as a dressing room, grabbed a clean tunic and put it on, along with the blank face that went with it.

The halls were quiet; most of the aristocracy had spent a late night dancing and wouldn't rise for a few more hours. They were more open while they slept, and Rialla caught a stray emotion here and there as she walked, far more than she usually could. Tension coiled in her, and she stopped in the empty corridor. Belatedly she realized that she'd been receiving scattered impressions since last night—as if the other empath's death had ripped apart some of the scarring that hindered her gifts.

With skills grown rusty with disuse, Rialla managed to raise a shield in her mind against the fragments of emotions that touched her. She could remove the protection if she chose, and explore the talent that was returning to her—but she wasn't sure that she wanted to do so.

She would never have thought she would be as frightened by the threat of her talent's return as she had been by its loss. Rialla swallowed and began walking, maintaining her outward serenity with an effort.

RIALLA BROUGHT LAETH BREAKFAST AND HELPED HIM into the gaudy full court dress. When he left, she set about cleaning the suite. Keeping busy kept her from terrorizing herself with thoughts of her former master. Energetically she folded clothes and hunted out the dark corners that tended to collect shoes and miscellaneous small items, so they wouldn't be left behind when they packed.

When she had done all she could do to their rooms, she sat cross-legged on the bed and dropped the barrier she'd imposed on her gift. With that done, she made herself relax and listen to the feelings passing invisibly through the stone and wood of the keep.

Since she first realized that the old scars that had shielded her empathy had been disturbed, she had felt exposed and vulnerable. That could not be allowed. Sitting on Laeth's bed with her empathy working better than it had since she'd been enslaved, part of her waited for the return of the pain that had destroyed her ability. By the time she'd finished with the exercise, her tunic was soaked in sweat, and she stank like old fear.

With disgust, she washed off with the water left in the basin by the bed and changed into a fresh tunic. She'd just pulled the end of the tunic over her hips when Laeth burst into the room to change for lunch.

He took one look at her and said, "Are you all right?"

Rialla nodded. Being Laeth, bless him, he didn't push her.

She helped him don his riding jacket for the scheduled hunt. Darranians changed their clothes five or six times a day, and the riding jacket was particularly ridiculous. It was cut so close that Laeth couldn't put it on alone, and once on it restricted his mobility severely. Just the thing to wear while riding spirited horses through fields and over fences at high speeds.

Laeth was so busy replying to her snide comments on Darranian fashions that he forgot his riding whip when he left the room, with an exaggerated swagger that left Rialla snickering. The whip wasn't necessary as far as the horse was concerned, but fashion dictated it be carried.

Rather than make him come all the way back to the room, Rialla snatched it up and trotted down the stairs to the entrance hall, where the riders would all gather and talk before they got on the horses.

Rialla kept her slave face on with an effort as she slid discreetly among the guests. She probably shouldn't have given Laeth such a bad time—most of the men were wearing coats that fit even tighter than Laeth's.

It took her two trips through the crowded room before she heard his voice. She came upon him and slipped the whip quietly into his hand without interrupting his conversation.

She was careful to keep her gaze down so she lacked warning when a familiar hand wrapped itself around the back of her neck and the voice of her former master said, "Where on earth did you manage to find this one, Laeth? I have been looking for her for years."

A thumb under her chin forced her gaze from the floor. He was taller than Laeth and stockier, though even after seven years it was muscle that filled the burgundy jacket he wore. His hair was still dark brown and tied neatly in a queue. The only sign of the passing years was the silvering of his narrow mustache.

"She was yours, Uncle?" Laeth's voice was carefully neutral, though Rialla couldn't see his face.

Uncle! She remembered the affection in Laeth's voice when he spoke of his uncle, Lord Winterseine. It would seem that her former master had high connections indeed.

Rialla kept her body relaxed, and focused her eyes somewhere past her old master's face. She took some comfort in knowing that her terror wouldn't be immediately obvious. His hand almost touched her tattooed cheek. The spymaster's mage had warned her that the illusion of the tattoo was visual only. If he slid his hand up farther he would be able to feel the scars.

The slave trainer released her neck, sliding his hand intimately to her shoulder, and Rialla fought back a sigh of relief. "Yes," he said. "She was a dancer in a small establishment that I own in Kentar. I trained her myself. It's been six or seven years since she escaped." He smiled and his voice took on a softness that she knew too well. "I believe that she killed the guard when she did. It will be good to have her back. She is a very talented dancer."

"Why, Uncle Iss, I didn't know you trained slaves." Laeth's tone bordered on insulting.

"I train my own horses too," his uncle replied. "I find the ones that others train pick up bad habits. It will take time to retrain her."

Laeth ran a hand casually down her back in a move as possessive as his uncle's hand on her shoulder. "I picked her up in the Alliance, near the sea, when I was guarding a merchant train across the wastes."

There was just the right touch of amusement in Laeth's voice. It would seem obvious that he was more interested in the abhorrence his uncle would feel at having a member of his family acting in such a menial capacity than in any claim that his uncle would have on his slave.

He continued in the same vein. "She was a gift for saving the merchant's son after he was bitten by a snake. I am afraid that I cannot return her to you, Uncle Iss—it has been longer than five years since you lost her, after all. I find I have grown," Laeth paused with a man-to-man look that conveyed a risqué meaning to his words, "fond of her attentions. She knows just how to please me." Laeth casually wrapped his hand around her neck, just as Isslic had. He pulled her away from Lord Winterseine's grip and twisted her casually around for a kiss.

Rialla complied with Laeth's demands, but it was his sorrow at discovering that it was his uncle who had hurt her, not passion, that slipped through the fraying defenses of her empathy. When the kiss was over, Rialla glanced unobtrusively at her former master.

Survival had forced her to read his face more easily than she could read a written page, and what she saw there worried her.

Laeth's uncle smiled and said lightly, "Very well, Laeth, the consequences be on your head, though. Remember that she killed a guard when she escaped; keeping her might be dangerous."

Laeth smiled back at his uncle and said, "She'll do me no harm, Uncle Iss. She knows that there are worse masters to have." He paused. The implication he'd just made *might* not have been intentional because he continued, "The merchant was free with his whip. If she isn't a good girl, I'll just send her back and she knows it."

Winterseine had started to say something else when they were interrupted by a man who looked several years younger than Laeth. He was handsomer than either of the other men and taller, but he lacked their presence. His voice was a soft tenor when he spoke to Winterseine. "Tamas says that the rest of our party is here."

Winterseine grunted, but Laeth stepped forward and reached for the younger man's hand and shook it warmly. "Terran, it's good to see you again. I see that Uncle Iss still has you organizing his travels."

The young man laughed shyly and nodded his head. "I don't know what I'd do if we stayed in one residence more than a week or so—perhaps get a full night's sleep without worrying if some vital piece of luggage got left at the last rest stop.'' Then he ducked his head and added, ''It's not that bad really; Father and I go mostly to the same places, so it's more like having many homes rather than none.''

Since no one was looking at her, Rialla examined Terran's face. She had forgotten about Winterseine's son: he had been as unobtrusive then as he appeared now.

Winterseine laughed, though there was an edge to it, and patted his son on the shoulder. ''I don't know what I'd do without him. He makes all the travel arrangements and I just follow and enjoy the trip. Ah, it looks like people are starting to leave for the stables. Shall we join them?''

Laeth turned Rialla around as if she were a child and patted her rump familiarly. ''Go clean the room and see that you find the other green slipper for your dancing costume. I want you to wear it to dinner. Check under the bed; I might have thrown it there last night. I want you ready to join me at dinner tonight.'' Rialla walked away obediently, carefully controlling the instinctive urge to run.

In Laeth's suite she stretched out on the bed and thought about Winterseine. It surprised her how angry Laeth had been. She would have been less surprised by an apologetic refusal to return her, though she found his unexpected defense warming. She closed her eyes and slept.

The sounds of the hunting party's return awoke her, and she got up hastily and began to dress in the emerald-green dancing costume she'd purchased at Midge's before leaving Sianim.

The green costume was surprisingly modest for being purchased from a brothel, quite suitable for a public dance. The veils covered her from hip to toe and from neck to wrist, almost concealing the skimpy top and bottom, allowing only faint glimpses of skin between the layers as Rialla moved.

She braided her hair into a neat crown that anchored

still more veils that covered her face and neck, leaving only her exotically pale midriff bare. The miniature gold bells that were scattered through the costume were its most unusual feature, and had been a lucky find at the bazaar in Sianim.

She searched through her packs until she found a leather pouch containing the jewelry of a dancer. Viciously long, sharp, golden nails slipped over the ends of her fingers, held on by slender golden chains that attached to black leather wristbands. Similar gold chains dangled from black anklets. A much heavier chain wrapped around her waist and slid down until it rested on her hips.

She put on the silk slippers that matched the rest of her costume. Normally a dancer performed barefoot; but feet were considered erotic and unacceptable for an audience that would include noblewomen. Lastly, she donned the heavy black cloak that covered most of her costume.

Dressed, Rialla descended the stairs and walked out to the dining hall, where she'd been commanded to wait for Laeth. She stood quietly, head down, outwardly ignoring the looks that the servants gave her; hers was probably the first dancing costume they had ever seen. Slaves were expensive—only the very rich could afford them—and dancers were more expensive than most. Most dancers were owned by businessmen, who used them to bring in customers to their taverns and clubs; dancers owned for private use were rare.

When Laeth entered, engaged in a loud, boisterous and not particularly sober conversation with his cousin Terran, who was frantically trying to quiet him, Rialla fell in behind. She held out Laeth's chair and helped seat him, then stood back against the wall so that she wouldn't get in the way of the servants. In their own way, the nobles were as fascinated with her as the servants had been. They were merely more discreet with their stares, so as not to appear too interested.

It was almost fun to pretend, knowing that she was

fooling all these people; especially since Laeth had already outfaced her former owner. It was odd, Rialla reflected, that she'd never felt less like a slave than now when she was pretending to be one.

She didn't notice Lord Winterseine until he spoke in her ear.

"You shouldn't have run away from me, Little One," he whispered. "You know what happens to slaves who run from me. Don't think the young whelp will keep you from my wrath. I have plans for him."

His rage boiled over onto her like molten lava when he gripped her arm . . . *These fools! Think that they can toy with me, do they?* . . . She was pulled out of his grasp and his mind by a strong hand on her wrist.

"Slave girl," said Laeth in slightly drunken tones, "get me the brandy that I brought from Sianim. Terran, here, said that he's never tried Rethian brandy, despite having visited Reth on numerous occasions." He shook his head chidingly at his cousin, as he shoved Rialla in the direction of the entrance.

She fled the room gratefully and darted up the stairs, not slowing until she reached Laeth's suite and shut the door behind her. As she tried to locate the brandy she'd just packed, she attempted to figure out what was bothering her about Lord Winterseine.

She had expected him to be angry, but his anger had been disproportionate. She had been valuable, but not irreplaceable. His rage had a hard edge of insanity about it, and of paranoia. From the little she'd caught, she thought Winterseine was angry most of the time . . . perhaps frightened as well.

When she'd speculated that her former owner was the man who called himself the Voice of Altis, she hadn't really believed it. She could now. He'd changed in more substantial ways than a few gray hairs in his mustache. Arrogance was necessary to a man who turned other humans into slaves, but Lord Winterseine's arrogance had grown tremendously.

Finding the bottle at last, Rialla started through the hall to the stairs. She stopped in front of the dining room to catch her breath, then strode in with studied grace.

Winterseine was on the other side of the room from Laeth, who was engaged in being thoroughly obnoxious. Rather than interrupting him, Rialla set the bottle on the table, well out of reach of his exaggerated gestures, stepped back to the wall and let herself be distracted by his antics.

In the middle of the serving of the hot cherry torte, Laeth, who had allowed Terran to keep him quiet through the previous four courses, suddenly jumped to his feet.

"I don't *care* who the princess marries; she can marry a donkey if she cares to: I just can't stomach a Darranian princess marrying that Rethian ox. The only thing good to come out of Reth in the last hundred years is this brandy." He grabbed at the bottle Rialla had brought down and missed. Giving it a puzzled look, he jumped on top of the table and managed to locate it near his ankles.

He swung the brandy toward his brother with such enthusiasm that even Rialla, who knew that he was about as drunk as she was, winced; but somehow he managed to hold onto the neck and keep from falling off the table at the same time.

"*You,* Karsten, are the reason that our poor princess is being forced to marry that brainless hunk of bear bait." His voice held such melodramatic sorrow that Rialla felt a grin tug at the corner of her mouth. So that was why he'd been making such a spectacle of himself.

After this performance, it would be clear that Laeth would be sympathetic to a plot that would halt the union of Reth and Darran. He was hoping that he would be approached by someone who would give them a suspect for the attempted assassinations—someone other than his uncle. Rialla was afraid that he wasn't going to find one.

Lord Karsten sat pale and composed at the head of the table, but Rialla thought that his lack of color was more from his recent poisoning than from the antics of his incorrigible brother. It was Marri who stood up and proposed that everyone retire to the music room for the evening entertainment. Terran and Lord Karsten, between them, managed to talk Laeth into getting off the table. Karsten poured several cups of something that a hastily summoned valet swore would sober Laeth.

Laeth allowed himself to be quieted and appeared almost normal, if sleepy, by the time he finished the drink. He was led cautiously into the music room and seated in the back. Terran was left with him to ensure his good behavior.

The music room was actually a small auditorium. Rialla felt a moment's panic at the thought of trying to fit three hundred people into it, but apparently an evening of amateur entertainment was not the highlight of the celebration. Although the room was not huge, there were still plenty of empty seats.

She found out why when the first performer stepped on the stage.

Two hours later Rialla had fallen into a comfortable doze that gave her some relief from the neophyte troubadour performing on a poorly tuned lyre. The performances weren't without merit. Marri was an acceptable alto, but Rialla's favorite was a middle-aged woman whose dramatic rendition of a classic monologue was eclipsed by an untimely rip in her overly tight gown.

Laeth, who had lapsed into a convincing drunken coma, sat up and rubbed his eyes and peered bleary-eyed at the stage. When it was obvious that no one was on it, he stood up and motioned Rialla to follow.

Rialla could hear her pulse pound in her ears, and adrenaline made her muscles taut and responsive. She'd almost forgotten how much she enjoyed performing. Before, it had been tainted by her slave status; this time she was performing by choice.

In the men's club in Kentar, there had always been a drummer to provide a beat for her, but here she would have to dance to her own music. Laeth stopped at the bottom of the stage and motioned her to continue up the stairs. She took off her black cloak and struck a demure pose, waiting for the audience to quiet. It took time for the people in their seats to realize what she was waiting for and quit talking.

She tested the chamber by a subtle movement of her foot, and the bells rang out with a clear and sweet tone. She had chosen her dance carefully, as the dances that she had used most often were unsuitable for public display. This was an obscure dance that one of the older dancers in the club had taught her; the story of a young girl who is lost in the woods at night and killed by a shapeshifter.

Rialla let herself become the girl, concentrating on the sweet refrain of the bells. Her movements were soft and furtive as she snuck out of her parents' house, then light and graceful as she dodged through the woods to find her lover.

He wasn't where they were supposed to meet; but she wasn't worried and danced to the night and the moon, accompanied by the musical babble of the tiny bells that she wore.

In the middle of an agile leap, she heard a noise. Landing, she crouched, momentarily frightened. She remembered that her lover should be coming. Her fear changed to excitement as she searched eagerly for him. He was not there.

With a shrug, she gave herself back to the dance. Her movements were lithe and willowy, but she was obviously tiring when she heard another noise. This time it was her lover in the form of a black cloak cleverly wielded in her hand. They danced together, laughing and passionate—until she noticed something on his clothing: something sticky that stained her hand.

She looked at him, questioning, and saw a great ravening beast in the place of her lover. She turned and ran, but he flew ahead of her and dropped over her, knocking her to the ground. She struggled uselessly and then they were still.

Rialla lay facedown on the cool wooden floor and panted, listening to the silence that was as much a tribute as the applause that followed.

Laeth stumbled up the stairs with exaggerated care and pulled her to her feet. He grinned and waved at the assembly, managing a credible bow that tested Rialla's ability to maintain her slave face over her laughter, and tugged her off the stage and out of the room by a side exit.

Safe once more in the suite, Laeth pulled off his alcohol-soaked shirt and undershirt while Rialla washed her face in the cool water in the ewer.

"How did you do that bit with the cloak where it flew up and then dropped?" Laeth's voice was muffled as he pulled a clean tunic over his head. "Is it weighted?"

"It's weighted, but it still takes a lot of practice to get it to fly just right." Rialla sifted through her bag and finally came up with a clean tunic. With it in hand she went to the changing room and stripped out of the dancing costume. The cotton tunic felt feather-light in comparison, though it was longer than most of its kind and hung well past her knees.

Barefoot, she returned to the bedroom and dumped the costume on top of her traveling bag. The bells protested her lack of care, but she ignored the noise as she knelt beside the bag and fought to snug the laces. "Shouldn't you have performed your drunken sot routine a little sooner? There's only one day left before we return." The bag taken care of, she sat cross-legged on the heavy carpet that padded the floor.

Laeth flung himself backward on the bed and said, "Seeing that the primary suspect seems to be my uncle, I suppose it was better to do it today then never. Maybe another slave-training worm will come crawling out into the open, and become the next suspect as Karsten's failed assassin."

Rialla could only see his legs from where she was sitting, but she didn't have to see his face to understand how he was feeling. "I'm sorry, Laeth. It might not be him. The slave girl could have belonged to someone else."

"No," he replied. "I told Terran that I had seen an unusually colored slave girl arrive, and he said she was Uncle's. She died last night."

"She might have been from somewhere that I've never been. There are a number of peoples in the far South, by the salt seas or over the sea, that I have never seen. My empathy is not so infallible that I could tell for sure she was from the East." Rialla was responding to the misery in his voice rather than out of any conviction of her own.

"I don't doubt that the girl was from the East. It's all right, Ria, you don't have to make excuses for him. Even if he isn't trying to kill Karsten, he is not the man I thought he was. He is not only a slave trainer, but a slave trader." He gave a half laugh. "You know, it probably wouldn't have bothered me before I met you."

Laeth sat up on the bed and crossed his legs underneath him, ignoring the damage his boots were doing to the bed tick. "I always wondered where he got his wealth, but I was never interested enough to find out. Before he inherited the Winterseine estate from a cousin, the only land he owned was a small property in the South, good for farming but not much else. Everything that Grandfather had went to Father, and then Karsten. If Uncle earns his money through slavery, it gives him a definite motive for killing Karsten."

Rialla reached up and touched him on the knee, a rare gesture from her. "Lady Marri might not have been far off when she claimed someone was trying to blame you for the assassination attempts. If Winterseine manages to pin the blame on you, then he gains control of all the wealth Karsten holds, as well as a good deal of the power."

He gave her a tired smile. "I suppose we'll just have

to see to it that my brother doesn't get killed. Then I won't have to worry."

THE GREAT BALLROOM HAD BEEN CLEANED AND POL-ished for the occasion. Even its healthy size was barely capable of handling the crowd of people who had come to celebrate the birthday of the most powerful lord in the realm. There was scarcely room to stand, let alone dance.

The gentry, and the more wealthy merchants and farm-ers of the surrounding areas, had been invited to mingle with the powerful aristocrats. Mostly, thought Rialla as she dodged through the crowd with the cool glass of ale she had brought from the kitchens, so that Karsten could house some visitors with the local gentry rather than try-ing to cram them even tighter in his keep.

She had gone on many such errands this evening, al-lowing her to mingle despite her slave status, but she'd managed to overhear nothing more interesting than a clan-destine affair. She'd managed to avoid Lord Winterseine, chiefly because he had not sought her out, but she found herself constantly aware of his presence.

Approaching Laeth, Rialla observed that his little group had been invaded by Lord Karsten and Lady Marri. Laeth's brother looked pale and had spent the better part of the ball sitting down on one of the couches set up here and there along the edge of the room. Marri kept her hand on his arm and her eyes lowered, like any good Darranian wife. Laeth's cousin Terran stood quietly in the back-ground with several other young men.

". . . lucky that the healer is as good as he is." Rialla caught the tail end of Laeth's statement as she handed him the vessel she carried.

"Indeed," agreed Karsten, "I sent an invitation to him this morning requesting his presence here so I could suit-ably reward him."

"Did you offer him enough of a bribe that he would show up? If you don't express your gratitude to him, peo-ple might think that you were lacking in manners."

Laeth's comment drew a gasp from someone, but his brother only laughed.

"As a matter of fact, I told him I wanted to talk to him about reducing the amount of payment that the village owes me," said Lord Karsten, exchanging a boyish grin with Laeth. "If that doesn't make him show up, I don't know what will."

"Lady Marri looks thirsty," observed Laeth laconically. "Would you care for something from the kitchens? Some ale, perhaps?"

"Please," she agreed. With a gesture, Laeth sent Rialla scurrying back to the kitchen.

She was almost to the door when some instinct caused her to spin around and look up. In a corner of the domed ceiling a shadow coalesced and condensed until it took on a monstrous, writhing, floating form that seemed to swim through the air as if it were buoyant.

Someone else noticed the thing and screamed. The creature, now fully materialized, slowly twisted through the air toward Lord Karsten like a giant snake with tentacles. Then it hesitated, as if something caught its attention. At the same time, Rialla felt a tentative touch on her mind; gentle and seductive, it froze her where she stood.

The thing shifted direction with a swiftness that something that size shouldn't have, whipping its tail behind it with an audible crack. Green and brown patches of scraggly fibers that looked remarkably like weeds hung here and there from its body, dropping off as if the creature had leprosy. The end of its tail was armed with sharp black spikes that glistened wetly in the light of the ballroom chandeliers. The only bright color on it was the red of its eyes, all six of them glittering like a king's ransom of rubies as they focused on its prey—Rialla.

Rialla absently took a step closer to it, as it hovered slightly in front and above her. While she was standing there, the better part of the crowd fled the room in a blind panic, until the space around her was unoccupied, leaving only a knot of people near Lord Karsten on the far side of the room. It stretched out one of its black, cordlike tentacles and touched her carefully, ruffling her hair.

There was no pain, only a slight tugging to indicate what it was doing, but the contact opened it to her empathic senses, and she knew its nature. Older by far than any creature she'd ever touched in that manner, it too was empathic. It fed on emotions until there was nothing left, then consumed the body of its victims—she could feel its anticipation.

The creature was too alien for Rialla to pick up any but the most basic of memories, but she could tell what its intentions were; finding an empath was an unexpected treat—something it hadn't fed upon before.

Casually, giving her no warning, it projected a stray thought, and Rialla screamed in terror that she could feel the thing absorb—but the terror broke her trance. Frantically, with a dancer's agility, she twisted out of the cord and ran. Grabbing a gilt-edged sword hanging from the nearby wall, Rialla ripped it from its mounting and held it in front of her with practiced ease. She could taste the blood where she had bitten her lip.

The sword was obviously made for decorative purposes—it was ill-balanced and unwieldy. It was also, unfortunately, dull. She thought wryly that she would more likely be able to bludgeon the thing to death with the sword than cut it.

Another black cord stretched tentatively toward her. When she struck out at it, it merely wrapped itself around the sword and tugged it gently away, dropping it carelessly on the floor out of Rialla's reach.

Muttering a filthy word, Rialla grabbed a black cast-iron candle holder and knocked the candle off the sharpened spike at the end. The candle snuffed itself out on the floor.

The candle holder was almost as good a weapon as the sword. The point was sharp enough to skewer almost anything, but it was only two hand-spans long. Judging from the creature's size, that was almost long enough to enrage it. The holder was also heavy; she could just manage to hold it if she rested the base on the floor. Unless the creature was as stupid as an enraged boar, her makeshift weapon wouldn't do her any good. From what she could sense, the beast was smarter than she was. Though she had strengthened her mental protection as well as she could, she felt the creature laugh at her.

Rialla dropped the end of the useless candle holder and stepped back to avoid its bounce. Then, with deliberate calmness, she waited for the creature to touch her again. There was one weapon she hadn't tried. Though she had never done anything like it before, she knew that it was possible to turn the creature's attack against it. If she were strong enough.

A slender cord wrapped itself around her neck so gently it almost tickled. Sweat trickled down Rialla's neck as she waited for its mind to touch hers. When it did, she welcomed it—luring it deeper and deeper. Then with a savage, desperate wrench she tore down the scarred barriers that kept the emotions of everyone around her out of her mind, and poured everything she could gather from the crowded ballroom into the creature's mind. Theoretically, if she could rid herself of it fast enough, only a token of the full effect would touch her.

Momentarily, she caught something out of the crowd . . . a voice in her head, Lord Karsten's . . . betrayal and surprise—hot pain that faded into the nothingness that she recognized as death. There were a jumble of emotions from people near Karsten's body. Ignoring the import of Karsten's murder, she fed his emotions and death into the mind of the creature that she battled.

The thing struck her with its tail, trying to break her concentration, laying open the large muscle in her thigh. She fed the burning pain back to it. The creature twitched and fought frantically, as if it faced a physical weapon, losing control of its thoughts as it tried to flee. She sensed the opportunity and thrust its own terror back into it.

When its heart burst under the adrenal surge, she frantically tried to close her mind. With an ear-shattering wail the creature fell heavily and lay silent and unmoving.

Rialla slowly became aware that she was on her hands and knees and that the floor was wet. The smell of half-rotten plants was thick in the air. As the minutes passed, she knew that she had to find the strength from somewhere to make sure that no one touched her. She could feel people moving closer as the stillness of the monster gave them courage.

If one of them decided to help her, they were likely to suffer the same fate as the creature that she'd killed. She didn't have the control to shield her empathy against such an invasion.

There weren't many people left in the ballroom, which made her condition slightly more bearable. Through her weak barriers she could sense Laeth and the tearing grief that he felt at his brother's death. Rialla could feel Lord Jarroh's rage and Marri's surprise at the depth of sorrow that she felt.

The healer must indeed have accepted the lure that Karsten had offered him. Rialla heard his voice ring clearly through the abandoned room, calmness in the insane clamor of the ballroom. "Lord Karsten is dead. The knife punctured his heart and left lung; he died almost instantly. I am sorry, but there is nothing I can do."

Someone was getting too close. Rialla managed to say hoarsely, "Stay away." He wasn't listening, so she added hoarsely, "It might not be dead." That made him back away fast.

There were too many thoughts in her head. She needed to rest before she could block everyone out. The stone was cold against her cheek, cold and wet.

"No. Stay back, Lord Laeth. Unless you want to end like that thing over there. Give her some time." The healer again. Tris. Someone who would keep the people away until she could pull up her barriers.

She relaxed and concentrated on retrieving her barriers,

but she loosened her control too soon. She should have known how well Laeth followed directions; she felt his intention just an instant too late. When he touched her, she screamed, trying frantically to shield him from the confusion of emotions, his and hers. Mercifully, she passed out just after Laeth did.

# FOUR

Rialla awoke with a smile. During the short space of time before full awareness descended, she savored the unusually strong sense of well-being like a sliver of ice on a hot day. She opened her eyes with reluctance as her memory returned.

Instead of the gray stone walls she'd grown used to, the room she was in was dominated by wood. The floorboards were varnished and lovingly polished to a high gloss. The walls were flatboard interlocked and darkened with oil. Across the room was a large window, extravagantly made of clear glass that flooded the room with light from outside.

The room was minimally furnished with the bed, a small table in the far corner and a small woven rug. The total effect was spartan and spacious: the warm colors of the woods and the red and yellow bedclothes kept it from feeling unwelcoming. It seemed obvious that she wasn't in Westhold, but she didn't have the slightest idea where else she could be.

Rialla sat up and caught her breath at the sharp pain in her left thigh. She remembered being hit by the swamp creature's tail, but at the time she'd been too caught up in the battle to assess the damage.

She sat up stiffly and tugged the unwieldy quilt off her leg, swinging both of her feet off the bed. A thick bandage of unbleached cotton covered her thigh from hip to knee. Underneath the wrappings, her leg throbbed painfully, though she hadn't felt it at all when she woke up. Rubbing her head, which was also starting to ache, she tried to reconstruct what had happened in the ballroom, so she could figure out where she was and what she was doing here.

It was difficult to sort out the mixture of other people's emotions and thoughts, but she could piece together a little of it. She knew that Lord Karsten was dead. She'd felt him die with a brief burning pain as a sharp knife slid between his ribs and into his heart.

Someone saw it happen, saw *Laeth slip the knife in*— Lord Jarroh, that's who it had been. His thoughts had a familiar touch; she could remember his rage from her days as a dancer at the club in Kentar.

Rialla shook her head in frustration. She *knew* that Laeth hadn't killed his brother; she had felt his grief and rage also when he saw his brother fall. Why had Lord Jarroh seen something that hadn't happened? Where was Laeth? Why was she here?

Ignoring her wounded leg, Rialla managed to set her feet on the floor, but that was as close to standing up as she was going to get. Frustrated, she reached empathically to touch Laeth and assure herself that he was well. It wasn't until then that she realized the scars that had limited her ability were gone, as if they had never been. The battle with the monster must have finished what the death of the Eastern empath had begun.

She found the mouse in the wall, and a deer eating grass in the forest nearby. But she couldn't touch Laeth—or anyone else for that matter. Experimentally, she constructed the shields that would protect her from unwanted contact. Her awareness of the deer and then the mouse faded. She dropped the shields again, to look for anyone she could read.

She touched something else. It felt familiar, as if she'd just been dreaming about it. Without willing it, a smile began to spread across her face. It wasn't what she was used to feeling when she touched a living creature. She received no emotions, no thoughts; just beauty—as if a sculptor had learned to work in a new medium and created something extraordinary. Something just for her.

Fascinated, she drew closer to it. She was so absorbed in her study that when the door opened and the healer, Tris, walked in, he startled her. She instinctively closed off her gift and assumed the blank face that slaves normally wear.

Now, where had he come from? With her barriers down and her talent free, she should have been able to sense him before he'd gotten that close. Although she couldn't read Winterseine without touching him, she'd been able to tell where he was. She must have let herself be distracted by the . . . whatever it was that she'd been sensing.

At least his presence gave her some clue as to where she was. From that and the herbal smells wafting through the room's open door, she concluded she was at the healer's cottage in the village of Tallonwood.

"Good morning," he said with suspicious blandness. "How are you feeling?"

She narrowed her eyes at him, trying to read his face. "I have been better," she finally allowed neutrally.

He smiled, humor warming his gray-green eyes as it animated his voice. "I bet you have. You'll feel better if you put your legs back on the bed." He made no move to help her.

She gave him a wary look, but since it was obvious that she wasn't going to be going anywhere soon, she painfully maneuvered back under the quilt.

He waited until she was settled comfortably, before sitting on the end of the bed and leaning against the wall.

He was a big man, and the end of the bed sank considerably with his weight.

"I don't know how much you saw of last night's events." He let the end of his sentence rise in a question.

"I was fairly busy," said Rialla, truthfully enough.

The healer grunted, then said, "Lord Karsten was killed by a knife in the back, while you were slaying the monster. Lord Laeth is locked in the guard tower at Westhold. The evidence against him is quite strong.

"Lord Jarroh himself saw Laeth stab Karsten in the confusion. A guard reported seeing the Lady of the Hold leaving Laeth's rooms late at night. He also apparently launched quite a verbal attack on his brother the night before Karsten died. The only mystery seems to be what happened to the dagger with which Karsten was murdered.

"Several people, including myself, saw it, but it appears to be missing. It was quite distinctive; the hilt was silver and shaped like a coiled serpent with ruby eyes— the one that Laeth was wearing the night Lord Karsten was poisoned. You have probably seen it."

"Yawan," swore Rialla with some heat, forgetting her role altogether. She was left with a real mess to clean up.

"Quite," replied the healer, Tris, relaxing even more against the wall. "It certainly looks as if someone has planned carefully to insure Lord Laeth is blamed for Karsten's death; unless Laeth is stupid enough to have actually done it."

"No," said Rialla. "It wasn't Laeth."

Tris nodded. "Lord Winterseine was anxiously explaining to Lord Jarroh that he had caught his young nephew, Laeth, playing with magic one afternoon when Laeth was a boy. *Obviously* the adult Laeth took magic up again while he was living in Sianim, and transported the monster from the Great Swamp.

"Indeed, I thought Winterseine knew a great deal about the unusual creature. He told Jarroh that the monster feeds on emotions and that you are an empath—not that anyone in the ballroom last night was in any doubt of that.

"*Obviously* Laeth intended the thing to act as a diversion while he killed Karsten. He needed you to draw the beast's attention—so it wouldn't kill anyone it wasn't supposed to. Winterseine explained that he had requested that Laeth return you to him and Laeth refused. Winterseine was surprised and hurt until he understood Laeth's motivation."

"All that you have is my word that Laeth didn't kill Karsten. Why doesn't all this evidence convince you?" asked Rialla finally.

Tris looked at her briefly, sincerity clear in his eyes, and then looked out the window, as if he knew how uncomfortable she was meeting anyone's gaze.

"Aside from my personal opinion of Winterseine?" he asked. "I was watching Lord Laeth while Karsten was stabbed. I didn't see who killed Karsten, but it wasn't Laeth. He was trying to get through the crowd and help you battle the monster."

Rialla looked out the window too, keeping Tris in her peripheral vision. His cordiality was making her nervous; he wasn't treating her like a slave. She liked people to be predictable; she couldn't understand what motivated the healer.

Deliberately, she looked at him until she drew his eye, wanting to watch his face. "Why do you think that I care about what happens to Lord Laeth? I am only his slave."

The healer smiled, and she could see a hint of a dimple under his close-shaven beard. Humor lit his eyes.

"Ah yes, a slave." He rubbed his jaw, as if in thought, and then snapped his fingers. "But I didn't finish telling you the rest of it. Lord Winterseine was here early this morning. It seems that with Karsten dead, he is Laeth's closest relative: as such he is claiming custody of Laeth's valuables, including you. I told him that you were currently too ill to move. Are you sure you are merely Laeth's slave?''

Rialla took an involuntary breath, forgetting momentarily the trepidation she had about the healer. She had been so worried about Laeth that she had forgotten what his imprisonment would mean to his slave. Ren had promised that she wouldn't remain a slave, no matter how the bones fell, but she'd rather not risk it. She also would rather not see Laeth executed for a crime he didn't commit.

The problem was that she couldn't do anything about Laeth or her impending return to slavery. She was effectively immobilized on the wrong side of the Darranian border, with a tattoo that proclaimed her property of Winterseine, who sounded as if he were intent on the death of her closest friend.

She looked at Tris, who had turned back to the window, giving her time to think about his words. She was unsure why Tris sounded so certain that she was not Laeth's slave, but at this point she didn't believe it mattered much. With Karsten dead and Laeth imprisoned, somehow keeping their investigations secret hardly seemed imperative—especially since they had failed so spectacularly at foiling Karsten's murderer. On the other hand, with Tris's cooperation, she might be able to stall Winterseine long enough to do something about freeing Laeth.

"Why are you so interested?" she asked. "I have spoken to you only once, and the only time you spoke to Laeth was to exchange unpleasantries."

Tris drew in a breath and spoke slowly. "I have my reasons," he said. "I don't think that I will tell them to you yet—but I mean no harm to you or Lord Laeth."

Rialla eyed him warily, but followed her instinct to trust him. "I used to be a slave, owned by Winterseine. I escaped years ago, and have been training horses in Sianim. When the Spymaster needed someone to play slave and accompany Laeth here, he recruited me."

When the healer turned to look at her, she lowered her eyes, but continued speaking. "The Spymaster had word that there was a plot against Lord Karsten. It didn't suit his purpose that Lord Karsten be killed, so he sent Laeth and me here to prevent it. As Lord Karsten's brother, Laeth was a perfect choice. As his slave, I was supposed to gather information on who was trying to kill Karsten and why." She shot Tris a quick, wry look. "Unfortunately, it seems that we only made the murder easier by giving the killer the perfect suspect. Laeth has always had a questionable reputation."

Lowering her gaze, she continued slowly, "I believe that the man who killed Karsten was his uncle, Lord Winterseine. He came here with an empathic slave, who died by her own hand the night she arrived. I can't be certain he intended to use her as a distraction for the creature in the ballroom, as he claimed that Laeth used me—I would have thought that she was too valuable for such use. Still, he certainly knew that she could be used that way."

She pulled the fabric of the bedcover tight and released it. "As for magic, I know that Winterseine is a mage. He makes his living as a slave trainer and trader—he was the man who enslaved me. If slavery were outlawed, as Lord Karsten proposed, it would reduce Winterseine's income enormously. With Karsten dead and Laeth blamed for it, Winterseine inherits all of Karsten's wealth and protects his current income as well."

Tris said, "I thought he was not at the hold when Lord Karsten was poisoned."

Rialla shrugged. "He wasn't there, but his servant Tamas was. It wouldn't have been much of a feat for him to slip poison into the food or drink. A trusted servant, even someone else's, is close to being invisible."

She rubbed her temples to alleviate her headache and continued, "There is also the matter of the missing dagger. Any decent mage can tell who wielded a weapon used for murder."

He had started to say something when she heard a

knock from somewhere else in the cottage. He pushed her flat on the bed and put a finger to his lips, then shut the door quietly behind him as he left the room.

She couldn't hear what was said, but she recognized the voice. When Tris, carrying what appeared to be a pile of bandages and a cloth bag, ushered Lord Winterseine into the room, she was lying down with her eyes closed. Winterseine touched her, and she moaned, channeling the pain from her leg to him through his touch, magnified enough that he didn't leave his hand on her for very long.

"He's right, Father," said a voice that she recognized as Terran's. "She still seems to be in much pain. The spikes on the tail of the swamp creature are poisonous. We should leave her here until she's healed or she'll be of little use to us. What good is a crippled dancer? From what I've been told, the healer is the finest in Darran. If she is recoverable, he is the one to do it."

Poisonous, thought Rialla. The healer must be pretty impressive when he can make a tainted wound feel this well in less than a night.

"Very well, Healer," said Winterseine's hated voice, and she felt him pull back the quilt so he could see the tight bandages on her leg. Though she was wearing the gray slave tunic, she still felt exposed without the covering to hide beneath.

"I will be back to see her tomorrow," he continued. "Don't worry about payment. If my nephew is not freed, I will cover the expense. She is a very valuable dancer and well worth the investment—especially if you are able to keep her leg from scarring."

"I will do my best, but not for the sake of your investment." Tris's voice was cold with dislike, and Rialla remembered that Laeth had said that the healer was not overly fond of aristocrats.

"Of course not, my dear man. A healer doesn't think of such things as money when he is curing the sick." Lord Winterseine's tone was amicable, disguising the dig in his words. Everyone knew that this healer was infamous for charging exorbitant rates.

Apparently the dig bothered Tris not at all. He said coolly, "My rates increase with the irritation that the case gives me. Yours have just doubled. You have seen her. The door is in the same place it was when you entered."

Winterseine laughed, but he left all the same.

Rialla and the healer waited until they heard the outside door open and shut. Tris stuck his head into the other room to make sure that they had left, then resumed his position on the foot of the bed.

"So," he said warmly, as if the frost in his manner had never been, "what do you plan to do now?"

"First," she said, "I need to get Laeth out of the guard tower. I suspect that unless Lord Winterseine makes a personal confession, Laeth will hang for the death of his brother."

"I can help with that," said Tris. He closed his hand and then opened it to show her the yellow rose that he held. Bringing the flower to his nose, he smelled it once; then he handed it to Rialla and continued to speak. "I have talents that might prove useful."

She looked at the rose, wondering if he used magic or sleight of hand. Deciding it didn't matter, she granted him a tentative smile. "Thank you."

"And after you free Laeth?" asked Tris thoughtfully.

"Gods," she said, "don't ask me. I'm a horse trainer, not a spy. I suppose I'll go back to Sianim with Laeth." Something about retreating to Sianim left a bad taste in her mouth, but she didn't know what else to do.

Tris got to his feet. "You're not going to be capable of anything unless your leg is ready to hold you, so let me take a look under the bandage."

He drew a knife from a boot sheath, and pushed the blankets to one side. With a brisk efficiency that said much for the sharpness of his knife, Tris cut away the bandage on her leg.

From the looks of the wound, a spike had hit just above

her knee and ripped through muscle almost to her hip. The flesh around the wound was mottled with bruises. There was a poultice over the torn area, a green mass that made the slice look even nastier than it felt, but what caught Rialla's attention was the smell.

She grabbed her nose quickly. "What is that stuff?"

Tris looked up momentarily from his perusal of the injury, unperturbed by the foul odor. "I'm not sure exactly what kind of poison the spirit-eater uses. This dressing should have drawn out most of it. Most of the odor is the poison, though the leaves have a strong scent of their own. I'm going to put the same dressing back on until it quits smelling, then I can start your healing."

He separated an oil-treated cloth from the rest of his pile and lay it out on the bed, then taking a small pair of pincers from the bag on the floor, he began pulling the large green leaves off her leg. Once he had most of the big pieces off, he carefully picked out the bits and pieces of greenery that remained. Sweat beaded on her forehead, and Rialla bit her lip as the gentle probing induced the pain she had expected earlier.

Tris gathered up the mess and left the room, returning shortly with two pans of steaming water which he set on the floor. He dipped a clean cloth in the water, then wrung it out and set it on her leg; he repeated his action several times as the cloth cooled down. When he was finished, the wound was clean and Rialla was trembling.

He took a carefully wrapped bundle out of the bag and unwrapped it, revealing dried leaves as long as Rialla's forearm and twice as broad. He took five or six and lay them in the clean pan of water to soak.

"Here now," he said, and his normally slight accent was thicker with sympathy. "I'm going to put a bit of this powder on the cut. It should help the pain in a bit." As he spoke, he sprinkled a yellow powder lightly on the wound, holding the torn skin open with one hand. "It's an anesthetic made from a plant I caught some local youngsters chewing on."

He started to put the softened leaves on her leg and chose to distract her with his story. "One of them had a bit too much, and I had a time keeping him from cutting off his hand. He thought that a maggot had gotten into it and was eating its way to his heart.

"I gave the whole village a lecture on the weed. In case that doesn't work, whenever I run into a patch of the stuff I make sure that the taste keeps anything with a tongue in its mouth from eating it. I've found and treated enough of the plants that most of the village young ones steer clear of it; but as a topical anesthetic it has few equals."

"You're a magician?" Rialla questioned, hesitantly. Darran was not a place where anyone admitted to being a wizard, but Tris's words had invited the question.

"Magic-user," he said as if he were correcting her, but as far as Rialla knew the two were the same thing. "Does that bother you? You are not Darranian."

She shook her head. "No."

He pulled the remnants of the old bandages out from under her leg, where they were keeping the sheets clean, and began strapping her leg with new wraps. "There, almost finished."

A bell rang stridently in the other room, and he called out, "Coming. No need to ruin my ears." He finished what he was doing, gathered up the mess and headed toward the other room. "You might try to rest up. I'll be back in to check on you when I am through."

Rialla shut her eyes and endured the throbbing of her leg for a few minutes before the pain started to lessen. As soon as the powder numbed the wound, she fell asleep again.

When she woke up, the small table had been pulled up beside her bed. The surface of the table was inlaid with light and dark wooden squares, forming a game board. The squares were occupied by small wooden game pieces carved in the shapes of animals, real and imaginary.

The pieces lined up on her side of the board had been

darkened by oil until they were nearly black. On the other side of the table, seated on a stool he must have pulled from another room, Tris was carefully lining up similar game pieces that were fashioned from a blond wood.

Without looking at her, Tris said, "This is a game that my father taught me, and now I am going to teach you. You would call it 'Steal the Dragon,' and," he held up a winged lizard carved with loving detail, "the object of the game is to steal the other person's dragon."

He explained to her in careful detail how to develop strategies, and the importance of stealth and deceit, following his lecture by saying, "Of course, you realize all I have just imparted to you won't help you at all. The only way to learn to play is by playing."

Rialla had noticed earlier that she was unable to stay wary around the healer; he simply wouldn't allow it. He ignored her silences and treated her as if they'd known each other for years.

After the first twenty moves of the game, Tris gave her bland face a piercing look under his heavy eyebrows and said in a menacing rumble, "*Woman,* who taught you how to play?"

In stunned disbelief, Rialla heard herself giggle. She had never heard such a ridiculous sound come out of her mouth, and she pulled the quilt up to her face to keep the silly sound from coming out again.

When she was sure that she had it under control, though laughter still pulled at the corners of her mouth, she said, "There is a woman in Sianim who has taught that game to everyone she can con into it. She hosts a tournament at least once a week. She says that it keeps the rabble off the streets and trains them to be devious, an important skill for a mercenary."

Tris growled at her and made his move. As the play progressed, the healer's face grew darker, and it took him longer to move his pieces. Rialla decided that he was playacting more than anything else, because his shoulders were loose and his movements easy.

She took one of his pieces. He glowered at her beneath his heavy brows, leaving her fighting the urge to laugh.

Darkness fell, and with an impatient wave of his hand the oil lamps on the walls lit themselves, and Tris returned his attention to the game, ignoring Rialla's start at the casual way he used magic. All the magicians she'd ever seen tended to use it sparingly.

Watching the healer, Rialla wondered why the thought of his anger didn't make her afraid the way other men did. If any other man, even Laeth, had growled at her the way Tris had, she would have been bristling with defensiveness, despite knowing he was only teasing. Why was it that when this total stranger glared at her, she laughed?

Experimentally she lifted her shields and stretched out the fingers of her talent. She'd already discovered she couldn't read him outright, but maybe she could learn something if she were focused on him. She reached out and touched—then drew back startled.

She *had* felt him before. *He* was the fascinating presence that she'd sensed when she woke up in the healer's cottage. The being so different that she hadn't even realized he was human.

"Your move," he said.

She closed her talent off again, reluctantly. Almost absently she moved a piece and went back to her thoughts. With Winterseine and the few other magicians that she'd tried to read, she'd been able to discern no more than their presence unless she was touching them. She'd concluded that the discipline required to control magic gave magicians involuntary shields against her talent. She wondered why Tris was different.

"Your move." There was a hint of satisfaction in his tone that caused her to turn her attention back to the game.

The last move she'd made had undone the strategy she had been working on for the past several hours. Any move that she made would leave her dragon for Tris to steal, and if she didn't move (also an option), he could steal her dragon anyway.

"Give up?" he asked, a little more eagerly than he should have, and she closed her mouth and returned her attention to the board.

"Not yet," she answered. There was something that she was missing; she stared intently at the board. There was nothing she could do to protect her dragon, but maybe there was something that she could do to get his. With a triumphant smile she took her rat and moved it to the same space that was occupied by his dragon. "Theft!" she claimed triumphantly.

"Thief," he acknowledged with a betrayed look at the board. He gathered the pieces and put them in the drawer of the little table with the same manner that a mother would use to put her children to bed. By the time he was finished, he had a broad smile on his face. "That's the first good game I've had since I came here. Rematch tomorrow. Now, you get some sleep."

She slid down the bed and pulled up the covers, and Tris waved at the lamps. Compliantly, the small flames extinguished themselves.

"If you need anything, just ask," said the healer. "I'll be on the other side of the door. Good dreams."

"And to you," Rialla replied with a yawn.

The next morning the dressing on Rialla's leg still smelled like rotten onions, so Tris replaced the old leaves with fresh ones and covered her thigh with a new bandage. When he was finished, he brought in two bowls of thick porridge and chatted lightly while they ate breakfast; then he left to go collect some herbs he needed.

Rialla waited until he was gone before experimenting with her newly recovered empathy. If she were going to use it to rescue Laeth, she needed to know how well it was working.

Releasing her shielding made her feel exposed. She shifted uncomfortably and pulled the bedcovers up under her chin, as if physical covering would make up for her lack of mental protection; but she didn't reestablish her barriers.

By the time she felt the healer near the cottage, she was sweating and exhausted—but she knew that she was almost as strong as she had been before Winterseine captured her. If she couldn't work as effortlessly, at least her shields were stronger.

When Tris came into the room to check on her, he frowned and felt her forehead. "How do you feel?"

Rialla shrugged carefully; the work that she'd been doing gave her a nasty headache. "Not too rough."

Tris grunted in acknowledgment and then said, "Lunch first, then a nap."

Rialla fell asleep before he got back with lunch.

RIALLA OPENED HER EYES SOMETIME LATER TO FIND THE oil lamps on and Tris muttering at the game board, apparently playing a game of Dragon against himself.

She watched for a while and then said, "Black wins. If you move the black sparrow to the left three spaces, then the black stag can take the white dragon in two moves."

Tris tilted his head at the board, then got up from his stool. He moved around the table to stand by the bed and look from Rialla's point of view. He rubbed his beard and slanted an assessing glance at Rialla over his shoulder.

He began to reorganize the board for a fresh game. "Are you ready for a rematch?" he asked.

Rialla gifted him with a lazy smile and sat up. "Ready to lose again?"

He raised an eyebrow, and with laughing eyes he bared his teeth at her and made his first move. "Enjoy yourself now, sweetheart. You won't feel like it later."

The room was silent and all but humming with intensity—Tris was as competitive as Rialla. After twelve moves Tris had it won. He sat back and relaxed while Rialla stared furiously at the board, looking for a way out.

"Tell me about Laeth," asked Tris while he waited for Rialla to move.

Rialla looked at him warily. But after another glance at the board, she decided that he wasn't trying to distract her. With a shrug, she moved one of her mushrooms and killed his rat, knocking the piece lightly off the board as she set the mushroom in its place. "What do you want to know?"

Tris moved a frog and said, "It takes an unusual Darranian to make a successful mercenary."

Rialla frowned at the game, still unwilling to concede. She poisoned his frog with her other mushroom before she spoke. "Laeth is . . . I suppose 'unusual' works as well as anything else. He's a genuinely nice person who takes great pleasure in shocking people, especially people he doesn't like.

"He's a decent fighter in practice, and I understand that he's better when the fighting is real—I stay out of the real battles. I'm a horse trainer, not a soldier . . . or a spy either, for that matter." Rialla paused to think, and then smiled. "He's also a diabolically clever practical joker." She shrugged, uncertain how to proceed.

Tris had waited for her to finish talking before he moved an owl to eat the mushroom that had killed his frog. Without looking up as he took her piece off the board, he said, "I take it that you are friends as well as associates."

Rialla gave him a keen glance and asked, "Why are you so interested in Laeth?"

Again a heavy, mobile eyebrow crept up toward Tris's hairline. "I only met him twice. Both times were under less than ideal circumstances. If I'm going to help you get him out of Westhold, as it looks like we'll have to, I'd like to make sure that I'm risking my skin for someone other than the arrogant aristocrat that I met when Karsten was poisoned. So, how well do you know him? Is he a lover, a friend, an acquaintance . . ."

"He's a friend, a good one," Rialla answered. She looked back at the board, and missed the subtle relaxation of the healer's shoulders that would have told her that her answer was far more important to him than he'd indicated. "He wouldn't make a good lover—he's too much in love with Marri."

"Karsten's wife?"

Rialla shifted her wolf an extra square since Tris wasn't paying attention to what she was doing. She nodded her head in response to his question and then explained, "Not that he'd do anything about it. He was in love with her before she was betrothed to Karsten. When he found out that she was to marry his brother, Laeth left Darran and turned up in Sianim. Marri came to Laeth's room to warn him that someone was trying to blame him for the attempted poisoning."

Tris nodded, took Rialla's wolf off the board and replaced it with his fox. Rialla objected hotly to the implicit accusation that she would try and take advantage of his inattention and move extra spaces, a practice that was legal only if your opponent didn't notice what you'd done.

Tris crossed his arms and held his position. Pouting, Rialla killed his fox with her remaining mushroom. The rest of the game was mercifully short; Rialla didn't enjoy losing.

RIALLA AWOKE SOMETIME IN THE MIDDLE OF THE NIGHT to the sound of violent pounding on the cottage door. She sat up and waited, unable to leave the bed.

She heard a woman's voice. The words didn't penetrate the door, but the tone was frantic. It was answered by a lower rumble that she assumed was Tris's. A moment later the healer entered the room, followed closely by the small, cloaked figure of the Lady of the Hold.

This time Tris lit the room more conventionally, by lighting a candle with flint and steel and using it to kindle the lamps.

Marri took off her cloak and looked around for somewhere to set it. Finally she simply dropped it to the floor. She looked as though she hadn't slept for several days. Her complexion was gray, and dark circles surrounded her eyes.

"Rialla," Marri said, her voice hoarsely urgent. "Laeth told me that I should come to you if I needed assistance. I don't know who you really are, or what you are doing with Laeth, but I need . . ." She stammered a little. "*He* needs help, and I don't have anyone else to go to. Lord Jarroh wants revenge, and he's convinced that Laeth killed my husband."

Rialla nodded and patted the side of her bed. "Sit down," she said briskly. Marri perched on the edge, as far from Rialla as she could.

Tris pulled up his stool and tried to appear innocuous.

"It doesn't sound like Laeth had much of a chance to tell you anything," commented Rialla. "Laeth is a good friend of mine"—she looked pointedly at the distance that Marri had left between them—"nothing more. We were sent from Sianim to prevent the murder of his brother. You can judge our success for yourself." Rialla shrugged and ran a weary hand through her hair. "I hope I'm more successful at preventing Laeth's hanging."

"They're not going to hang him; they're going to draw and quarter him," said Marri in a small, shaky voice, "tomorrow morning."

"What?" exclaimed Rialla, throwing her blankets back and jumping to her feet. Tris's hand was there to catch her when her leg failed. "Whatever happened to a 'fair and deliberate trial'?"

"Lord Jarroh has declared that there isn't any doubt of his guilt. Lord Winterseine will swear he saw Laeth stab my husband," she replied, shrugging hopelessly. "So I came to you."

"Scorch it," said Rialla in frustration, "how in the name of Temris am I going to be able to help him with this plaguing leg?"

Tris abandoned his mild demeanor and pushed Rialla back down on the bed, saying, "Stay there. Now, miss," he turned to look at Marri, "can I trust you to keep your tongue to yourself?"

Marri nodded mutely.

"Well enough, I suppose," Tris said, turning to Rialla.

He reached down, pulled his knife and sliced the fresh bandage off her leg. The leaves smelled as bad as the last set he'd removed. The healer's face was grim as he peeled the dressing away.

"I can heal your leg enough that you can walk on it, but you're chancing your life. If that poison isn't out of your system, it could still kill you," he said.

"If it's my time to die, this is a good night for it. Better that than sit idle while Laeth is killed," replied Rialla briskly.

"Your choice, lady," acknowledged the healer in formal tones, as if this were a ritual of some kind.

He placed his hands over her leg and closed his eyes. Rialla's leg tingled and went numb, so she could no longer feel the touch of his skin against hers. Her heart rate picked up until her pulse raced as if she were running in terror and she gasped for breath.

His hands glowed orange in the shadows of the night, as if lit by some inner fire. She could hear Marri's gasp but was too distracted to take notice. If he could heal her like this, Tris was definitely not a common magician; everyone knew healing was difficult for wizards.

Tris pulled his hands away, leaving only a half-healed scar on Rialla's leg, saying, "That's the best I can do and still leave you enough energy to get out of bed."

Experimentally, Rialla got up and flexed her knees to put some strain on her thigh muscles. The leg hurt, but it held under her weight. She flashed a quick smile at Tris and turned to Marri. "What do you know about the tower? How is it set up? How many guards are there, and where are they?"

Marri looked for a minute at Rialla's leg; the angry red scar was invisible behind the tunic that hung to her calves. "Laeth is being held in the top of the tower." She closed her eyes, as if it would help her envision the tower more clearly. "There are four floors on the tower. The lowest level is underground and contains only weapons and supplies that are not being used. There is usually a guard at the stairs that lead down to the weapons room. Besides him on the main floor there are two or three others. The next floor up is where they question the prisoners. They don't always station a guard there, but with a prisoner in the tower there are sure to be several."

Tris grunted and turned to Rialla. "If I get Laeth out of the tower and back here, can you get your horses? You'll need them to get away."

"What do you mean, 'If *I* get Laeth out'? You aren't planning to do this all yourself, I hope. Laeth and I can buy horses here, or at the next village. I'll come with you," stated Rialla.

The healer shook his head. "It will be easier for me to get Laeth out by myself. That healing has tired you more than you apparently yet realize. If Laeth and I have to run ahead of the chase, you won't have the stamina to make it.

"The horses are necessary," he continued. "There are none to spare in the village. Even if there were, Lord Jarroh is not the most reasonable of men and likely would hold the owners responsible even if you steal the beasts. If you try to make it on foot to Riverfall, which is the closest village, the guards will overtake you before you have traveled half a league. The horses are probably going to be more difficult to get out than Laeth is—at least he can climb over the wall."

Rialla frowned at him. "Why are you doing this?"

The healer gave her an enigmatic smile and replied, "If you wish to, you can ascribe it to a hearty dislike of both Lord Jarroh and Lord Winterseine. Given a chance to annoy either or both, I'll take a little danger in exchange."

Rialla had the feeling that it was the best answer she was going to get.

"What can I do?" Marri asked.

"Just what you have done," replied Tris. "If someone sees you out and about tonight, you'll be held responsible for Laeth's escape. That is a crime that holds the death penalty as well, even for nobility. If you would like, you can wait here and see him off, then I'll get you back in with no one the wiser."

She looked mutinous but finally nodded her head. Rialla suspected that it was the knowledge that she would be more of a liability than an asset and not any ideas of self-preservation that made Marri agree.

"Do you have any weapons here?" Rialla asked. "The only thing that I brought with me from Sïanim was a knife, and that is in Laeth's rooms in the hold."

"Anything my lady desires," he answered grandly as he walked to the flatboard wall.

He touched it gently, and a section moved in just far enough that he could slide it on hidden tracks behind the rest of the wall, revealing a small closet. A packing trunk occupied most of the floor, but the rest of the closet was dedicated to weaponry, most of it projectile weapons.

Rialla shot Tris a look under her eyebrows. "It looks like a poacher's dream come true. I always thought healers were law-abiding citizens."

He shrugged. "I haven't always been a healer. Poaching has become a favored hobby of late. Most of this is useless for combat, but there should be a knife or two and I think that there might even be a sword."

There was a sword, heavier than Rialla was used to wielding, but it would work. She had to borrow one of Tris's belts so she could wear the sword sheathed. She struggled with the braided leather before finally wrapping it twice around her waist. The sheath was too high for an easy draw, but she couldn't afford to be too particular.

She also borrowed a dark-colored tunic and trousers since her slave's garb was too light-colored to skulk around in effectively. Although everything was too big, a few lengths of rope tied here and there, as well as Tris's belt, made the outfit workable.

Tris took a wicked-looking staff, as tall as he and studded at both ends with metal points, and pulled the door back into place. Even knowing that it was there, Rialla couldn't detect any sign of the door once it was closed.

Rialla followed Tris out the door, leaving Marri alone in the bedroom.

The workshop was as busy as the bedroom was spartan. Large windows were cut into the three outer walls, letting in the dim light of the waning moon. All of the wall space not devoted to windows was covered with shelves of various sizes, which were in turn stacked with neatly labeled clay and wooden containers. So many bundles of plants hung from the ceiling that it looked like a jungle, and Tris had to bend his head to avoid the flora.

Once out the door, Tris motioned her behind the cottage where the woods began.

"There's a path to the hold through here," he explained shortly.

Rialla concentrated on her footing until they reached the better surface of the path. "How are you going to get Laeth out?"

"Subtlety and a bit of magic," he replied. "Have you thought about the horses?"

Rialla nodded. "I'll get them out through the herald's gate."

"Without alerting the guards?" he asked.

She smiled at him. "You do your part, let me worry about mine."

They quit speaking then. Rialla wished she had taken the time to find where their horses were in the stables, but she'd been too intent on maintaining the appearance of a slave.

They reached the wall of the hold before she was ready. It loomed high over their heads, more of Karsten's improvements. Rialla ran her hands over the freshly cut pale blocks of stone, fingering the edges. The wall was meant to keep back armies, but it was unfinished. Small gaps between the stones made the wall as easy to climb as a

ladder. Rialla raised her hands and got a firm grip in preparation to climb.

"Wait," said Tris in a soft voice that wouldn't carry
to anyone who happened to be on the other side of the
wall. "Your red hair makes you too identifiable. Stay a
moment, and I'll take care of it."

She released her hold on the wall and took a step nearer
to the healer. He touched her hair lightly and closed his
eyes. When he opened them, he looked closely at her and
then nodded. Rialla pulled a strand of her hair to where
she could see it, then let the dark-colored mane fall back
to her shoulder.

"Illusion," he said. "Simple, but it will hold for the
night."

Rialla nodded, and began again to climb; Tris chose
another section of wall and did the same. On top Rialla
noted that the catwalks that were meant to run the entire
length of the wall hadn't yet been built here—making the
descent a simple climb down the inner side of the wall.

Once on the ground they were much safer. Although it
was still too early in the morning for much activity, it
would be easy enough to come up with a reason for legitimate occupants of the castle to be wandering around
in the darkness.

"I'll get the horses and meet you at your home," suggested Rialla softly.

Tris nodded, and replied in a voice as quiet as hers,
"That is as good a place as any. If I'm not back before
dawn, take the woman and go to Sianim. Luck be with
you, dancer." He turned toward the tower.

"And with you"—she wasn't sure why she added the
next word—"shapechanger."

He stopped in his tracks, spinning to look at her. For
an instant she saw a glimpse of something . . . wilder in
his face. But it was only for an instant, and then he was
scowling at her with laughing eyes. "You know so much
of shapechangers you can name me so on such short acquaintance?"

Rialla shrugged and said easily, "The woman who taught me how to play Steal the Dragon is rumored to be a shapechanger. She calls it *Taefil Ma Deogh*." Rialla knew that she couldn't twist her tongue around the syllables so that they sounded correctly, but she thought that Tris would get the point. "She's never *said* that she was a shapeshifter, but she's never denied it either. I've also been around human mages long enough to know that healing is not something that human magic works well on."

"I am not a human wizard," he acknowledged. "Nor am I a shapechanger, though my people are distant kin. *Taefil Ma Deogh* is a very old game, and well known amongst us."

"What are you then?" she asked.

Again he shook his head. "Nothing that you would know. We have been too few for too long. If we live through this night, perhaps I'll tell you about my people."

Rialla turned on her heel and began stalking in the general direction of the stables, murmuring to herself, "If that man makes one more cryptic remark, he may *not* live through this night."

She decided she would look more suspicious if she tried to sneak around, so she strode boldly past the makeshift pens that had been erected to house the animals of the lesser nobles. There was a pair of guards making their rounds, but they paid her little heed.

By the time she reached the main stable, she was perspiring from fear and vowing never to do anything other than train horses again. Before she entered, she drew a deep breath.

Horses were empathic themselves. If she walked in feeling fear, it was bound to cause an uproar in a stable full of warhorses. Rialla closed her eyes and drew in a deep breath of horse- and hay-scented air, trying to pretend she was in one of the barns at Sianim.

Rialla knew the general layout of the stables from her earlier visit. There were stalls along both outer walls and small loose pens in the center. The tack was set in the middle of the aisle between the stalls and the pens, far enough away from either that the horses couldn't nibble at the sweat-salted leather. Rialla suspected the pens were where she'd find their horses, since generally the stalls would be assigned to the hold animals.

The stable was dark inside, and Rialla waited just inside the door, hoping her eyes would adjust to the darkness. A few of the horses nearest to her began shifting as they noticed her unfamiliar presence. Carefully she extended her empathic touch to them, reassuring them that she meant them no harm.

When her vision had gotten as adjusted as it was going to, Rialla stepped forward cautiously until she rested her hand on the top bar of the inner pen. The horses were only darker shadows in the night. Rialla counted on her empathy to help her find the right animals. Rialla had herself trained Laeth's gelding, Stoutheart, though not the mare she'd ridden here. She could have taken the first horses she came to, but both of the Sianim animals were conditioned and of high quality.

Most of the horses ignored her, resting comfortably in the clean straw bed. An aged gray mare walked with Rialla the length of her pen, hoping for an apple. Rialla rubbed the mare's cheekbone where it itched and silently apologized for coming without a treat.

Her horses were in a pen near the end of the barn. The mare stood in a three-footed doze, but Stoutheart whickered softly in greeting. By touch Rialla located saddles and bridles, then readied the horses while they were still in their pen.

Leading the horses out quietly required Rialla to send out a constant reassuring babble to all of the horses they passed, and she released a sigh of relief when she finally made it out of the building.

There was only one way to get horses out of the hold. The main entrance was kept shut and barred at night, but on the other side of the gatehouse was the herald's gate. The gate was actually a narrow tunnel through the base of the wall, designed to allow the passage of messengers when the main gates were closed. Heavy metal doors, locked and barred, were set into the wall at either end of the tunnel.

Rialla was able to lead the horses unseen along the wall, due more to luck than any skill on her part. When they neared the gatehouse, Rialla extended her senses and found each of the guards on duty there and on the nearby wall. If they had been alert and ready for trouble, she would have had to find another way; but they were bored and drowsy. It only took a nudge to send them over into a sound sleep.

She yawned herself before leaving the horses waiting while she searched the guards until she found a large ring of keys.

Rialla opened the first door and continued through the tunnel to open the outside door as well; it would be easier to convince the horses to enter the tunnel if they could see the light on the other side. As she stepped into the tunnel, she noticed that the floor was covered with a metal grating suspended over the ground by a pair of heavy wooden beams. Getting the horses across it was going to be quite a feat of persuasion—and loud in the bargain.

The mare put her front feet into the opening, but backed up quickly at the strange sound of her metal-shod hooves on the grating. The whites of her eyes gleamed in the darkness and her ears were flattened with displeasure. Even with Rialla's gift, the mare wouldn't budge.

Sending soothing thoughts, Rialla backed the mare away and tied her reins high on her neck so that she wouldn't trip on them. Though the mare wasn't trained for a verbal command to stay, as the gelding was, her instincts would keep her near the other horse.

Rialla had tried the mare first because she was smaller. Even throwing the stirrups across the back of the saddle to reduce the gelding's width, she was afraid that the bigger horse's barrel was going to rub the sides of the tunnel all of the way through.

When Rialla led Stoutheart to the mouth of the tunnel, he dropped his nose and blew a puff of air at the strange floor. Using her empathy and soft coaxing sounds to encourage him, she took a step back, tugging once on the rein and then relaxing the pressure.

The gelding put a foot tentatively on the metal floor, flattening his ears at the odd sound as well as the slight flexing of the grate. But Rialla had trained him, and he trusted her to know what would hurt him and what was safe. Deciding that the floor was going to hold his weight, he followed her almost placidly. When he reached the far side, he found a small patch of grass and began to eat.

She commanded him to stay, and started back to the tunnel. Before she reached the opening, the mare bolted through, clanking and snorting, anxious to rejoin her companion.

The open door was sure to send searchers out as soon as the guards woke up enough to notice it. If she closed it and got out over the wall, it could be dawn before anyone realized that Laeth was gone. There was work currently being done on the wall here as well, and the scaffolding on the outside would offer an easy enough method for exiting the hold.

Rialla slipped back through the tunnel, locking the doors behind her. She tucked the key ring back into the guard's pocket and started over the wall.

Unlike the part of the wall that she'd crossed to get into the hold, here there was a newly built, though obviously temporary, catwalk. The guard who slept on the newly constructed stone stairway shifted uneasily as Rialla started up the stairs. He was a veteran, and not one to sleep on duty no matter how tedious. She turned back to the base of the stairs and reinforced her suggestion to give her time to get over the wall before he woke up.

Just as she lowered her protective barriers to project sleep onto the guards again, someone nearby died in an unpleasant, terrifying manner. Rialla tried to shut it out, but was unable to stop before she'd projected what she'd felt. She heard the guards cry out with their comrade's death throes. So much for escaping unnoticed.

She would have sworn if there had been time for it.

The first guard who saw her and attacked was inexperienced, and slowed her only minimally as she staggered for the stairway, and left him to wake up with a headache in the morning.

Before she could gain the stairway, where the veteran soldier waited patiently, two more guards came out of the gatehouse. They moved apart to flank her, one quickly climbing the first few stairs to gain the advantage of height. She ran directly at the one on the stairs, then quickly changed direction, ducking under the stroke the other guard had intended for her back.

Failing to find the anticipated target for his sword, he lurched forward, trying desperately to regain his balance. Using a neat backhand, Rialla hit him on the head with the pommel of her sword and flashed a bright smile as she turned to face the second guard, still standing on the third stair.

He had obviously expected an easy victory and stood peering at the still, silent shadow of his associate. He quickly shifted his attention to Rialla and began to descend. Before he could close with her, she set him on his backside by sweeping his feet out from under him with the flat of her blade. She didn't have to knock him out— he did it himself. Breathing harshly, Rialla ran up several steps to face the warrior who waited for her there.

The first three men had been inexperienced, and unaware of what they were facing. This man had watched her take out his comrades and knew that she was Sianim-trained—it didn't take Rialla long to discover that he was too.

He was good, but she was better, just not enough better that she could get behind him and knock him unconscious. Several times she could have wounded him fatally, but she couldn't force herself to take the opening and end it. Not because she was overly squeamish, but because she remembered what it felt like to kill a man when her empathy was barely functional. She had no intention of killing when her gift was working well.

If she killed this one, there was a fair probability that the act would kill her too. She already had a thundering headache thanks to the three prone forms strewn behind her.

The guard knew as well as she did that she was the better swordsman, and she could feel him thinking of the fate that would fall to his family if he died. His young wife had just given birth to their first child. The widow of a guardsman would have no one to care for her, and he worried.

She might be the better swordsman, but he was stronger than she was and she was beginning to feel a deep weariness—perhaps the effect of Tris's healing, as he had warned. If she did not finish this fight soon, she might not win it.

Her face grim with concentration, she began to force the guard backward up the stairs. While she fought, she reached out lightly and touched the presence that she knew to be Tris—later she would wonder why she found him easier than Laeth.

Sweat trickled down her neck, and she worried that she wouldn't have the stamina to do what she was going to try. The guard reached the top step, and stumbled when he reached for a higher step that wasn't there.

He caught himself quickly, but his stumbling gave Rialla a chance to press home her advantage, until both of them were on the battlement. The wooden boards of the walk creaked underfoot. If they fought too long, someone would look over and see them.

She waited anxiously for Tris to leave the hold, aware that her thigh was beginning to show definite signs of weakening. Her sword arm ached with the force of the guard's blows. He was starting to believe that he might face another day, though he was puzzled that she hadn't finished him when he stumbled over the nonexistent step.

The wall was crenelated to allow archers to fire through the low sections and dodge back behind the higher merlon. Though the top of the wall was well over Rialla's head, the crenels were only hip high. When she knew that Tris, hopefully towing Laeth behind him, was safely out of the castle, she feinted. The guard drew back, giving her the room she needed to jump onto the crenel wall and, in a step, over the other side, landing some distance below, on the slanted platform of the scaffolding.

She slid and stumbled to the ground and called Stoutheart to her by focusing her gift. Only when she was mounted and heading for the cover of the woods did she look to see if the guardsman had followed her leap. Seeing no one, she assumed that he had realized that his heavy mail shirt would hamper his leap, and had retreated to sound a warning.

The clear tones of the alarm bells followed her into the woods.

# FIVE

After Rialla left for the stables, Tris made his way carefully through the courtyard, taking advantage of each bit of cover as if he were stalking game in the forest. He was too well known at Westhold to strike out boldly as Rialla had, but stealth was second nature to him, and his progress was only minimally slower than hers. He was amused to discover that he was enjoying the challenge of this adventure as much as a boy half his age.

The tallest structure at Westhold, the tower stood midway between the hold wall and the keep, overshadowing the squat structure of the nearby guardhouse. It was half again as high as the great wall. Although the tower was older than any other structure in the keep, having been part of the main building of the original fortress, the ancient stones still rested squarely where they had been placed.

He was crouched in the shadow of the guardhouse when the sound of men's voices caused Tris to freeze where he was. He kept his breathing shallow and his body still against the rough-finished wooden wall as three guardsmen passed close to him. Too close for Tris, who wrinkled his nose at the sour smell. He waited until they were safely inside their living quarters before he moved from the darkness and crossed the short open area that separated the tower from the guardhouse.

There was no door into the tower, only a wide opening onto the main floor. One guard stood just inside the door, staring at the night. He was a young man, with the nervous air of a green recruit. His hand rested on the wooden hilt of his sword, clasping and unclasping slowly.

Tris called to his magic, humming under his breath to lend power to his summons. When the magic came, he pulled it around him in a curtain of silence and shadows. He slipped cautiously between the guard and the edge of the aperture.

The inner room of the tower was cramped and bare; the high ceilings made it appear almost empty. It was lit by a number of slow-burning torches that sent shadows dancing against the gray stone walls.

In the center of the room was a circular stone pillar with another doorless entrance, through which Tris could see a narrow, winding stair reaching upward. Just past the central stairway, a man, obviously more experienced than his fellow guardsman, sat on the floor, leaning against the banister of a descending staircase. Patiently he ran a stone in small circles against the edge of a knife blade.

Tris followed the wall, moving slowly to put the stone of the wide pillar between himself and the older guard. He froze motionless when the man looked up and stared directly at him, some instinct alerting him that the atmosphere of the room had changed.

"Nar!" called the younger guard. "There's something outside."

The veteran sighed, laying aside his honing stone. He rolled lightly to his feet and walked without hurry to the younger man's post. Tris took advantage of the guard's distraction to sprint across the room and into the safety of the enclosure that housed the central stair.

The surface of the staircase was worn unevenly, and he was glad of his soft-bottomed shoes that allowed him to feel his way. The twisted stone steps and the enclosing stone walls made Tris, who preferred wood to stone and open air to either, feel uneasily confined.

As the ceilings were high, it took two revolutions of the stairs before another doorless aperture opened into the second floor. From what Tris could see of it, the dimly lit chamber seemed to be a duplicate of the one below. Faint light entered the room from window slits near the ceiling, but most of the light seemed to be coming from a small oil lamp.

A guard sat at his ease on a bench placed near the outer wall. He was carving a small piece of wood by the lamplight. The lamp itself sat on the arm of a chair equipped with thick leather straps. The room was littered with devices of various sorts needed for "persuasion."

Tris continued up the stairs, which narrowed until there was less than a hand span between Tris's shoulders and the stone wall. The last light from the rooms below faded until even Tris's acute night vision ceased to be of service and he climbed by feel alone.

The stairway ended with a trapdoor set into the wooden floor of the upper level, which Tris discovered by slamming his head into it. His spell was sufficient to absorb the noise, but it didn't help the knot on his head. He felt around the edges of the door with his hands until he found the simple wooden latch and released it, catching the door before it hit his head a second time.

Climbing the last few stairs, Tris arrived in a very small circular room. He stepped onto the floor and pulled the trapdoor shut behind him. There was a latch on the upper side as well, though this one was made so a strong pull from below would break it.

Satisfied that the door was securely closed, Tris divested himself of both shadows and silence and called a magelight to allow him to see.

Four oaken doors, heavily barred and framed with iron,

stood at regular intervals in the wall of the room. He opened his mouth to call out, but shut it before a sound escaped.

There was no reason to assume that Laeth was the only one imprisoned in the tower. The less noise that he made finding the Darranian the better off they would be.

Tris moved to the first door and set his forehead against the wood. Stone was cold and dead to him, but wood was like an old friend. When he asked, the oak gave up its secrets to him, allowing him to descry what lay hidden behind the door.

The first room was empty, and Tris moved on to the next. As he lifted his hand, the magic in the cool metal reached out to him. A human mage had ensorcelled the locks; no green mage could have done such a thing with iron.

The magic was so foreign to Tris that he couldn't even discern its nature. He *could* tell that the magician hadn't tainted the oak with his spell. Laying his forehead against the old wood, he ''looked'' inside.

If it wasn't Laeth, it was someone of his height and weight wearing the clothes of a noble. He was shackled hand and foot. He must have put up quite a fight, judging from the care someone had taken that he not be able to move more than a finger.

Tris placed his open hand on the door and sang softly in his own language. With a soft, sighing sound, as if it were very tired, the wood disintegrated into a pile of sawdust, leaving both the lock and the metal structure that had framed the door intact.

Laeth looked up at the light too quickly, and had to duck his head into his shoulder to wipe his eyes free of the light-induced tears.

For all that Laeth was a useless Darranian noble chained hand and foot, he was still a trained warrior. Tris had dealt with enough predators in his life to know that they were at their most defensive when they were trapped. It would, he decided, be wise to wait until Laeth knew that he was a friend before attempting to remove the bindings.

Laeth opened his eyes cautiously, took in the missing door and the magelight hovering behind, and came to the wrong conclusion.

"I'm surprised that even the Spymaster of Sianim found out about my imprisonment so quickly," said Laeth in a soft voice that wouldn't carry far.

"As far as I know, he didn't," replied Tris as quietly, pulling the hovering light source around until Laeth could see him clearly.

The Darranian's eyes widened as he realized, for the first time, who had come to his rescue. Before he could say anything, there was a loud crashing noise from the floors below.

Tris froze, noticing that Laeth held himself still as well. They waited, but no further sound reached them.

Finally Tris stepped over the sawdust and into the cell, his magelight following closely. He propped his staff against a convenient wall and crouched beside the battered Darranian to examine the chains more closely.

As was usual for such objects, they were made of low-grade iron. Iron and its refined cousin were exceedingly resistant to natural magic. Given enough time, the healer might have been able to destroy them with his magic, but time was a scarce resource.

Tris pulled a ring of keys out of his belt pouch and found one that worked on the wrist cuffs.

One night, not long after Tris had come to Tallonwood, a man had knocked on his door in the middle of the night, obviously suffering from a severe beating. He stayed with Tris for two days before leaving as suddenly as he had come. Tris found the set of keys on his worktable the morning after the man left, set out obviously as a payment. When the word came that a notorious thief had escaped his imprisonment at Westhold, Tris had not been surprised.

The set of skeleton keys had proven to be useful several

times since then, and he carried them with him more often than not.

The shackles had been overly tight, restricting the circulation to Laeth's hands and feet. While Laeth worked at returning the feeling to his limbs, Tris looked him over carefully. There were a few abrasions and bruises, especially where the rough metal had cut into his wrists and ankles, but the worst of it seemed to be the swelling.

Tris reached for Laeth's hands. Instead of rubbing them, as Laeth had been attempting to do, he held them gently and began to heal the abused tissue.

The Darranian jerked his hands back and stared at them—probably, thought Tris with some amusement, because he'd never seen them glow before.

"What . . ." Laeth visibly caught himself. The less talking that they did the better; there would be time for that later, if they made it through the night alive. The Darranian gave Tris a frustrated look, then held out his hands again.

Tris worked on Laeth's hands and feet. The healing wasn't as complete as it could have been; Laeth was still having problems moving with any ease. Bruises and stiffness were difficult, and they had already taken too long.

By levering a shoulder under Laeth's arm, Tris managed to get the Darranian through the doorway. He balanced Laeth against the wall, went back for his staff and then touched the sawdust with a finger, and concentrated.

Slowly, the dust shimmered yellow and restructured itself. Like a living creature, it slithered up the iron frame that had reinforced the wooden edges, until a saffron curtain hung where the door had been. There was a snap, as if someone clicked his fingers, and the oak door stood as solid as ever. If a guard came up to look, he would have to open the door to notice that Laeth was gone.

Tris dismissed the magelight and opened the trapdoor again. The tower was quiet below them.

The healer had to help Laeth down the first few steps. Between the heavy staff and the heavier Darranian, negotiating the narrow, dark stairway was awkward work. As soon as the noble seemed steadier, Tris pushed in front.

After they had descended six stairs, Tris gestured for Laeth to wait, and continued down alone. He intended to deal with the guard on the second story himself, leaving only the two on the bottom. As he stepped carefully down the stairs, he noticed that the room was different.

The oil lamp was no longer burning. Faint moonlight from the three windows high in the side of the tower allowed Tris a clear view of the empty bench where the guard had been. The rest of the room was lost in darkness.

He had hoped that he could take on the guards separately and minimize the risk of an outcry, but the guard who had been here had left. He would have to get Laeth and—

He had taken a step back toward the stairs when something caught his attention.

He held very still, listening for the faint noise that instinct told him would come. Something bumped into a piece of furniture, pushing it a short distance across the floor. Tris dropped to a low crouch, hoping he'd escaped detection. His new position allowed him to see under the table and past it to the source of the noise that had first alerted him.

A square of pale light from one of the windows illuminated a pair of rough boots—boots that moved limply forward and back, scuffing the floor lightly. It had been this sound that he'd heard first.

A small gust of wind from the window brought with it the peculiar rotting smell of the swamp and the sweet smell of fresh blood. It appeared that another swamp creature was loose in Westhold: someone wanted to make sure that Laeth didn't miss his appointment with death.

Balanced in a kneeling position, with eyes slitted so they wouldn't glisten in the faint light, Tris waited. The guard's body shifted suddenly across the floor as the killer changed its hold, and the healer got a clear view of what he faced.

Someone had told him once that many creatures of the swamp were things created by one of the old human wizards—the ones who had very nearly destroyed the world with their uncontrolled use of magic. The creature that suckled the neck of the dead man certainly had unnatural origins; Tris could sense a wrongness in her that a natural animal, be it ever so vicious, had never inspired.

From a distance she would appear to be a voluptuous naked woman. Tris was close enough to see the pointed ears, the flesh-colored gills on her neck, and that her long, silky hair grew from her back as much as her head.

The inch-long nails on her hands and bare feet were retractable, sliding in and out as she ate. Her eyes were closed as she concentrated on her meal.

Something around her neck was starting to glow purple; the light grew stronger even as Tris noted it. It was a collar of some sort, and she reached up to bat at it without taking her mouth from her prey.

As the glow intensified, she growled and hissed, jerking back from the body, a bead of blood trickling from the corner of her mouth like a teardrop. She tore at the collar, but it held firm.

To Tris's surreptitious examination, the collar reeked of human magic. If he had to guess, he would have bet gold that the collar contained some geas that forced her to find Laeth and kill him.

Sullenly she left the body and started toward the stairway, not noticing Tris frozen motionless only a length away. He would have let her go if it hadn't been for Laeth—weakened, unarmed, and waiting on the stairs.

When she passed him, Tris rose to his feet and held his staff at ready in one hand. He would wait as long as he could before attacking. The more he knew about her, the better chance he would have.

Tris saw her stiffen as she caught sight of Laeth, seated on the stair and momentarily unaware of the drama that was taking place. She hissed. Tris couldn't see Laeth, but he heard the sounds of the Darranian backing up the stairs quickly.

She made a soft barking sound that might have been a laugh before unleashing her magic. The wordless call that she sang was potent enough that even outside the focus of her magic, the healer could feel the pull.

As Laeth stumbled down the stairs, she backed away before him, leading him into the room with the rest of this night's meal. She was intent on her prey, and didn't notice the healer sinking back into the shadows on one side of her, aided by his own magic.

Laeth took two steps forward, then stopped. He pulled his hands slowly to his ears. She increased the intensity of the summoning, making the tones evocative of sex and need. Sweat beaded on the Darranian's skin as he fought to stay where he was.

Enough, thought Tris, and struck at the side of her head with the metal-strewn end of his staff. It was a blow that would have killed any human, and it knocked her across the room and into an assortment of tables and implements whose purpose was lost to the dark. She returned to her feet in a silent, powerful rush.

Remembering Laeth's earlier reaction, Tris closed his eyes momentarily and called a brilliant flash of magelight, just long enough to blind her, and took two quick steps to one side. She hit the table next to him, reducing it to kindling, and he swung again with his staff, connecting with her shoulder.

She seemed less hampered by the darkness than he was, so he recalled the magelight at a bearable level.

Her fangs were impressive but thin and sharp, more suited to opening the neck of her prey than fighting. Her eyes were slitted, like a cat's, telling Tris that she was indeed more comfortable in the dark room than she would have been in the light. He'd hurt her; one arm hung limply at her side and blood from her head blinded her right eye. The hard, slick floor bothered her; he could see her testing it warily with each step. He had just come to the conclusion that he held the advantage in this fight, when she threw something at him with her good hand.

He raised his oak staff, and it caught the spell, absorbing most of it; the remainder flung him against a wall.

The creature laughed, and she sounded like a young girl. She drew her hand back again, but stopped midgesture. She looked surprised, and blood trickled out of her mouth. She coughed once before falling face forward. Laeth stepped out of the shadows behind her, holding a bloodstained metal bar with a sharp point. Tris assumed that it was something the guards used for torturing prisoners.

Laeth looked at the dead creature and said, "I don't suppose that we have to worry about any more guards."

Tris shook his head. "Not unless we've made enough noise to wake the men in the guardhouse. We'd better get moving." Laeth nodded in agreement and followed, walking only a little stiffly.

On the first floor they found the bodies of the other two guards lying near the entrance. Tris stepped around them and into the darkness, with Laeth behind him.

The healer led Laeth to the outer wall of the keep, near the place where he and Rialla had entered. Laeth climbed the wall slowly, but without incident. Tris waited until the Darranian had reached the top before securing his staff and following him up and over.

They had reached the protective cover of the forest when the alarm bells began to sound. Laeth hesitated, and Tris grabbed his arm and pulled him deeper into the forest. Laeth waited for explanations until they were immersed in the heart of the woods. Then he stopped and leaned against a convenient tree to rest.

"My thanks for your timely intervention, healer," he said, with a wary look. "You'll have to excuse me for wondering why you did it."

Tris shrugged and made himself at home on a fallen log. "Do you believe in prophecy?"

"What?" Laeth asked.

"I was given a riddle . . . a path to follow that might lead to something necessary to me."

"This riddle requires that you risk your life for someone that you have shown every sign of disliking? A man, moreover, who is being held for killing the Lord of the Hold?" questioned Laeth incredulously.

Tris smiled slyly. "Well, now, Laeth of Sianim," the healer said, "my actions tonight might reflect the fact that your associate is the only person I've ever met who can beat me at Steal the Dragon."

"Rialla?" Laeth's voice was suddenly intent. "Where is she? Is she safe?"

Tris nodded. "She's fine." He hesitated, and honesty compelled him to add, "I hope. She should meet us at my cottage with your horses. Your lady is there as well."

"Marri?" There was relief and surprise in the lord's voice.

"She came to let Rialla know that they intended to draw and quarter you in the morning," said Tris.

"Did she tell you that Lord Jarroh intends to prosecute her for conspiracy to commit murder? That she is supposed to be locked in her room? The stupid chit came to warn me of something that any idiot would have noticed and someone saw her—as you've probably already heard. Then she compounded the crime by insisting on seeing me in the tower." Laeth shook his head in exasperation, but there was admiration in his tone as well.

Tris smiled and shook his head, saying solemnly, "That's too bad then. You'll have to take her with you to Sianim."

Laeth looked at the healer for a minute before donning a return smile. "Isn't that too bad? Poor girl." Straightening, Laeth sent an inquiring look at Tris. "Shouldn't we be going, in case someone institutes a door-to-door search of the village? I seem to recall that is the first procedure the hold follows after a felon has escaped."

"They'll wait until dawn; it's too easy to miss

someone hiding in the night,'' said Tris, getting to his feet anyway. ''I imagine she's worrying herself into a frenzy, though. Shall we go and relieve her anxiety?''

WHEN THE TWO MEN REACHED TRIS'S COTTAGE, THERE was no sign of life, except the healer's gelding dozing quietly in its pen.

Cautiously Tris opened the door and slipped in, followed by Laeth. The dim light of the waning moon caught Laeth's bruised face.

A gasp was the only warning Laeth had before a shape launched itself over the counter and hit him with enough force to make him stagger back. Some part of him must have recognized the voice because he grabbed her and spun sideways, deflecting Tris's staff with his shoulder.

''Ouch, plague it! I thought that wizards were supposed to be able to see in the dark. It's only Marri.''

When Laeth was sure that no additional blows were forthcoming, he turned on the lady. ''By the Lord of Death and all his minions, Marri! Don't you know better than to throw yourself on someone without identifying yourself first? If the healer's staff had fallen where it was aimed, it would have knocked the few brains that you have out on the floor; as it is, I think that he broke my shoulder blade.''

His anger would have been more believable if it hadn't been for the fact that he held her close throughout the tirade, his hands gently smoothing the sobbing woman's hair. His voice softened remarkably. ''It's all right, my heart. Don't carry on so. I'm safe now and so are you.'' He looked up to say something to the healer, but Tris had tactfully and silently withdrawn to the back room.

WITH THE ALARM RINGING IN HER EARS, RIALLA TOOK the horses to the high road, where the guards would be sure to see their tracks. Riding Stoutheart and leading the mare, she kept them to a brisk trot they were capable of maintaining for several hours.

When the side road to Tallonwood appeared she trotted on past it, waiting for a dirt road in the opposite direction that would show her tracks well. She wanted no suspicion to fall on the heads of the hapless villagers or their healer.

She also didn't know what shape Laeth was in. It was possible that he was unable to travel on his own. By misleading the guards, she might be able to steal some time for Tris to get Laeth to the cottage.

Just as she turned off the road, she heard the thunder of a mounted party that was rapidly decreasing the distance she had won. Rialla tied the mare's reins so there was no chance that they would cause the horse to fall and left her to follow without being led.

When Rialla leaned forward and asked for a faster pace, the dun gelding responded by stretching its neck flat and breaking into a hard gallop that the more heavily laden and lesser quality beasts of the guardsmen would not be able to match for long. Though she wasn't as well bred as Stoutheart, without lead line or rider to hamper her, Rialla's mare had no trouble following.

When a hunting horn was sounded behind her, Rialla knew that the guards had seen her. She made sure that she stayed just within their eyesight, wanting them to chase her, rather than wandering through the countryside, where they might chance upon Tris and Laeth.

As the guards' mounts tired, Rialla slowed Stoutheart, giving her horses a well-deserved breather. She guided the gelding onto a narrow game trail through the woods. Relaxing slightly, she settled deeper into the saddle, resting her back and legs. She glanced behind her occasionally to make sure that the guards didn't fall too far back.

The trail took a sharp turn through some bushes and over a narrow creek. Rialla looked back to see how far behind her pursuit was, just as her mount pushed through the brush and into a meadow. On the other side of the meadow was another party of guards.

With a series of startled shouts the fresh group broke

into a hard gallop and Rialla turned the dun sharply to the left. She rose in her stirrups and leaned forward as her horse charged through the meadow and crashed headlong into the bushes on the other side, followed by the loyal little mare.

She decided that she'd given Tris enough time and concentrated on losing her followers—if she could. The new party was mounted on fresh horses and hers had already had quite a run. Stoutheart's shoulders were wet with sweat, but both he and the mare were still moving easily.

She could hear the men cursing as they fought through the brush. They were losing most of the advantage of following where her horses had already broken the branches, because there were too many of them; they tried to follow her as a pack instead of one at a time.

Most of the second party were falling behind, but there were a few who were more determined. At least one of them was mounted as well as Rialla—probably a nobleman who had decided to relieve his boredom by chasing criminals.

Stoutheart stumbled to his knees in the rough footing, but recovered quickly. Rialla couldn't see any sign of lameness, so she stayed on him. Time enough to switch mounts when the gelding showed signs of weariness.

They broke through the last of the undergrowth to find themselves on a well-traveled road. Rialla pulled her mount to a trot and looked back to see if there was anyone still behind them.

The nobleman was still in pursuit, but she didn't see anyone else. Turning the gelding in a circle, she aimed him at the stone wall that ran the length of the road, and hoped that there was enough light from the sliver of moon that the horse could see to jump.

Rialla had carefully chosen the horses that she and Laeth took from Sianim. They were grain-fed and in fighting shape, lean and tough as only rigorous daily riding could make them. Rialla blessed that toughness as the gelding cleared the wall with a snort and the mare followed closely on his heels.

She looked back and swore silently. Despite their mad run across the salted field and the leap over the fence on the opposite side, the noble was still gaining ground.

She turned back into the forest, where skill played a greater role and minimized the advantage his fresher horse had. In the rough going, he quit gaining on her, but he didn't fall back either.

Rialla wasn't familiar with the area, and it seemed that the other rider was. Several times he took advantage of shorter, easier routes through the terrain that was rapidly becoming rougher as they raced away from the cultivated areas. The thought that he might be herding her occurred to Rialla just as the gully they were running down deepened and narrowed.

Rialla was afraid that the trap had already closed. The sides of the gorge weren't much taller than the trees that grew here and there along its length, but they were sheer and soft. Rialla searched frantically in the dark for an exit, certain that the canyon would end in another precipitous embankment.

Finally, she found a section of the ravine wall marred by a recent rock slide which had carved a path of skree and detritus that was marginally less steep than the rest of the wall. The trail was not inviting, but Rialla was desperate.

She sent the riderless horse up first, urging it with a swat and an empathic demand. The little mare leapt up like a deer and made it to the top.

Her scrambling hooves kicked loose the rocks, and slowly the whole slope began to move again. When the mare was safely up, Rialla turned Stoutheart at the tide of moving rocks that was their only way out.

True to his name, the gelding dug into the tumbling rock, his breath labored and clearly audible. A lesser horse would have failed, but wild-eyed and sweating, Stoutheart plunged to the top of the rubble and made a tremendous leap upward to solid ground. Dust rose as the slide rumbled to the bottom, leaving behind silence and a sheer wall that no horse could negotiate.

Rialla let the horses catch their breath. She wanted to get a clear look at the man who was so intent on catching her. It was only a moment later that the pursuing horse thundered down the ravine. His rider pulled him up when he saw the silhouette of his intended prey on the top edge of the bank.

She heard him swear. The only way that he was going to get his big horse to where she sat quietly watching was by backtracking to the entrance, and by that time she would be long gone and lost in the darkness.

She recognized his voice, but even if he hadn't spoken a word, she would have known him. Lord Jarroh had a way of carrying his muscular body that was unmistakable at this distance.

His fury caused his horse to half-rear, before it was ruthlessly controlled.

Lord Jarroh raged at her, his voice rough with grief, "Why did you do it? He loved you, damn you. He was proud of the way that you defied the family to train in Sianim. He used to talk about how much he missed his clever brother. But he wasn't as clever, was he? He trusted those he loved too far. He didn't know that the bitch he married wanted his brother's bed. He didn't know that his brother wanted the wealth and power that he possessed."

Rialla had forgotten Lord Jarroh's tendency to make speeches. He obviously thought that she was Laeth. If he knew that Laeth had escaped tonight, then it made sense.

She and Laeth were about the same height, her newly darkened hair was a similar color and length, and she was riding Laeth's horse. A Darranian would never believe that a woman could elude two parties of guards and a Darranian lord—much less that a slave could.

Rialla looked down at the man who had beaten the little slave to death that long ago day in Kentar. Stoutheart shifted restlessly under her and she forced herself to loosen the reins. She was glad that she wasn't carrying a knife or bow, because if she had been, he would be dead—and she had a use for him.

With Karsten dead and Laeth discredited, Lord Jarroh was the only one who would stand a chance of securing the alliance between Reth and Darran: the alliance that would mean an end to slavery in Darran—if Winterseine didn't gain the power of Karsten's estates.

She kept her voice low and husky when she spoke. If Lord Jarroh knew that it was a woman who spoke, he would simply dismiss her words.

"I am not Lord Laeth, merely a compatriot of his from Sianim. My task was to divert pursuit from him, and by now he is safely spirited away. Still, I have a few thoughts to share with you.

"First, why should Lord Laeth choose to murder his own brother in a manner that was sure to put suspicion on him? If he can work magic, why not stage an accident? A misspent arrow or a slip down the stairs should have been easy enough for a man who can control a thing like the creature at the ball.

"Think about the man who is pushing so very hard to accuse Laeth. Who benefits if Laeth and Karsten are both dead? Who depends on income from the slave trade that would cease if the marriage between the princess and King Myr takes place?

"Perhaps you might turn your inquiry in other directions, since Laeth is now well beyond your reach." With a small salute she turned her winded mount into the mountain country at a slow canter.

As soon as the trees hid her, she let Stoutheart drop into a walk. The mare followed as faithfully as any puppy, rubbing her sweaty head against Rialla's leg to relieve an itch under the leather bridle. Rialla only had to find her way back to the healer's cottage before morning, without running into anyone else, and the rescue would be complete.

She was forced to huddle in a thick copse of brush

when she ran into some of the guards resting their horses. She couldn't tell if it was one of the parties that had been chasing her or not. There were probably stragglers scattered all over the woods. Luckily the guard's horses were too tired to bother to whinny a greeting, and Rialla kept hers quiet.

The enforced rest allowed her time to think about her speech to Lord Jarroh. Blowing at an errant strand of hair, Rialla shook her head at the idea that was presenting itself; but neither went away. The hair was an annoyance; the idea a possible solution to this disaster.

The guardsmen left eventually, and Rialla mounted the mare and set off in the general direction of the healer's cottage. She narrowly avoided another group of riders, and heard a third before she found Tris's home.

Cautiously, she waited to be sure that there were no guards nearby. When she was satisfied that she was the only one lurking in the nearby woods, Rialla tied the horses in a thicket of lilacs that grew on the edge of the woods. The heavy perfume of the flowers followed her as she crossed the log spanning the creek that ran behind Tris's home.

"Laeth? Tris?" she called softly as she opened the door.

A quiet-voiced reply led her into the back room, where she found Laeth, Tris and Marri waiting in the dark. They'd left the lamps unlit so they didn't attract the notice of the patrols.

"Greetings," Rialla said wearily, leaning against the door. "It's good to see you in one piece, Laeth."

"It's better to be in one piece than four," he agreed gravely. "What took you so long?"

"I was keeping Lord Jarroh and his men off your tail, so don't take that tone with me," she told him.

Laeth grinned at her unrepentantly, and Rialla smiled back, picking a leaf out of her hair. She took a seat on the floor next to Tris's stool, since Laeth was sitting on the bed with Marri.

"The horses are waiting in the grove of lilacs by the edge of the forest," Rialla said, fighting the urge to close her eyes and sleep. "You'd better get going; it's almost dawn, and if you're found here, innocent people will suffer."

"Aren't you coming too?" asked Laeth.

Rialla shook her head, having come to a decision as she rode through the night. "I'm going to try to prove that Winterseine killed Lord Karsten."

"How?" said Marri with a frown. "No one is going to listen to Laeth's slave."

"No," agreed Rialla, "but they don't have to. I intend to get the proof of Wintersiene's involvement to Ren in Sianim. If he can persuade me to come back to Darran as a slave, he can convince the regency council to convict Winterseine."

"Where are you going to get this proof?" The healer's voice sounded tired, softer than usual.

"Winterseine wants his slave back. If Laeth disappears, he will have legal claim . . ." She noticed that there was a damp spot on the floor near Tris's chair, where she was resting her hand. She touched her fingers to her mouth and said, "Did you know that you are bleeding, Tris?"

"No, am I?" He sounded intrigued. "That creature that we bumped into must have caught me—I didn't notice."

A faint light appeared cupped in one of his hands. As he bent to examine his legs, Rialla noticed that his sleeve was suspiciously dark.

"It's your arm."

Tris pulled the knife from his boot and twisted to tuck the point of the knife under the material of his tunic.

"Here, let me," offered Laeth, who'd crossed the room when Rialla first noticed that Tris was wounded. He took the knife and split the sleeve from shoulder to wrist.

"Just a cut," said Tris after a quick look. "I've got some brandy and bandages out front."

Laeth stayed where he was while the healer left the room.

"By the gods, Ria, I wouldn't take my brother's estates if they were offered to me," he said intently. "I enjoy being a mercenary much more than I ever did being a Darranian lord. Let Winterseine have the plague-ridden land. Don't do this."

Rialla leaned back against the wall and shook her head. "I'm not doing this for you, Laeth; proving your innocence is a side benefit, but that's all it is. If Winterseine gains the power of your brother's estate and title, what happens to the alliance?"

"It fails, as he intends it to," Laeth bit out angrily. "Slavery remains a part of Darranian culture. That's tragic, but slavery has been around a long time. Eliminating it in Darran isn't going to stop it elsewhere. Plague you, Ria, it's not worth the risk of your freedom."

"What freedom?" asked Rialla intensely. "I am a slave. I spend all of my time trying to prove to myself that I am not."

"Nonsense," commented Tris. Rialla hadn't noticed when he entered the room; he had dispensed with the magelight. "You were supposed to come straight here, not engage in a series of highly unnecessary heroics, and lead the hold guards on a white stag hunt all over the countryside while we sat here and worried. A slave does as she's told."

Laeth snickered. "I keep trying to tell her that, but she doesn't listen."

Rialla smiled, enjoying the exchange—but not accepting it. They didn't know how insidious the slave mentality was, the fear of being beaten or worse: the need to please the Master.

"Did you clean your arm?" she asked.

Tris nodded. "I can't get the bandage tight, though. It's in an awkward place." He handed a long, narrow cloth to Rialla.

She hesitated then said, "I'll need some light."

He produced another light, and she wrapped the cotton tightly around his upper arm.

"This looks like you were raked with claws," she commented.

"We ran into something in the tower," said Laeth. "I didn't notice whether it had claws or not."

"Something that smelled like it came from a swamp," added Tris. "Apparently someone wanted to make certain that Laeth would die."

"I told Lord Winterseine I was going to stop Lord Jarroh," said Marri hesitantly from the bed, "even if I had to sleep with Jarroh to do it."

Laeth started laughing. "I bet you had him convinced that you were a mouse all this time. Did you call him a stupid mule too?"

"No," said Marri, "I called him a murderer. I knew that you hadn't killed Karsten: you don't have it in you to commit such an act. The next most logical suspect was Winterseine. Especially since he was working so hard to convince everyone that you were the guilty one."

"I wonder what he sent after Marri," mused Rialla. "I think that you'd better take her with you to Sianim, Laeth."

"Yes," he agreed, "I had intended to do so. I wish you would come with us."

Rialla shook her head again. "No."

"I'll tell Ren what you are doing. He ought to be able to find you and get you out, if you can't do it on your own." Laeth obviously wasn't happy, but he knew her well enough to understand that he couldn't change her mind.

"Thank you," said Rialla.

"I suppose, then, that we had best be out of here," said Laeth briskly.

"Let me get some things together," said Tris, heading to the front room. "I've got some sturdy clothes that might fit the lady, if she's not too choosey. I wondered what I was going to do with them when the farmer gave them to me for healing his ewe. I've traded bread as well. It should only take me a moment to find everything."

True to his word, Tris took only a short time to pack a pair of large saddlebags. He hefted the load and handed it to Laeth.

With the bags over his shoulder, Laeth took Rialla's hand and kissed it with a courtier's grace.

Rialla patted his cheek gently with her free hand, and then shoved him on the shoulder hard. "Get going before they find those horses. Keep it to a walk if you can; they've had a hard night. If you bear northeast into Reth, you should be safe enough; most of the soldiers are searching in the southeast, toward Sianim."

"I'd planned on it," he said. "I have some friends in Reth that we can stay with and rest the horses. Luck to you, Ria."

"And to you," she replied.

Laeth turned to Tris. "Thank you for your aid this night."

Tris shrugged it off. "If you and your lady reach Sianim in safety, that will be thanks enough."

Tris followed them out, saying that he could conceal the obvious tracks and if anyone saw him wandering around in the dark, they would think nothing of it. There were several plants that were more potent if picked at night.

Alone in the cottage, Rialla went back to the bedroom and fell on the bed with a moan; she couldn't believe how exhausted she felt. She closed her eyes and couldn't seem to open them; she groaned when Tris roused her again.

"Sorry, I know," he said apologetically. "But I have to get you cleaned up before someone wonders why a badly wounded slave is covered with mud and tree limbs." As he spoke, he pulled off her borrowed clothes.

She was just far enough out of her stupor to know that she should be objecting to his actions, but couldn't seem to find the energy to do it. He wiped her down with a damp cloth and put her slave tunic back on with minimal help from her.

It worried her to be so sluggish, and she fought free

long enough to say in a frantic voice, "What's wrong with me?"

"Shh, it's all right. Healing is very wearing on the body. Normally after what I did, you would sleep for a whole day rather than leading a pack of hunt-mad guards on a will-o'-the-wisp chase." As he spoke, he took a comb and began working it through her hair, ignoring her irritable complaints when he tugged too hard. "We've got to get the rest of the leaves out."

Finally he laid her down in the bed, but he didn't cover her. Instead he sat beside her and said, "Rialla. Wake up, just one more time. Come on, sweetheart."

Responding to the urgency of his voice, she just managed it. The dawn lit his craggy face, and she could read the reluctance in it.

"If they see that I've healed your leg, they're going to be suspicious." He seemed to be having trouble with what he was saying.

"We need to give them a slave with a wounded leg," she said.

Tris nodded.

Rialla worked up the energy to smile. "If you have a knife, I'll do it."

He shook his head. "No need for anything so crude, but it's still going to hurt."

Her eyes closed again, but she laughed anyway. "Give me a minute and I doubt that I'd feel it if a mule kicked me."

She was wrong. When he reopened it, she cried out—too tired to be tough.

He carefully set stitches to keep it from scarring, then covered the wound with a numbing salve and wiped the involuntary tears from her cheek with his thumb.

"All right now?" he asked.

She nodded and closed her eyes and didn't open them again for several hours.

# SIX

The sun was almost finished with its journey to the west when Rialla woke up. She still felt tired and her leg ached. With the instinct of the hunted, she knew that some noise had roused her from her healing slumber. She closed her eyes again and listened.

Someone was in the outer room; she could hear them talking. As they came closer to her room, she distinguished Winterseine's voice. She sat up and waited for the door to open.

Terran led the way, followed by Winterseine and Tris.

"May I see the wound?" asked Winterseine. "Not that I doubt your skill, healer, but I want to see it for myself. If she is going to be badly scarred, she will be of no use to me."

Without a word Tris threw back her covers and cut the unbleached cloth off her leg. The inflammation was gone and neat stitches ran the length of her thigh. It wasn't healed, but it was obviously no longer serious.

Winterseine looked impressed. "You do good work, healer. What did you use to draw the poison?"

Tris stared at him long enough to be insolent, then said, "A poultice."

Winterseine smiled, but it didn't reach his eyes. "We all have our trade secrets, don't we?"

"When will she be able to travel?" asked Terran, breaking the tension in the room. Rialla had forgotten that Terran was there; he had a way of fading into the background.

"It depends on how you are traveling," answered Tris civilly enough. "She can ride in about a se'ennight. If you have a wagon, you could try it in two or three days, though five would be better. In a se'ennight the risk of infection will be significantly lower."

Lord Winterseine nodded and ran a finger down the stitches, pushing to test for hidden infection. Rialla knew that her face retained its slave-impassive expression, but she could feel Tris's sudden rage. Startled by the first specific emotion she'd caught from the healer, she shifted her gaze momentarily to look at him. There was nothing more in his face than there had been a minute before; it appeared that she wasn't the only one capable of hiding emotions. She lowered her protective barriers, but the brief flash of anger had faded and he was as veiled as ever.

"Very well," said Lord Winterseine, "we'll be back in a week for her. It will probably take at least that much time before everything else is cleared up anyway."

"Remember, Father," said Terran's meek voice. "We have to leave soon," he continued. "There is a shipment expected at Winterseine hold a fortnight from now. We can wait a week easily enough, but no longer than that."

Rialla started and stared at Terran, forgetting her role for a moment—luckily no one noticed. She focused her gift tightly and probed, but the results were the same. Lord Winterseine was opaque, but she could sense his presence. Tris she was aware of on another level, but she couldn't sense Terran's presence at all.

"Of course." Lord Winterseine turned to the healer and

said, "I hope it is not an inconvenience for you to keep her here until we leave."

"No," replied Tris. "I'll total your bill and have it sent to you. When you have paid it, you may have your slave back."

"Certainly," said Winterseine. "Send it in care of my son." He walked out, followed by both Terran and the healer.

Rialla stretched thoughtfully. She'd never met someone whom she couldn't sense at all. She was running into several things that were odd: first the healer and now Terran. It could be that her abilities were not as functional as she'd thought. They certainly seemed to have a few quirks.

Tris had started through the doorway from the other room when another knock sounded. He smiled and shrugged, closing the door behind him.

Rialla listened as he put salve on a little girl's injured puppy, set a farmer's broken arm and arranged for someone to help the farmer out until the arm healed. A woman came in mumbling something about her kid (Rialla wasn't sure if it was a goat or a child) and Tris left with her.

Rialla slept as long as she could, then set up imaginary games of Steal the Dragon until she grew bored. Tris stopped in briefly as the sun was setting, but was called out again by the smith, whose wife was having difficulty delivering her third child.

Rialla threw the covers back restlessly and limped to the window. The sill was as wide as a narrow bench; she perched on it and stared into the night sky. It was nominally better than counting the fifty-seven boards that served as the ceiling, held down by four hundred and twelve nails.

Rialla fidgeted and finally got up to gimp across the floor again. She lacked any method of lighting the lanterns on the wall; she knew that Tris had flint and steel around, but it was hidden well enough that she couldn't find it.

She searched both rooms twice, more for something to do than because she needed light. The moon was shining through the window, giving her almost as much illumination as a lantern would have.

Finally, she went to the wall in the bedroom. It took her a while to find the catch for the hidden closet, but not as long as it took to overcome her scruples and look. She salved her conscience by reasoning that if Tris were worried about her rummaging around, he wouldn't have shown her the secret door in the first place. At last the door slid open, divulging what it hid.

Most of the weapons she had used or at least seen used, but she was mystified by a short, forked stick with a strip of catgut connecting each prong of the fork.

"It's a spear thrower." Tris sounded weary as he observed her from the open door and waved on the lights. "The man who made it for me called it an atladl. If you look in the closet, you should find five small spears that match the design on the haft. The end of the spear fits on the thong, and you throw it almost the way that you'd throw a javelin. It's not quite as accurate as a bow and arrow, but it's faster to use and easier to hide from the gamekeepers."

Rialla nodded, trying not to look as guilty as she felt, and slipped the weapon back into the closet. She got to her feet easily, though she grimaced when her weight was on her bad leg.

"Have you had anything to eat?" she asked, when she got a closer look at his face. "I took the liberty of raiding your larder. There's a plate of cheese and sausage on the foot of the bed."

"Thanks," he said, sinking down beside the plate and looking at it with faint interest. He must have washed off in the creek, because his linen shirt was wet on the sleeves and collar.

"How did the birthing go?" she asked, sitting on the floor when it became apparent that he wasn't going to move for a while.

"Not good," he said and shook his head, staring at the piece of cheese he held in his hand, as if it had turned green. "There were twins and the first one was a breech. It died before I got there. The second one is small, but the smith's cottage is clean and warm; he should be fine."

Rialla could see that the death bothered him more than weariness. She took a piece of goat's cheese and nibbled at it while she tried to think of something to say to distract him.

"Tell me," she asked, "how did you become the healer here? All the stories say that shapeshifters keep to their own kind."

He looked at her, and faint amusement crept into his weary eyes. "I am not a shapeshifter. Shapeshifters get their amusement by eating innocent young virgins who stupidly wander alone in the forest. Mind you," he said, taking a bite of the cheese with more enthusiasm than before, "that's not to say that they don't deserve it. Stupid young girls who get caught alone in the forest fall prey to anything that crosses their paths, be the beast animal, human or shapeshifter. The moral of the story is," he took a piece of sausage, "don't be a stupid young virgin."

She grinned at him and said, "Thanks for the advice. I'll remember that. So what are you, and why are you here? I'd think that if you were going to fraternize with humans, you would at least pick a group of people who weren't liable to burn you at the stake if they caught you working magic."

He snatched another round of sausage and shrugged. "I'm healing people."

She rolled her eyes and grabbed the plate, setting it behind her. "No more food until you tell." Playing was a long-forgotten art, but the twinkle in his eyes encouraged her.

He looked forlornly at the remains of his piece of sausage and whined, "I'll starve."

She showed no signs of softening, especially since he was looking less tired now, the grim lines around his mouth fading. "Not if you tell me what you're doing here."

He leaned back against the wall and crossed his arms behind his head. "Torture will never make me divulge the secrets I keep."

She took a piece of cheese and waved it invitingly. "How about bribery?"

"That might work," he conceded. "Why don't you try it?"

It took her three times before the food that she tossed at him made it to his mouth.

"All right," he surrendered. "I am a sylvan."

Rialla waited but he didn't elaborate. "What's a sylvan?"

"Where's my bribe?" he replied.

She hit him in the nose with a piece of cheese. He caught it before it hit the bed and examined it with satisfaction before eating it.

"Sylvans are users of natural magic like the shapeshifters, though our talents lie in different directions. They are closer to the animals of the forests, while we are guardians of the greenery. We are a simple folk, and it is easy enough for us to blend in with the humans, so our enclaves are not hidden the way those of the shapeshifters are." He paused and closed his eyes, leaning against the wall, but he caught the small piece of hard sausage she threw at him anyway.

"There are not many enclaves, though," he said finally, rubbing his beard. "Over the centuries they have died out, one by one. The enclave that I belonged to is the only one left in Darran. We claimed to be a religious order, worshipping Naslen, lord of the forests—I suppose that the story is more true than not. There are many such groups of humans, caught in the past, holding to the old ways and the old languages. They are tolerated, even in Darran, because they have always been there. The sylvans blend in with the others.

"My enclave is in a minor estate of a great noble—so

minor that in three generations the lord had not visited it. The old lord died, and his son decided to visit each of his new holdings; I believe that he had some debts, and was evaluating his lands for later sale.

"I was walking alone, and I came upon a child; a human girl-child that some of the lord's friends had found earlier. Her body was badly broken." Tris looked grim.

"I knew her, had watched her grow from a toddler to an explorer. Her mother was an excellent weaver, and I had often gone to the human village to trade food for cloth. They had four grown boys, and this girl-child. You have to understand, Rialla. The reason that our enclave had survived as long as it had was that it was forbidden to work magic around humans. Absolutely forbidden. I knew this, and understood the reason for it."

His voice dropped almost to a whisper as he continued. "But this was a child, a child that I knew and liked. She was dying as I watched. So I healed her body, until there was no evidence that any violence had occurred. Rape is as much a wound of the soul as a wound of the body, and I gifted her with forgetfulness. With luck no one would have ever known, not even the child.

"When I was through healing her, I woke her, teased her about sleeping in the woods and escorted her home. Her father I took aside and warned that I had seen one of the lord's guests eyeing her. He assured me that he would keep her in the cottage until the lord and his entourage were gone.

"When I returned to the enclave, I found that someone had seen me violate our law. I was tried and sentenced to banishment. They took me far from the enclave and bound me with magic and rope. If I managed to free myself, I could live—but never be welcomed in any enclave."

"You broke free?" asked Rialla.

He shook his head, smiling at the memory. "No. I struggled for a while, but the man who'd tied the rope didn't want me to live. I was contemplating my probable fate when an old woman came upon me. She poked her finger in my face and said, 'Look you, I have a bargain for you. You are a healer, and I have need of such. I have a knife, which you need as desperately.' " Tris grinned at Rialla. "She was so scared her finger trembled with it, but she didn't let her fear stop her. When I agreed to help, she cut the rope; so here I am."

"How did she know you were a healer?" asked Rialla.

"She has a gift that occasionally allows her to see such things."

Rialla nodded, accepting his answer. "Do you like it here among humans?"

He nodded slowly. "Better than the enclave. They were wrong. It is an evil thing to have the power to help others, and not to do so."

"Is that why you helped rescue Laeth?" asked Rialla.

Tris gave her an enigmatic look then shrugged. "Part of it."

He rose restlessly from the bed and gave Rialla a hand up off the floor. Her leg had stiffened, so he helped her hobble to the bed. Then he slid the closet door closed, picked up the plate and waved the lights down.

"Good dreams, healer," said Rialla.

He nodded and pulled the door closed behind him.

"SO WHAT WILL LORD WINTERSEINE DO WITH A NEWLY recovered runaway?" They were deep into a game of Dragon that Rialla was winning when Tris spoke. Over the past few days, they had played a game whenever Tris had a moment to spare; not that Rialla minded. She enjoyed the game as much as he did—even if he won most of the time.

"You're just trying to distract me," she complained at his interruption. "This is the first time I've had a ghost of a chance of winning since the first game we played, and now you want to take even that away from me."

"You *are* getting paranoid, aren't you?" He commiserated with deepest sympathy. Rialla flashed him a rude hand gesture before she turned back to the game board.

Tris laughed, then said, "Seriously, Rialla, he's not going to hamstring you or beat you, is he?"

Rialla moved her frog to an empty square on the board, and shook her head. "No. That happens sometimes in Ynstrah and some of the provinces in the Alliance where they depend on slave labor in their agriculture. Occasionally they'll hamstring a runaway here, but only one of the less valuable slaves—more to serve as an example than to keep the slave they've crippled from running again. A dancer is too valuable to damage that way."

She smiled dryly at Tris. "That's not to say that he'll let me go unpunished. The Master has an aptitude for creative retribution."

Tris was staring at the game, but Rialla had the feeling that he wasn't really seeing it. He finally moved a piece and looked up. "Are you sure that you want to go back? You're paying an awfully high price for a chance at vengeance."

Rialla nodded, moving the frog again. "It'll be worth it if it works. If it doesn't . . ." she shrugged. "There are other reasons as well. You told me that you've traveled. Have you ever been on the other side of the Great Swamp?"

Tris shook his head.

Rialla shifted on the bed, trying to find a comfortable position for her leg. "Did you ever wonder why Sianim is so anxious to stop the fighting between Reth and Darran?"

He raised an eyebrow and shook his head. "I should have. It is hardly in Sianim's best interest to prevent wars."

"Exactly. When the Spymaster called me in to persuade me to accompany Laeth here, he explained his reasoning. Apparently there is a good possibility that there will be an invasion coming from the eastern side of the Great Swamp."

"There are always wars among humans," commented Tris. "I would have thought that Sianim, with its mercenary hoards, would be delighted at the thought of another one.''

Sometimes Tris had a way of making the word ''human'' sound like a name that gutter-bred children called each other to start a fight. Since he seemed not to hold her humanness against her, Rialla let it pass unremarked.

''I would have thought so too,'' she agreed readily. ''But this isn't just any invading force. It's an army that has conquered all the nations in the East in something less than a decade. The leader of the armies is a man who calls himself the Voice of Altis. He claims to be a prophet of the god Altis, and the religious revival is spreading faster than his armies. The Spymaster thinks that the only way to resist the invasion will be to unite all the Western countries against him; and he has a nasty habit of being right.''

''So he supports the alliance of Reth and Darran,'' said Tris.

Rialla nodded and continued, ''None of this would have much bearing on what I'm going to be doing at Winterseine's hold, except for one thing. The people of the East apparently do not believe in magic; it's been so long since they've had wizards that they've long since dismissed the existence of magic as a child's fable.

''The 'miracles' the Voice of Altis performs as a prophet of the old god bear a striking resemblance to the accomplishments of a trained magician. The Spymaster believes that the Voice is a trained mage from this side of the Swamp.'' Rialla met Tris's gaze. ''And I think I might have found him.''

''Winterseine,'' said Tris.

She nodded her head. ''If it's true, then maybe something can be done to prevent the invasion altogether. Laeth and I discovered enough of a link between Winterseine and this self-proclaimed prophet that even if he's not the Voice of Altis, he almost certainly knows who is.''

"I'm going with you," Tris announced calmly, as he moved his snake a space beyond her frog.

Gods, she thought, wishing she could accept: to have someone she trusted with her, to have the healer's steady presence, to not be alone.

"No," she replied, her voice steady, maneuvering her bird to take his snake if it tried to eat her frog.

"I'm afraid you don't have any voice in this," his tone was matter-of-fact as he moved the snake out of danger, taking her stag as he did so.

"What about your bargain with the old woman?"

"I've been at Tallonwood a little over two years," he replied. "The bargain was for one."

She opened her mouth to protest, but saw the resolution in his eyes. "Plague it, Tris. What are you doing this for?"

He gave her an odd smile, and she was abruptly reminded that he was not human. "I told you the woman who rescued me had a gift for seeing things others cannot. She told me I should help you accomplish your task."

"She just told you to help me, so you are?" asked Rialla incredulously.

"Nothing so neat. The future is not unchangeable, Rialla. Trenna gave me a goal, a hint of the possible results of a course of action. Enough to persuade me the goal is worth pursuit."

"You're not going to tell me why you are doing this, are you?" Rialla accused, but there was no heat in her voice.

"Of course," Tris said blandly, "as I explained to Laeth, I am loath to give up the first person I've found in a long time who is capable of defeating me at Dragon. Your move."

She gave the board a surprised look. "I thought I just moved; you must not have been watching."

He didn't take his gaze from her face. "I was watching; it's your move."

She shrugged and said, "I choose not to move."

He shook his head. "You chose that five moves ago; you can only do that every six moves. Your move."

She smiled, moved her sparrow two spaces to the right and said, "Fine. Theft."

He looked at the board. Her sparrow sat on the space with his dragon.

She raised an eyebrow at his exaggeratedly forlorn expression. "I *told* you that it wasn't my move, but when you insisted, you made it my move anyway."

"What did you move after I took your stag?"

She smiled sweetly. "Your dragon."

He laughed and raised his hands in mock surrender. "Thief. Your game."

"It was about time," she said darkly, helping him replace the pieces in the drawer.

"Now you only owe me two kingdoms, five horses and twelve pigs."

"Four horses," she contested hotly.

"Five," he corrected. "You wagered five horses against the twelve pigs you lost before. It was supposed to be six horses, but you whined and I let it stand at five."

"Well," she said, "at least I got my fifty chickens back."

He started to answer, but the sound of the outer door opening and the frantic crying of an infant called him back to duty.

Alone, Rialla picked absently at the stitching on the bed covering. The week had passed far too quickly. Her leg was almost healed; Tris had taken the stitches out that morning. It still pained her when she used it too much, but every day it improved. Tomorrow morning she would leave with Lord Winterseine.

Perhaps, she thought, it was a good thing that she would soon be going. If she spent much longer with the healer, it would be too hard to go back to being a slave—and to survive, she had to be a slave again—not a Sianim horse trainer pretending to be a slave.

She raised her hand to her cheek, feeling the scar beneath the illusion. She couldn't feel the tattoo, but she knew it was there: nose to ear, jaw to cheekbone. Sometimes she had felt as if it were tattooed on her soul, that she could never be anything but a slave.

She allowed herself to be drawn out of her bout of self-pity by the sound of a loud, angry voice and the healer's quiet reply. The front door shut with a slam, and Tris stalked into the bedroom with a black scowl on his face.

"What's wrong?" she asked.

His glower deepened. "I just finished setting a broken bone for one of the hedgefarmer's sons."

"Hedgefarmer?"

"The hedgefarmers work the land in the hills and lower mountain slopes. It's poor land, and gives a marginal living at best—but that's no reason to break a child's arm. At least once a month I treat one of his children or his wife for miscellaneous bruises and broken bones. I've talked to him twice about it, and told him this was it. Next time he hits someone weaker than he is, I'll see to it that he won't be in any condition to do it again."

"Will he listen?" she asked as he paced back and forth.

"No, he'll probably just not allow them to come to a healer for treatment, plague it! It was stupid to lose my temper. I'm sorry that I did it in front of the child too. That boy has to live with enough violence in his life; he doesn't need mine as well."

"You are needed here." Rialla spoke softly. "Who will set their bones and heal their animals if you aren't here?"

He stretched and shed his anger as if it were a coat. When he looked at her, there was nothing of it left in his eyes. "These people survived without me for most of their lives. The headman's mother is a decent healer, as is her new daughter-in-law. I've already informed them that I will be leaving shortly."

Rialla opened her mouth, and he held up his hand to forestall what she would have said. "Rialla, if I stay here too long, someone will eventually notice I work magic, and that could be worse for the village than the lack of a healer. I was preparing to leave soon anyway.''

Tris sat down on the end of the bed. ''Tomorrow, when Lord Winterseine takes you, I'll follow. It shouldn't be difficult to track a large group of humans through the woods.''

Rialla snickered and Tris stopped talking.

''I'm sorry,'' she said, ''I've just never heard anybody say 'human' when they meant 'mindless stinking mass of waste left undigested by a pig.' You do it well.''

He made a half-bow and gave her the sweet smile that he used when he'd made a particularly devious maneuver in Dragon.

''There is one more thing I need to take care of before you go.'' He reached over and pulled off her earring. ''This comes off too easily. If Winterseine takes it off and your tattoo comes off as well, he's going to start wondering about you.''

He pulled a small, very thin piece of kidskin out of his belt pouch. ''I got this from the tanner this morning.''

He closed his eyes, humming softly, folding the kidskin around the earring and tucking the resultant bundle neatly into his hands. After a moment he opened his eyes again and shook the fine leather open, displaying it for Rialla. The earring was gone, and the tattoo that had covered her cheek now covered the kidskin.

Leaning near her, he pressed the skin against her face and resumed his humming. Rialla's cheek grew cold. When he took his hands away, she touched her cheek. Her fingers detected smooth skin where her scars should be, and her cheek felt numb.

''The tattoo?'' she asked.

''Is on your face. I'll contact you at night, when the others are sleeping. You are an empath, but you've spoken about being able to read people's thoughts as well as their emotions. Can you contact me that way if you need me?''

She shook her head. ''Most people I could, but I can't

even read your emotions—let alone project a message to you.''

He raised an eyebrow, then nodded with an odd smile. ''No, of course you couldn't.'' He hesitated momentarily and then said, ''But I know a way to help.''

He slipped his boot knife out and examined it before he ran his thumb almost casually over the finely honed edge. Rialla didn't realize that he was working magic until he said something in a foreign tongue and touched her mouth with the fresh wound. Involuntarily she licked the blood off her lips. She felt as if she'd sipped distilled alcohol; it burned its way deep into her body, leaving her toes and fingertips buzzing and her vision blurred.

Before she had time to react, he touched the knife to the side of her neck and bent his head. She felt the soft, quick touch of his lips and the brush of his beard before he backed away. He touched her neck again briefly, this time with his fingers, and the sting of the cut disappeared. Staring at him, she touched her skin where he and his knife had touched. The wound was gone.

''Try it now,'' he said and his voice sounded different to her—shadowed with magic and moonlight, though the sun still lit the trees outside the window.

She reached out to him with her gift, carefully, not knowing what difference his magic had wrought. At first it seemed as though nothing had changed. As before, she could touch him, but it was like touching a solid object with her thoughts: she could see him, but not what he was. She pushed gently, but he remained opaque. Just as she started to back away, Rialla was sucked in.

It was too far, too fast. She was dizzy, cut adrift among memories and feelings that she couldn't distinguish from her own. She was accustomed to receiving emotions from most people, but from Tris she was getting memories, thoughts and dreams as well.

*Rialla.* His mindspeech seemed too strong, but it gave her something to balance herself.

Rialla pulled herself back until the contact was not so

strong, his warmth soothing rather than burning. His thought-voice was tightly formed, arguing that he had communicated mind to mind before.

She had been able to reach her father in this manner, but she wasn't used to the communication being two-way. *Tris,* she said, *what did you do that allowed me to touch you this way?*

She caught faint nuances of emotion that were quickly tucked away, but not before she caught a hint of guilt and excitement.

*I'll tell you sometime. You can contact me now?*

She tested her gifts on him warily. *Anytime. I don't know how close I have to be, but this is easier than any other mindspeech I've ever attempted.*

*Sylvans speak with each other in such a manner,* he said.

*Like this?* asked Rialla in surprise. She sent him a picture of the intimacy that this form of communication offered her—the complex emotions and thoughts that she picked up when he talked.

*No,* he said, startled. *Can you see so much?*

Sensing his unease, she withdrew even further, the memory of Laeth's outrage at her empathic gift fresh in her mind. Usually she had no trouble leaving the subjects of her touch their privacy, but Tris's stray thoughts tended to brush against her without warning. Finally she removed herself altogether, reconstructing her barriers until he was once again opaque.

Tris gave her a particularly enigmatic look and said, "Now if you need help, you can contact me."

She wasn't capable of doing more than moving her head to indicate her agreement. When the sound of a woman calling from the front room pierced the intimate atmosphere that somehow had developed, Rialla felt extremely grateful. She desperately needed time to figure out what Tris had done.

✝     ✝     ✝

THE MORNING DAWNED CLEAR AND WARM. RIALLA WAS waiting quietly when Lord Winterseine entered her sanctuary. Her face was impassive, and it didn't change when her master set the heavy training collar around her neck.

She didn't flinch when chain-linked metal cuffs were closed on her wrists, pulling her arms behind her. A second chain was run from the wrist chain to the collar, further restricting her movement. Winterseine attached a leather leash to the front of her collar and led her out.

It was easy not to react to the restraints; she'd had them on before and had expected Lord Winterseine to use them. What she had not expected was the hot rage emanating from the healer, though he appeared calm and remote, as he always was with the Darranian nobles. She tried to close his reaction off, before it affected her as well, but it wasn't as easy as it should have been.

Apparently, whatever channel Tris had forged between them was not easily closed. She sent a surge of reassurance to Tris, and then tried to reestablish her privacy.

Terran gave her a hand in mounting. It was difficult under the best of circumstances to get on a horse without the use of hands. Since Rialla was distracted with the task of suppressing the persistent connection with Tris, she appreciated Terran's help.

As they rode away, she could feel the healer's eyes following them into the trees.

THERE WERE MANY DARRANIANS WHO HAD LOST EVERY-thing in the wars with Reth. They roamed the forests extracting tolls from those foolish enough to venture through without sufficient force. Winterseine's entourage was large enough to discourage most raiding parties. Besides Winterseine and his son, there were a score of fighters, more or less, and two servants—one of which was the man who Rialla suspected had poisoned Karsten. His name, she recalled, was Tamas. Apparently the dark-skinned girl was the only slave they'd brought to Lord Karsten's hold, because Rialla was the only slave in the party. Four men rode in front, followed closely by Lord Winterseine and his son Terran. Rialla and the servants rode next, then the rest of the party.

Rialla knew that Winterseine was a formidable warrior: it was one of the reasons for his success as a slaver. Looking at his son, she decided that Terran might be as good. Certainly he bestrode his battle-trained stallion with the ease of long practice, and the easy way that he'd tossed her on her horse argued that he had strength.

Winterseine's man Tamas held the lead rein for Rialla's horse. Like her, he was mounted on a lighter-bred saddle horse. He wasn't armed with anything more formidable than the heavy whip that was coiled on his saddle, but Rialla had seen such a whip wielded at Sianim, and didn't underestimate the damage he could inflict with it.

They traveled south through the rolling hills of southern Darran. Everywhere, Rialla could see the toll of the last war. Many of the farmhouses had been recently constructed over old foundations. Several times she saw the burned-out remains of dwellings that had not been rebuilt, perhaps because there was no one left to do so.

They stopped near one of the charred cottages shortly before sunset. Camp was set up with a minimum of fuss. Winterseine used the leash on the training collar to stake Rialla to the ground near the fire, where she would be easily visible throughout the night. He didn't remove the bindings from her arms.

None of the restraints were overly tight, but her arms had been in the same position for the better part of the day and her shoulder was beginning to ache. Between that and her throbbing leg, Rialla decided that a decent night's rest was doubtful. Adding insult to injury, she had the choice of lying with her face in the dirt, or with her weight on her awkwardly bound arms.

*Rialla.*

She thought she must have jumped, but if she had no one had noticed. She wasn't used to someone speaking in her mind. *Tris?*

*Yes. How is your leg?*

She tested it cautiously. *It hurts, but no more than it did.*

*Good.*

She waited, but he didn't say anything more. With a resigned sigh she rolled on her face. To her surprise she fell into a restful doze that lasted through the night.

THE NEXT MORNING, TERRAN WAS BUSY ELSEWHERE, SO it was the servant Tamas who boosted Rialla onto her mount. She hadn't paid much attention to him the first day of the trip, but his touch forced his emotions and some of his thoughts onto her, leaving her feeling unclean. It wasn't simple lust he was feeling, but something more bestial—he fed his desire on degradation and pain. Even after she was on the horse, he found a thousand reasons for touching her.

By late that afternoon the sky had darkened, and Winterseine increased the pace to a trot to avoid the threatening storm. The horse Rialla was riding had a trot that threatened to rattle her teeth loose, and what it did to her aching head wasn't pleasant—but the faster speed limited Tamas's fondling, so she felt it was a vast improvement.

They sheltered for the night in a monastery dedicated, ironically enough, to the god of storms. Most of the worshippers of the old gods were confined to a few old temples like this one. It was a primitive fortress made of the dark native stone and rendered even more dismal by the gloominess of the darkened sky.

Several monks came to take their horses, and Rialla dismounted easily enough by throwing one leg in front of her and sliding down her horse's side. She hoped to avoid Tamas's help at all costs.

The storm god disliked women in his sanctuary, but the good monks had built a small outbuilding as a concession to secular parties who needed shelter and would pay the monks generously for the privilege. The hut locked from the outside, so that there was no chance of females wandering into the main buildings and desecrating the temple.

The building was barren and windowless. Rialla supposed that if she'd been a noblewoman, a cot would have been found for her and burned when she left. As it was, she would have to make do with the stone floor. There wasn't much chance to look around before the door was shut, leaving her in the darkness. She heard the unmistakable sound of the wooden board being slipped into place on the door.

Rialla sat on the uneven stone floor and closed her eyes with a sigh of relief that she was alone. She'd feared that Tamas was going to be left to guard her, and she didn't want to spend all night fighting him off.

She wasn't sure the actual moment she realized she wasn't alone in the room, or what first alerted her. Before she had time to panic, she realized that she knew who was here.

"Tris?"

"Mmm?" he answered absently, and the collar jerked around her neck as he began unbuckling it.

"How long have you been here?"

"Not too long. You smell like wet horse." He removed the bands on her arms and Rialla stretched gratefully, almost moaning in the relief of moving her arms freely.

"My favorite scent," she replied.

One of Tris's magelights illuminated the barren little chamber.

"Not exactly cozy," he commented.

"It is clean, which is better than the men's accommodations in the sanctuary are likely to be," she said, patting the stone beside her in invitation.

Instead, Tris sat facing her and took off the pack he carried on his back. He rummaged inside it and then pulled out a checkered board and placed it between them.

It was not as elaborate as the one he had at his cottage, but it was functional and they whiled away the afternoon with several games of Dragon. He won them all, but she managed to make him work for it. After the third game he set it aside with visible reluctance.

"I have to turn out the light now," said Tris. "Though this building is sturdy, I don't doubt that there are enough holes in the mortar that someone might notice the light coming out. You don't want to try to explain how you managed to produce light in here." He waved his hand and the magelight disappeared.

"I noticed that Winterseine's rat-faced servant was having some difficulty keeping his hands to himself today," Tris commented. "Now, have you thought about giving the little lecher leading your horse a thorough disgust of you? I would think that empathy would prove useful that way."

She laughed, grateful that somehow his remarks had turned Tamas from threatening to absurd. "I'm afraid anything vile I can think up will just excite him more."

"There is that possibility," he agreed in thoughtful tones.

Rialla laughed again and found a more restful position. The silence continued comfortably between them until she began to drift asleep.

"How do you intend to prove Winterseine killed Karsten?" asked Tris abruptly.

She roused herself slightly. "You mentioned that the dagger that killed Karsten disappeared. If I can find it, any decent wizard can tell who used it."

"Who are you trying to convince?" asked Tris.

"What do you mean?" Rialla said. Then she added, "Gods, I never thought of that. What Darranian is going to believe anything a wizard says?"

She thought for a moment then said, "What if I approach it differently? What do you think the regency council's reaction would be if I proved that Winterseine was a mage? It wouldn't prove Laeth's innocence, but I don't think that Winterseine would be allowed to inherit Karsten's lands either. That would leave Lord Jarroh as the most powerful man on the council."

"How are you going to prove that Winterseine is a mage?"

She shook her head, though in the dark he couldn't see her. "I don't know, but I'll find a way."

TRIS WOKE HER EARLY IN THE MORNING TO REPLACE THE restraints before someone came in. Just as he finished the last buckle, they heard the bar being removed.

"Tris," hissed Rialla urgently.

He smiled at her and took a step back until he was against the wall, then made an odd gesture and his features blurred and darkened. Rialla watched fascinated as Tris blended into the wall, the stone coloring overshadowing his own. It altered in subtle tones until the shadows hid any sign that he stood there. Tamas opened the door, pulled Rialla up by one arm and escorted her out, oblivious to the observer left in the stone hut.

It was a cold and miserable day, and the horses were spooky because of a stiff wind that brought strange smells uncomfortably close. Rialla huddled under her cloak and wished vainly that Tamas weren't holding the lead line on her mare.

The sun rose, a dim disk in a gray sky. By the time it had reached the middle of its journey, it was totally obscured by black clouds. When rain began to fall in sheets, the party halted while Terran and Winterseine conferred briefly.

Tamas took advantage of the rest stop to force his horse next to Rialla's.

"I like the pretty ones, the soft ones like you," he said. "Lord Winterseine says if you are not good enough to dance, I can have you before he sends you to his brothel. You wouldn't like it there, but if you pleased me I might keep you."

As he spoke, he rested his hand on her sore leg. Her horse shifted restlessly, dislodging his grip as Rialla's unease communicated itself. Tamas smiled and kneed his horse sideways, following hers.

"Now, what's getting you all upset?" He pressed his hand against the wound again, this time harder.

It hurt, but Rialla knew her face didn't show it. She knew that her lack of expression disappointed him. She also knew that somewhere nearby, Tris was getting *very* angry.

Lightning flashed, followed a few seconds later by a low rumble. Her horse and Tamas's reacted with similar violence to the sound—aided by a touch of empathically projected fear. The other horses danced and jumped, their herd instinct overwhelming training.

Rialla's horse jerked its lead free of Tamas's loose hold and, free of any constraint, put her head between her front legs and kicked. Rialla leaned back, pushing her feet forward. As the mare's hindquarters fell to the ground and propelled the horse sideways, Rialla shifted her weight appropriately. Her empathy let her know what the horse was going to do a moment before the animal moved.

One of the guards caught the flying lead. His firm grip discouraged Rialla's mount; it gave a few halfhearted hops before settling down.

The courser that Tamas rode was more successful at ridding itself of its rider than Rialla's had been, tossing him into a thicket of thorn apple. When he was extracted from the inch-long thorns at last, his wounds were not limited to punctures and scrapes—his arm hung visibly broken at his side. One of the guardsmen had caught Tamas's horse, and it danced nervously, scattering mud on anything nearby.

*Nicely done,* commented Tris. *I hadn't thought of using the horses.*

*Thank you,* she replied lightly as her horse danced away from Tamas's, dragging the man holding the lead several feet. *I . . .*

As her horse turned another circle, Rialla got a clear view of Tamas flexing the arm that had been clearly broken only a moment before. Ignoring her distaste, she probed him briefly, but the only pain that Tamas was feeling was from the thorns.

*Tris,* she asked, *did you do that?*

*Do what?* he asked.

*When Tamas was thrown, he broke his arm.* She sent Tris a picture of what Tamas's arm had looked like. *Someone healed it. Was that you?*

*No.* There was a pause and then Tris said, *I don't think that anyone here can use green magic; we can usually recognize it in each other. I can usually also tell if someone has used green magic recently, but I don't see it here. Human magicians can set a bone, using magic as a splint, but it requires much power. Inefficient magicians, humans.* Then he added thoughtfully, *Just how strong is this magician of yours?*

*He trained with the former ae'Magi,* answered Rialla slowly. *Can you tell if a human mage has healed Tamas's arm?*

*A human mage can't heal the arm,* explained Tris, *he can only set it, like a splint made of magic. He would have to constantly reinforce the spell, and if the magician fell asleep, the magic would cease functioning—unless he used runes, and I could feel those. I can't feel any magic at all now, but the only human magician I've been around was Trenna, the woman who bargained for my service. She was only half-trained; I don't know if I could tell if a human mage was working magic.*

Rialla thought about what Tris told her. She wondered why Winterseine would be so concerned with Tamas's broken arm that he would drain his magic and pretend to heal it when there was no one to impress but his servants—it seemed out of character from what she remembered of her master.

Rialla shivered, and speculated uneasily about magic, human and green. What kind of power, she wondered, would the prophet of a god wield?

# SEVEN

The stone walls of Lord Winterseine's keep loomed darkly over the party of tired riders. Moonlight glinted off the ivy gathered at the base of the outside walls, lending an eeriness to the hold's appearance.

As they crossed the drawbridge, Rialla glanced down into the dark waters of the moat that surrounded the keep. The moat wasn't as rank as most of its kind; Winterseine had it drained once a year and cleaned of debris so it smelled mainly of algae and rotting plants, rather than less wholesome sewage.

The aged boards of the drawbridge creaked under the weight of the horses. The heavy chains that had been used to lift the bridge in times past had fallen limply into the moat, where they rusted and grew long strings of algae.

The entrance to the keep was adequately defended by the heavy iron portcullis that blocked the entrance. As far as Rialla knew, the ancient drawbridge had not been lifted this century. The keep was small and strategically unimportant, so it had escaped most of the ravages of the Rethian wars. Few robbers were desperate enough to take on the experienced fighters that manned the keep now that the war was over, and Winterseine preferred to avoid the petty bickering and feuding that took up so many land-holders' time and resources.

Rialla was unable to repress a shudder as the heavy ironwork of the portcullis dropped behind them, trapping her inside. For a moment she felt a frantic urge to fight against her bonds. She found herself reaching for Tris's reassuring presence; knowing he was nearby made it eas-ier to continue.

They rode directly to the keep entrance, where grooms waited to take the weary horses. While Winterseine and the rest of the party stopped in the entrance hall, one of the guardsmen escorted Rialla down the stone stairway that led to the holding cells. After making sure she had bread, water and straw in the small room, he removed the wrist manacles and left her alone.

Moonlight drifted in through a small window near the ceiling; its deep-set iron bars crossed the pale stone floor—a constant reminder of the room's purpose. The sound of water lapping against rock drifted faintly up from the deep hole underneath the sanitation grate in the far corner of the cell.

Rialla looked around with dawning recognition. She'd been given the same holding cell that she'd had when they brought her here the first time. For confirmation she knelt by the door and ran her fingers over the stone nearby. Her searching fingers found the crude letters scratched in the granite. It was too dark for her to read what was written there, even if some of the scratches hadn't been too faint to see—but she didn't need to read the words.

"*Isst vah han ona faetha,*" she spoke them softly, pro-nouncing them carefully, as her father had. "Without faith there is nothing."

Until she'd become a slave, they were the only written words she knew, although she had spoken several lan-guages. Her father had worn a gold disk on a chain; inscribed in the disk were those five words, the motto of her clan.

"This was the cell that they put me in the first time," she said without looking up, knowing that Tris was behind her. "How did you come in?"

"Through the wall."

Rialla twisted to look at the solid stone wall. Raising her eyebrows, she looked at Tris.

He shrugged. "Stone is not as easy for me to pass through as wood, but if you know how to ask it is not impossible—just slow."

She nodded and rose to her feet, uncomfortable with her vulnerable position. "I'm glad you came."

"Glad I followed you here, or glad I came to your cell tonight?"

She smiled. "Both actually. I needed to talk to you about Tamas's arm. Can you think of any reason Winterseine would heal it? I don't remember him ever working magic that . . . casually."

It was difficult to see details in the dark little room, but Rialla saw him lift his arm to his face and knew Tris was rubbing his beard.

"If he were trying to pass himself as a servant of Altis, he might do it to reinforce his position," he said thoughtfully at last.

"In front of a group of guards, a servant and a slave?" questioned Rialla.

"Even so," answered Tris. "If I wanted to know something about a noble, the first people that I would ask would be his servants. If he has declared himself the Voice of Altis, then the people who must believe in his position most fervently are his servants."

Rialla felt something inside her relax with Tris's explanation: facing Winterseine was sufficiently daunting. She would rather not worry about prophets and gods.

"Where did you leave your horse?" she asked, kicking at the straw until it padded a section of floor.

"What horse?" Tris replied.

"You ran?" hazarded Rialla doubtfully, looking at the heavily muscled healer. In her experience, runners weren't built like blacksmiths.

He smiled. "No. In the forest, there are other ways opened to those who know how to use the doors."

"Magic?" asked Rialla, hiding a yawn behind her hand.

"Indeed," he nodded.

THE SUN WAS JUST UP WHEN A PAIR OF GUARDS CAME and escorted her to Isslic of Winterseine's unoccupied study. They attached her leash to an elaborate bronze ring set in the wall and left her alone.

She sat on the floor and leaned against the wall. As with the holding cell, she'd been in this room before. When a slave was misbehaving, Winterseine had her brought here to his room for sentencing—but first he made the slave wait.

The sounds of advancing footsteps woke Rialla up from her nap—she had stayed up too late talking with Tris. She was thankful that she awoke before Winterseine had come into the room—the wait was supposed to make her nervous, not sleepy. She didn't want to enrage him pointlessly.

She was on her feet when the door opened to admit Winterseine. Docilely she kept her eyes on the floor and her hands at her side.

"Well," said Winterseine, his voice almost a purr, "it's nice to have you back, Dancer. Tell me, why did you run away in the first place? You knew that I would find you."

Rialla answered meekly, "Yes, Master. I knew that you would find me. I am sorry that I ran—I was frightened."

"What frightened you, Little One?" Again his voice was soft, like a predator stealing up on its prey.

Rialla felt the first twinge of fear—but it was a slave's fear and she was here by choice. The thought steadied her. Just as she started to answer his question, Tris attempted to contact her.

*Rialla, where are you?*

*Later,* she snapped at him, and closed her mind tightly to his presence.

To Winterseine she said hesitantly, "One of the other slaves there, in the upper rooms of the tavern in Kentar . . . she was killed that night. I saw them bring her body out." She paused and framed her words carefully out of truths. "The day before, the man who owned her was asking the barkeeper how much it would cost to buy me."

It had been idle speculation, a common question rather than serious intent, but the thought of being sold was frightening to a slave. Better the known evil, which one has gotten used to, than the unknown. Slaves are taught to be afraid of the unknown.

"So you ran away, killing one of my people."

"He startled me," Rialla said tremulously, remembering the shock of the man's death. "I pushed him and he hit his head on something on the floor. It was dark and I couldn't tell what it was." She had hit him as hard as she could with a mallet that had been left in the stables. She'd set the mallet near the body, and left. But Winterseine would expect her to lie and she had to stay in character.

There was a squeak as Winterseine settled himself into the big, leather-covered chair behind his desk. "You killed him with a hammer."

Rialla shook her head and looked frightened. A slave would never admit such a crime and Winterseine knew it. "No," she said. "He hit his head."

"You killed him," said the voice of the Master implacably. He might know that she wouldn't admit it, but he still needed her to realize that she couldn't get away with lying to him. He didn't wait for her reply again. Instead he asked a different question. "Where were you going?"

Rialla shrugged helplessly. "I don't know. Away, anywhere." That was true enough.

"Laeth said that he picked you up in the South. How did you get there?"

"After a few days, I don't know how long exactly, a man found me hiding under a bush. He took me and sold me to a merchant who smuggled me out of Darran and sold me to another merchant who worked the countries in the Alliance." Though selling an escaped slave was illegal, it was commonly done.

"I can't have slaves escaping, Dancer." Winterseine's voice was stern, but there was regret in it as well—a father talking to an errant child. It made Rialla want to retch.

"No, Master," said Rialla submissively, and the slave master sat back to contemplate her punishment.

THE GUARD LED HER THROUGH A MAZE OF HALLWAYS until he came to a place where there were two half-sized doors set into the wall at waist height. Rialla could hear soft sobbing sounds coming from behind one of the doors, and she watched apprehensively as the guard slid the bar off the other one. The door opened to reveal a dark hole even smaller than the door itself. A cobweb covered one corner and the guard brushed it aside.

"In with you," he said. His manner wasn't threatening, but Rialla had no doubt that he was willing to enforce his command.

She entered the darkness as slowly as she could, wanting to give any insects the chance to get out of her way. The opening wasn't quite tall enough for Rialla to crawl on her hands and knees, so she had to squirm forward until her feet slid through. The guard closed the door behind her and threw the bolt. Rialla stretched out her hands and felt the end of the cell; it was little bigger than the coffin the Darranians used to bury their dead.

For a normal human, such confinement would have been frightening. Rialla's awareness, though, wasn't limited by the stone around her. She could tell when the guard left to find lunch, she could touch the terror of the slave occupying the other cell, and she could feel Tris's impatience as he waited for her to tell him what was happening.

*Rialla!*

*Yes*, she answered.

*Are you all right? Where are you?*

She caught his worry and sent back reassurances as she responded. *I'm in solitary. It's not so bad; he had to do something for discipline and he doesn't like damaging his slaves if he can help it. I thought that it would be worse.*

*I'll take your word for it*, Tris answered, *I feel trapped inside these stone buildings humans like to build; I wouldn't care to be enclosed in a smaller area. I think I'll go exploring today and see what I can find out—call me if you need some company.*

*Where are you going to explore?* Rialla asked curiously. His face was known to Winterseine and a fair number of his guards. If someone saw Tris wandering through the castle, his presence might be questioned.

*Illusion is a simple enough magic*, replied Tris, apparently having little trouble following her thoughts. *Not many people notice one more bench or decorative plant.* A picture formed in her mind of a plant, similar to those scattered about Westhold, and a battered bench.

*What if someone tries to sit on you?* questioned Rialla, still feeling uneasy at Tris's ability to read thoughts that she wasn't actively projecting.

*That's why I prefer the plant when I can, but the bench has a rotted leg to discourage anyone who might want to rest.*

*Luck to you, Tris*, Rialla said. *Be careful.*

*I will*, he assured her, withdrawing to a less intimate level.

The other slave was beginning to get frantic in the enclosed dark space. Out of a latent sense of compassion and a desire to test her empathy further, Rialla decided to see if she could help her fellow penitent.

Patiently she worked through the fear of the other slave, sending peace and reassurance. Gradually rid of her fear, the woman was rocked by another emotion: hatred. Her emotion was strong, and it gave Rialla a clear picture of the focus of her hatred: Winterseine—hardly a surprise.

Unable to bear the contact any longer, Rialla withdrew and struggled to rid herself of the residue of the slave's fear and hatred. When she was calm, she steadied herself and projected the soothing peace that would allow the other woman to sleep. Gradually the other slave allowed herself to be pacified and fell into a light stupor.

It was late in the afternoon when Winterseine and two guards came to get her out. She crawled out of her hole and stood blank-faced for his inspection. He narrowed his eyes at her thoughtfully before leaving her with the guards.

Rialla watched as Winterseine slid out the bar that held the other slave captive in the coffin-shaped hole. In the relative light of the hold hallway, Rialla could see that the other's skin was so dark it looked as if it were carved from oiled ebony. Her features were fine-boned and her thick copper-colored hair hung past her waist—another Easterner.

As Rialla looked at the other slave closely, she realized what Winterseine had seen to make him look so thoughtful. Though the other slave's face was as blank as Rialla's own, it was lined with exhaustion and her hair was matted with sweat. Slight tremors shook her shoulders as she struggled to maintain the passive stance that Rialla had adopted. Rialla knew that she herself looked as if she'd been sleeping in a cot all afternoon.

"Take them to the baths and have them cleaned. Return the dark one to her classes in the blue room. Take the dancer back to her cell," ordered Winterseine briskly, and the guards led the slaves away.

In a clean tunic and freshly washed hair, Rialla found herself back in the little cell she'd spent the night in. There was a meal of bread and fruit waiting for her. She left the food where it was, waiting for Tris to come and eat with her.

Daylight came in from the high window, and the bars left their shadows on the walls rather than the floor. Rialla paced for a while before retreating to the accustomed discipline of the exercises that had become second nature to her as both dancer and horse trainer.

If she were going to have to dance very often, she might as well be in shape for it, she decided ruefully. Her bad leg was tight and she babied it through, hoping that she wasn't doing it more harm than good.

When she was finished, there was sweat running down her back, but she wasn't overly tired. Into her right hand she poured a little of the cool water from the ewer that had been left with her food. She splashed the water on her face and dried it off with the bottom of her tunic.

Bored, she sat beside the fresh straw and began to braid it as her mother had taught her to fashion horsehair rope. The straw was bulkier and not so strong, and the rope kept breaking before she got very far, but it was something to do.

She was beginning to eye the bread wistfully, when she realized that Tris was very near. She noticed a change in the stone near the top of the cell by the window. It looked at first as if the stone were growing. The granite blocks and the mortar between them bulged out in a lump roughly the size of a man's body. The lump slid gradually lower until the bottom of it rested on the ground. Slowly Tris pulled free of the rock, his body and features became distinct. The color of the stone gradually left his skin and clothing, and Tris stood brushing dust off his tunic and breeches.

"Better you than me," commented Rialla.

"What? You mean passing through the stone? It's not that bad—granite's kind of scratchy, though. I prefer marble or obsidian, but granite's more common."

Rialla laughed at his serious tone.

"So," she said, "how did your explorations go?"

"Fine," he replied, rubbing his beard as if it itched. "I

didn't see anything unusual except the number of cats here.''

Rialla nodded and grabbed a piece of fruit. ''Most castles have a lot of cats. They keep down the rat population.'' She bit into the tart apple and sighed with appreciation. Sianim was too warm to get really good apples.

''No, I mean *a lot* of cats. Someone here really likes them.'' Tris sat with his back against the wall. ''How was your day in solitary?''

Rialla gave a rueful shrug. ''Not bad, better than tomorrow will be. There was another slave from the East there, but I didn't get any useful information out of her.''

''What do you mean better than tomorrow?'' Tris hadn't been moving before, but now he was still, like a predator who has scented his prey.

Rialla finished the apple and put the core back on the tray. ''Do you want something to eat?''

Tris shook his head without losing his air of intensity. ''I'm fine. What about tomorrow?''

She tore off some bread and stood leaning against the wall. When she was through with her piece, she said wryly, ''I'm in for it. I was stupid and forgot that I was supposed to look abused after a day in solitary. Now he's got to find another punishment.'' She sighed drolly, trying to soothe him as she felt his anger rise. ''I guess I was never meant to be a spy.''

''What will he do?'' asked Tris again, grim-voiced.

She shook her head. ''I have no idea. Don't worry, it probably won't be anything too painful—he doesn't want to ruin his slave. He has to maintain a fine balance: too little discipline is disastrous, but too much discipline will break the spirit and ruin a dancer.''

Tris looked down at the floor and asked, ''Does it bother you to be a slave again?''

Rialla glanced at his hands, which were clenched around his left knee. He was having a harder time with her enslavement than she was. She paused thoughtfully for a moment before she answered, hoping that she could make him understand. "I would have thought it would, but it doesn't. I guess it makes a difference that it was my decision to come back. I choose to act like a slave, so they can't make me feel like one. Does that make sense?"

He looked a bit baffled so she added, "A slave has no power to make decisions; I do." Thinking about tomorrow, she smiled with little humor. "I have to live with the results too."

THE NEXT MORNING, WHEN THE GUARDS CAME, RIALLA was awake and ready for them. She wasn't taken to Winterseine this time, but to the castle punishment chamber.

The chamber was in a light and sunny area in the corner of the main floor of the castle. Both of the windows were low enough to get a nice view of one of the walled gardens behind the castle. Clear glass was expensive, so the windows were barred and open to the air.

Rialla supposed that the windows were there to remind the prisoners that there was a world outside, and to keep them from succumbing to the hopelessness that made them die too soon under the torturer's knife. From the despair she read in the few moments before she pulled her shields all the way up, she could have told Winterseine that he was wasting his windows.

The guards attached her tether to a wall and left her alone with the other prisoners, none of which were slaves. She had never been in this room; Rialla had been a tractable slave before she escaped.

The leash was a formality without the arm restraints—she could have taken it off with very little effort—but she was supposed to be a good slave. There were no guards, just the prisoners attached to the wall with heavy manacles.

Heavy canvas curtains blocked off the business end of the chamber. Rialla was just as glad not to have to look at the arcane devices responsible for the human wrecks that moaned pitifully where they hung like so many car-casses at a butcher's shop.

As she waited, Rialla became more and more agitated. The unpleasant emotions that pervaded the chamber were so strong she couldn't block them completely. They served to reinforce her apprehension. She got to her feet and paced back and forth to relieve her tension and keep her from tearing her collar off and running to Sianim as fast as she could.

Several men entered the chamber talking and laughing. One of them came up to her and unfastened her lead from the wall. He stank like sweat and other people's terror, and couldn't keep his hands to himself.

Rialla didn't struggle, and eventually he tired of his fun and blindfolded her with a strip of cotton cloth stained with dirt and dried blood. She followed the tug on her leash, stumbling blindly over the uneven floor. She hit her shin against a piece of wood and decided that it must have been a stair, because she was lifted up a short distance and put back on her feet on top of some sort of platform.

He pushed her backwards until her shoulders pressed against a bar of wood that moved slightly when she touched it. She felt the jerk at her neck as he attached her collar tightly to the bar. Her arms were pulled up over her head and tied to another bar that seemed to be both higher and farther away than the first. A thick strap was secured around her waist.

Rialla heard a groaning sound as the bars took her weight and her feet were slowly drawn off the floor. As her back arched against her support, she realized that she was tied to a large wheel. It stopped turning and her legs were pulled back and attached to another bar on the wheel.

When the man was satisfied that she was secure, he groped her one last time and went on to his next job. She couldn't close her ears to the noises in the chamber nearly as well as she could close her mind to the suffering that spawned them. She found herself wishing that they would punish her and get it over with.

Finally, there was a creak as the mechanism that turned the wheel was unlocked. Slowly she was pulled up and over the top of it. The wheel made an odd noise, but before Rialla was able to figure out what the sound was, her head was immersed in cold water.

The shock made her gasp, and she came out of the water choking and spitting out the fluid she'd swallowed. She was disoriented, and her head hit the water again before she was ready. She was underwater the third time when she realized that the wheel wasn't being turned at a steady rate that she could gage. She gagged and spat out the water that she had tried to breathe. The distraction caused her concentration to fail, and the strength of the shield that kept out the emotions flooding the chamber faded.

As soon as her barriers weakened, Rialla got a full dose of the torment of the other victims in the cell. She started to scream and her head was forced underwater again. This time the trip through the water was so slow that she started to black out before her nose broke the surface again. The wheel stopped to let her catch her breath, and she managed to close most of her barriers again as she choked and fought frantically for air.

*Tris.* She didn't really expect to be able to touch him without dropping her shields more than she could in this room. She was surprised when she got an answer.

*Rialla?* She could read the concern in his reply as he caught the edge of her desperation.

The wheel began to move again, and involuntarily she struggled against the ropes that held her. She started to tell him what was going on, but she couldn't form any coherent messages before she was under the water again.

*Rialla!* The demand in his tone brought her back to herself, and she struggled to communicate what she needed.

*Talk to me . . .* The struggle to keep from breathing the icy water grew more difficult. *Please . . . I need you to give me something to concentrate on . . .* Her face was numbed by the cold, and it was getting hard to tell when she was out of the water.

It wasn't until her forehead started under again that she realized that she'd held her breath too long. She managed to grab a quick breath before water closed over her mouth.

*Rialla? What . . .* He stopped, and she could feel him forcibly restrain himself. Slowly, as if he were reciting out loud, he sent her what she'd requested. *Black cherry root, otherwise known as nightshade or belladonna, can be used as a sedative or pain reliever in small enough doses . . .*

She grasped onto his words like a lifeline, using them to calm herself, much as a monk chants himself into a trance. She didn't care what he said, as long as he kept talking.

He seemed to sense what she needed and kept up a steady flow of information. She found that she could use him to block out the feedback she was getting from the other occupants of the chamber. Once she was calmer and not feeling other people's emotions, Rialla could tell when she was about to be submerged.

Tris kept talking, but she didn't really hear the words. Gradually, she was able to sense the water before it touched her. There was something odd about that, but she was in no state to decide what that was. Once she thought that Tris warned her, but that was ridiculous—she could tell that he was somewhere in the upper levels of the hold.

When they finally pulled her off, she was too dizzy to stand up, and the guards carried her back to her cell. She didn't stop Tris's steady voice in her mind, drawing strength from his presence. There was a towel and dry clothes waiting for her on the straw. Shaking with cold, she rubbed herself with thick cotton material until only her hair was damp, then put on the dry tunic.

*. . . acids that the flowering coralis uses to digest its prey can also be used to dissolve warts and . . .*

*Tris?* Rialla interrupted wearily as she stumbled to the

pile of straw. *Thanks. You can stop now. I'm back in the cell.*

To her surprise he didn't ask anything, just said, *I'm coming.*

Rialla drew up her legs and wrapped her arms around them, resting her cheek against her knee. She couldn't seem to get warm. She didn't watch this time when Tris came through the wall—once was enough.

"Are you all right? Is this the end of it?" Tris's voice sounded soft and dangerous, but when he touched her shoulders, warmth flowed from his hands.

Rialla turned her head to give him a tired smile and said hoarsely, "I think so. There's no reason for anything more. Thanks for the help."

"Good," he said, ignoring her thanks.

As she quit shivering, he pulled away and began pacing restlessly. Rialla could feel his agitation, but only distantly through the curtain of her exhaustion. She lowered her head to her knees and closed her eyes. Somehow it wasn't worth the effort to open them again. She fell asleep and woke up alone early in the morning.

SWEAT GATHERED IN THE SMALL OF RIALLA'S BACK AS she worked with fourteen other slaves to perform the combinations called out by the dancemaster. This man was new to her, although he seemed experienced. When the slaves were through with his workout, they would be warmed up and limber, but not overly tired.

Deliberately taking deep, even breaths through her nose, Rialla pulled her good leg behind her, until the heel touched the back of her head, and counted the drumbeats silently, trying to ignore the burning in her bad thigh as it supported her weight.

She switched legs, but couldn't make her bad leg stretch the few extra inches to touch. The burning increased and she was afraid that she would tear the wound open, so she let it relax a little further, aware that the dancemaster stood near her. When the combination was finished, the master called for a rest and the slaves dropped to the mats.

He examined the narrow red line that marked her leg where the swamp beast had slashed her.

"Bend it," he said shortly.

At his command, she flexed her leg as far as she could and released it.

He grunted, "Winterseine says that you are already a fine dancer. That being the case, I would keep you off that leg for another month, but he has decided that you are to dance with the advanced group. I want you to take it easy, but if Winterseine is watching you'd better not be favoring it. He doesn't believe in giving wounds time to heal; says that it makes for easy excuses."

Startled that the dancemaster would criticize Winterseine to a slave, Rialla merely nodded. She watched him walk to the center of the wooden floor and clap his hands once, and the workout resumed. Minding the dancemaster's words, she babied her left leg and kept a sharp eye out for Winterseine.

The other girls were wary of her and made no move to greet her on the rest breaks. Rialla sat quietly a little apart from the others, but close enough to listen to the other slaves gossip softly together.

Most of what they said was unimportant; they were too conscious of Rialla to talk about Lord Winterseine or anything else interesting enough to get them into trouble should the Master hear about it. If she continued being unobtrusive, they would forget her, but it was going to take time.

With a sigh, Rialla relaxed and closed her eyes. Carefully she lowered her defenses and reached out lightly. As she did so, she heard one of the slaves giggle. She focused on that one and caught a picture of Terran, altered by the slave's perception of him—Rialla knew he wasn't *that* good-looking.

The slave had seen him recently in intimate circumstances and enjoyed every minute. Rialla withdrew hastily before she received a touch by touch outline of the slave's experiences at the hands of Winterseine's son. Just before she pulled back completely, she caught something, an image . . . of a cat, a blue cat.

It was dark when she was returned in a clean tunic to the holding cell. Although practice was done in a one-piece garment that left most of the body bare, it was too cold to wear all the time, so a clean tunic was also supplied daily. Her hair was freshly washed and braided neatly, brushing the top of her shoulders.

As soon as the guard left, Rialla lay face down on the cool stone floor.

"Tired?" asked Tris in a voice that didn't carry beyond the room.

She didn't bother lifting her head, just slid it back and forth against the floor. "I'm too old for this. The other girls are just babies, and they're in much better shape than I am. Let's go back to Sianim and I'll sit in a rocking chair and embroider tablecloths."

Two hands touched her back and caressed the sore muscles there. She moaned weakly and folded her arms to cushion her face as the stiffness eased with magical swiftness.

"Do you embroider?" Tris asked with interest.

"No," she replied, "and maybe, just maybe, if you keep that up I won't have to learn."

He laughed, started on her lower back and said in conversational tones, "I found out some interesting information today." He stopped kneading and began thumping her with the sides of hands instead.

"From what I've overheard," he continued, "Lord Winterseine has indeed been traveling to the other side of the Swamp. He keeps a ship at a small harbor near the Southern Sea that he uses to sail to the East. For the past six years he has spent at least four months a year there, except last year, when his son made the journey alone. What was that?"

"Mmpft," she said obscurely, then managed, "Tri . . . hiss . . . sstop . . . it!"

He quit pounding on her and sat on his heels.

She gave him a narrow-eyed look, twisting her head so she could see over her shoulder, and said with mock affront, "Thanks. Maybe we should have sent you here on your own. All that I've managed to learn today is that I'm out of shape."

"Touchy aren't you?" he protested with a hint of laughter. "I thought a hold of this size might have some work for a journeyman woodcrafter." Abruptly his features sharpened, and his beard disappeared; his clothing changed, becoming heavier to keep out sawdust. Tris never paused in his speech, but his accent vanished. "It seems that the old one died last season and his apprentice left for the city. I spent the day repairing cabinets in the kitchens. The cook likes to gossip, especially with a near equal."

Rialla eyed him with some respect. If she hadn't seen it herself, she would have sworn that she was talking to a middle-class Darranian craftsman.

"How did you explain your lack of tools?" she asked.

He looked sad. "I was stopped by bandits on my travels. They took everything I owned. Isn't it miraculous that the old woodcraftsman died without heirs, so his tools were left here?"

He dropped the illusion and continued, "I also accidently hit my thumb with my hammer; even the best craftsman does so occasionally. I swore, using a certain god's name, and was hushed by a number of horrified people, including the spit boy."

Rialla stilled. "I thought I was insane when it first occurred to me that there might be a connection. But I can't imagine another household in Darran that would be worried if a stranger used Altis's name as a curse." She looked at Tris. "Don't look so smug, it doesn't suit you."

He laughed and went to work on her legs.

"Tris?" she asked.

"Hmm?" he grunted absently, working on the back of her bad leg.

"Did you say something about there being a lot of cats here?"

"Hmm," he said again. "Yes, not just in the lower floors, but all over the castle. Why do you ask?"

She shook her head and closed her eyes. "I don't know . . . but one of the slaves was thinking about cats today. It was in an odd context . . ." She shrugged. "It was probably nothing, but it seemed strange."

THE NEXT DAY WAS MORE OF THE SAME. WHEN RIALLA returned from the long day of workouts, Tris told her what he had learned as he loosened her muscles. He was much better than the masseuse that had a turn at all the slaves before they bathed. Part of that was because, although he never commented on the various bruises acquired from the dancemaster's staff, he healed them partially, so they were much less painful.

Tris had spent most of the day listening to servants' gossip. He'd found that, though Lord Winterseine had earned a great deal of money from training slaves, he brought back even more from his trips east. The exotic dark-skinned slaves were in demand, and in Darran they brought in two or three times more gold than other slaves.

For her part, Rialla had learned nothing new. Working slaves might be a good source of information, but dancers in training had limited exposure to the world outside. The dancemaster might have known something, but his emotions were spared for his obsession with dance, and his unemotional thoughts on other matters were his own.

When Tris finished with her massage, Rialla felt like a boneless mass of relaxed muscles resting facedown on the straw. Tris seated himself against one of the walls and snatched an apple, biting into it with obvious enjoyment. At the sound, Rialla sat up and took a hard roll from the basket out of which Tris had gotten his apple.

They ate in companionable silence for a while. Tris finished the apple and threw it down the corner grate.

He slanted Rialla an oddly solemn look and then said, "I haven't spent much time among the nobility in Darran, much less around slaves. You have an expression that you use when you are impersonating a slave, but it is different from the expression that the slaves in the keep use."

The bread in Rialla's mouth was fresh and sweet, but she had to force it down to talk. She bowed her head and knew that the slave's mask that he'd asked her about was frozen on her face. Finally she said, "Winterseine would tell you that there are two kinds of slaves in Darran. The first is a pleasure slave, a bedmate. Most men prefer to have their longtime bedpartners compliant and smiling, acting as if their duties are pleasurable. Force is fine occasionally, but it takes energy. Pleasure slaves are punished if they do not at least feign enjoyment of their duties."

She swallowed, feeling Tris's focused attention. "Dancers, like me, are usually not owned by an individual for his personal use; the term that slave trainers use for them is 'exotics.' Dancers are expensive because they take time to train and require a certain amount of ability. They are owned by taverns, clubs and brothels."

Rialla looked at her half-eaten roll without interest and continued to speak. "Slave trainers believe that a slave that has been turned into a pleasure slave has no spirit, no individuality. A dancer requires a certain amount of independence and arrogance."

"You said that slave trainers believe that. What about you?"

Rialla shrugged. "A slave has no spirit, no individuality. It doesn't matter if she is a dancer or a pleasure slave. A slave feels what she is told she feels, and does what she is told to do. Dancers follow the pattern established for them just as the pleasure slaves do. The pattern is no better or worse, just different."

"I'm sorry," said Tris softly.

Rialla tossed him a lopsided smile, and took another bite of the bread. "Don't be. It's hardly your fault."

AFTER A COUPLE OF DAYS OF WORKING OUT, RIALLA found that she wasn't quite so worn out at night, but Tris continued to act as masseur. Under his ministration, the stiffness was leaving her bad leg, until she could stretch it out almost as far as her good leg. They had been discussing what he found while he kneaded and pulled until she was as limp as a lump of bread dough left to rise, but this night he was quiet.

"What's wrong?" she asked finally, keeping her face in her arms. She could feel his distress at the edge of her awareness, but didn't want to pry without permission.

"Nothing," he said. "This place oppresses me. The cold stone keeps out the sun's warmth and light." He paused. "I thought about what you told me last night."

"Do your people own slaves?"

"No," he said. "But we knew about it. A slave came to the enclave once, seeking sanctuary. I understand that some of the religious communes offer a hiding place for slaves. Mine did not. The slave was held until the owners could collect her."

"Was that your decision?" questioned Rialla, trying to get at what bothered him. She could sense his guilt, that he'd violated his sense of right and wrong, but she didn't know how to help.

"No. I opposed the decision—for the wrong reasons." Straw rustled as he moved away. "I felt that the commune had come to its decision from fear of discovery rather than out of any reasoned discussion. I was right, but too young to understand that there was never any other motivation for what the enclave did. The elders had offended my belief in them. I was more concerned with that than with the poor girl who rode off in chains."

That bothered him, she could tell, but it wasn't the cause of his disquiet.

"You're doing something about it now," she said, finally sitting up so she could see him. "Even if slavery continues for another five centuries, you are doing something about it."

He stood with his back to her, in the faint area of fading light.

"Am I?" he said in an odd tone. "Yes, I suppose I am."

He swung around and approached her, gesturing for her to take her former prone position. "I'll loosen that muscle in your back and tell you about what I learned today. Do you know the ideograph that belongs to Altis?"

Rialla rolled facedown again. She could feel his pain, guilt and remorse churning strong enough to make butter; but she didn't know what to do about it. She wasn't sure that he knew how easily she read him—it wasn't deliberate on her part. She didn't want him to think that she was impinging on his privacy, so she allowed him to change the subject.

"I don't know anything about Altis, except that he was one of the old gods."

"Shame on you," he reprimanded in his best healer voice. "Altis was the lord of the night. It's in his shadows that the hunted escapes the hunter's dinner table. He was one of the benevolent gods. Not only did he refrain from tormenting humans when he was bored, as a fair number of them did, but he actually was known to interfere with other gods at their sport."

"What of the folk that weren't human—the shapeshifters, the selkies, and the . . . the silfs."

"Sylvans," corrected Tris dryly, as he started to put pressure on the muscle in her lower back. "We were the children of the gods themselves, and better able to defend ourselves. We could call more readily on our parent god. Naslen, the lord of the forest, fathered the sylvans; Torrec, the huntress, bore the shapeshifters; Kirsa, goddess of the waves, bore the selkies. All of them minor powers, but strong enough to keep the others from lightly playing their games with us. Now, where was I . . ."

"Altis," said Rialla, in a voice that was more of a moan as he caught just the right place.

"Yes, Altis. His ideograph is that of a stylized cat sitting on its haunches with its body in profile, and its head full face and lowered—"

"With a five-pointed star in the middle of its forehead, and in the center of the star a large emerald," interrupted Rialla.

"I don't know about the emerald," said Tris, "but there is a five-pointed star. Where did you see it?"

"One of the slaves," said Rialla. "She was thinking about it."

"One of the slaves you dance with?" asked Tris.

"Yes" replied Rialla, smiling at the floor. "It was easy to pick up since she remembered it with some . . . er . . . fervor."

"The slave was a follower of Altis?"

Rialla laughed despite herself. "No, actually I'm not sure how the cat came into it; she was remembering a glorious night of passion. I can assure you that it had *nothing* in common with religious devotion."

Tris snorted. "You obviously haven't met the same sorts of religious zealots that I have."

"You did have something in mind when you brought up this cat?" asked Rialla.

"Yes, though it has lost what little import it had. I was asked to evaluate the chances of saving a wooden screen in one of the rooms on the upper floor of the castle. Once past the public rooms, there isn't a room in the castle that is free of that cat."

Rialla thought, then said, "To convince the servants? As with Tamas's broken arm?"

"Then why would they be only on the private floors?"

"I can answer that," said Rialla. "As a slave trader, Winterseine deals frequently with Southerners, merchants who would sleep in the guest quarters on the first floor. There is a new religion in the South; it was beginning to evolve when I traveled there with my clan. They worship someone they call the All-Mother. I don't know much more about them, except that they would certainly not do business with a heathen who worshipped dead gods.''

A peaceful silence descended, and Rialla relaxed into the rhythm of Tris's movements as he loosened her tight legs. "Tell me something about your people, Tris."

She could feel him hesitate. "It is forbidden for one of us to tell an outsider about . . . Ah, well now, I suppose that I no longer have to listen to the dictates of the elders." He thought for a moment.

"Long time past, humans were only a minor part of a world ruled by green magic." His voice took on a classic story-telling rhythm, though a bit hesitant, as if he were translating as he spoke. "There were the little folk: the butterfly-winged people who played over the winds, and the stone workers who preferred the shadows of evening to the light of day. The forest people, sylvans, dryads, shapeshifters, haunted the woods and fought for territory. They all spoke to the spirits of the trees and the animals.

"The green folk, though, like the gods whose children they are, do not propagate well, and humans began to overrun their part of the world. As they spread into our territories, the dryads welcomed them as they did all things, while the other folk retreated and watched. First came the traders, then the wizards who sought to learn the secrets of our magic, but it was the farmers who spelled the end of the reign of green magic.

"They tore up the land and cut down the forests; the spirits of the trees cried out, crippling those tied too closely with earthmagic. They settled the land, driving the little folk underground and forcing us further and further into the forests of the far north, where green magic ruled the strongest. There was not enough room there for all. The earthmasons retreated below ground. The shapeshifters retreated into themselves. The sylvans hid where no one would think to look: among the humans themselves. Only the dryads remained, the few the rape of the land had left. For them came the slavers, and the dryads disappeared into the East.

"When the human wizards began to vie with one another for power and Nevra Forest became the glass desert, the last of the dragonkind vanished in the winds."

Tris allowed his voice to darken dramatically. "But sometimes, empath, among the humans is born the legacy of the dryads. Green-eyed or amber-eyed like their distant kin, these can touch the spirits of the trees and the beasts and the deepest souls of mankind."

Rialla turned and narrowed her clear, green eyes at his gray-green, innocent gaze.

He laughed, unimpressed.

Something that had been nagging at her for a while chose that moment to crystallize.

"Tris?" she asked softly. "In your story you said it was the Wizard's Wars that destroyed the dragons. Is that true?"

"I don't know . . . not having been there myself. The legends say that dragons are creatures *of* magic rather than just users of it. The wars disturbed the flow of magic and dragons were no more . . . or so say the legends."

There was something in his voice that prompted her to ask further, "You don't seem convinced that the legends are true."

"Well, you see," began Tris, starting on her other foot, "I saw a dragon once."

LATER THAT NIGHT, TRIS STOOD ALONE IN THE DARKNESS of the forest that stood near Winterseine's keep. He leaned his forehead against an oak, but could draw no comfort there, for the oak couldn't change the impulsive action that caused the cold breath of guilt on his conscience.

# EIGHT

The labyrinth that served as the government building in Sianim was deserted at this hour of the night, but when Ren stepped inside his office, he waited until the door was shut behind him before removing the shade that muted the light from his lantern.

Pushing aside a few books, he cleared space on his desk for the lantern. Before leaving this evening at the usual time, he'd taken the precaution of pulling the heavy curtains across his window so that no one would see the light from the outside. He wasn't really concerned with secrecy or he never would have chosen his office as tonight's meeting place, but it was his nature as well as his profession to keep as much information to himself as possible.

A disturbance in the air currents, and a whiff of sweet perfume informed the Spymaster before he turned around that his visitor was here.

Kisrah ae'Magi, once a minor Rethian lord and now the Archmage, made an impression upon everyone he met. Ren had never actually seen the Archmage before, but he had heard enough about him that he wasn't unduly surprised by the magician's distinctive appearance.

Kisrah's hat was a deep purple that contrasted neatly with the light pink of the long fluffy feather that curled from the hat's brim to his shoulders. The sleeves of his lavender overcoat were heavily embroidered with gold thread, as were his shoes and gloves. A gold-and-amethyst earring pierced his left ear.

He looked young to Ren's jaded eye, too young to hold the power he wielded, but many of the more powerful wizards were that way. Someone less observant than Ren might have dismissed the Archmage as an overdressed fop, overlooking the keen intelligence that lurked in his dark eyes. Lord Kisrah had made good use of his power in the decade he'd been Archmage.

"Lord Kisrah," said Ren in a welcoming tone. "It is most kind of you to agree to come here."

"Spymaster," replied Lord Kisrah with a touch of humor in his voice. "How could I refuse when your invitation was so unique? I had no idea that my mistress's gardener was a Sianim spy until he invited me to meet with you here. Not that I am offended by it. I had begun to worry that you did not deem me important enough to spy upon."

Ren smiled at him, a remarkably open expression on the Spymaster's face. "I do have other spies in your household; otherwise I would have found another method of getting a message to you. The wizards' council would not have called you as ae'Magi if you could be so easily disregarded."

"I *am* flattered," returned Kisrah, with an answering smile. "I suspect that you had another reason for asking me here."

Ren nodded and gestured Kisrah to a chair that he had cleared of debris earlier in the day. The Archmage ignored the dust and sat, crossing his extended legs at the ankles. Ren pulled his chair out from behind his desk and sat facing Kisrah.

"Are you familiar with what is happening on the other side of the Great Swamp?" questioned Ren.

Kisrah nodded. "You are not the only one with spies. Unfortunately, I did not become aware of the situation until someone started expending a great deal of magic at the Swamp with the intention of clearing the old road.

"My sources say that there will be an invasionary force through the road by next spring at the latest. There was some thought that the wizards' council should force a confrontation before the road is cleared, but I vetoed it." The magician leaned forward. "I reminded them of the Wizard Wars and the destruction that they caused. Whoever is opening the Swamp is very powerful. A direct attack on him before we know what he is capable of could have disastrous results."

"What do you know of the Eastern magician?" asked Ren.

Lord Kisrah shook his head. "Not much. He claims to be the speaker for one of the old gods and uses religion to ease his conquests."

"Then I might be of some service," offered Ren.

Lord Kisrah leaned back in his chair and said, "How much will it cost?"

"Nothing," answered Ren in slightly affronted tones. "If you can take care of the wizard, you are welcome to all the aid that I can give you."

The Archmage raised his brows in mock astonishment. "This must be a new policy. We'll be paying Sianim for cleaning the Uriah out of the ae'Magi's castle for the next twenty years."

Ren shrugged. "That was different. The Voice of Altis is a threat to us all."

"And Uriah aren't?" muttered the Archmage, but he'd regained his smile. "So, what knowledge do you possess regarding this man?"

"He's from this side of the Swamp," said Ren. "My informants in the East have confirmed it. I didn't contact you then, because I had no idea who it was. Yesterday, though, one of my people returned from a mission in Darran. While he was there, he inadvertently ran across some information indicating that the sorcerer we are looking for might be Lord Winterseine."

"*Isslic?*" asked Lord Kisrah incredulously, then he nodded his head more thoughtfully. "He is powerful enough in his own right, and I've heard rumors that he dabbled in forbidden magic—the only thing that kept him out of the council was those rumors."

"I had heard"—Ren coughed discreetly: the wizards' council was infamous for its obsession with secrecy— "that if you knew who the renegade wizard was, you, as Archmage, could control him."

"Now, I wonder where you heard that," commented Kisrah, but with no real offense. "I am sorry that in this instance your information is incorrect. The Master Spells might have allowed me to control him, but they have been lost."

Ren drew in his breath in shock. "*What?*" It had been a long time since someone had managed to shock the Spymaster.

Lord Kisrah shrugged, leaning back in the chair and closing his eyes wearily. "In the spellbook of the ae'Magi there are symbols that cannot be redrawn. These are necessary to the spells' castings. After Geoffrey, my predecessor, died," Kisrah's voice echoed with remembered sorrow, "we found the Archmage's spellbook, but someone had been there before us and removed the pages that held the Master Spells."

The Archmage opened his eyes to look at Ren. "It is possible that Isslic, Lord Winterseine, took the pages. He was a friend of the late Archmage, and would know where to look."

Ren drummed his fingers on the arms of his chair and swore softly to himself. "What you are saying is that someone else, possibly Winterseine, could cast the Master Spells and hold all the wizards under his power?"

Kisrah shook his head. "No. Not yet, at least. The council holds the method of working the spells in another *grimoire*. As soon as we found that the symbols were missing, we hid the rest of the spells in a safe place. No one can get to them now without alerting the council. It's been ten years and no one has tried to get to the second book.''

''Why not destroy the second part of the spell?'' asked Ren softly.

''The spells were developed to keep magicians from each other's throat. Without them, there is no check on the behavior of the mages. I don't think that we need another glass desert,'' replied Kisrah.

Ren snorted. ''I think you magicians exaggerate the importance of the Wizard Wars. It can be more dangerous to have the wrong person command absolute control of all magicians than to have the possibility of a battle between wizards.''

'' 'You magicians'?'' queried the Archmage softly. ''Don't you mean 'we magicians'?''

Ren stared at him for a minute, then smiled reluctantly. ''So that's why you chose to tell me so much. How did you find out about it?''

Lord Kisrah returned the smile. ''Old Aurock used to brag about you. She said that you were one of the few apprentices she'd ever had who knew when to quit. I will see what can be done to confirm Winterscine's involvement. The council will then decide what to do about him. I'll keep you informed.''

He was gone with the slight disturbance of air that accompanied magical teleportation. Alone, Ren looked into the shadows in the corner of his office for some time, before he left, shutting the door quietly behind him.

RIALLA LAY FLAT ON HER BACK, PRETENDING TO BE more winded than she was. No one would bother her if they thought she was resting, and she could tap into the emotions around her without worrying that she would be interrupted.

She'd been here long enough that some of the other slaves had made overtures of friendship, though nothing obvious enough that the dancemaster would see: a wink while she listened to the dancemaster's impatient scolding, a hand helping her find a towel to wipe her face in the bathhouse. She'd forgotten how warming such small acts of support could be; she'd wanted fervently to forget everything about slave life.

Though in most respects the classes were not as bad as she had expected, in some ways they were worse. The hardest memory of slavery that Rialla had to bear was not the lack of freedom; it was the lack of desiring freedom.

By the time that Rialla had been a slave for a year, she lived for the dance, and practiced far into the night. She'd known that she owed obedience to any freeman, but among the society of the slaves she'd been special. She'd been the best of the dancers that Isslic owned, and she'd taken pride in it.

Lying on her back with the sweat drying slowly in the heat of summer, Rialla supposed that she owed a debt to Lord Jarroh. If she had not felt his slave's painful death on the night of her escape, she would probably still be dancing in one of Winterseine's clubs. A wry smile twisted her lips: now she was a spy dancing at Winterseine's home estate. The sound of the dancemaster's hands clapping together brought her to her feet before she opened her eyes.

The dancemaster was working one of the standard dances that the slaves would be expected to learn. It was common fare, something that even the Darranian ladies could watch. It was also impressive and, with the right costuming, highly erotic; a useful addition to any slave dancer's repertoire. He'd been teaching sections of it all week; today he called on Sora to dance it from beginning to end.

Sora reminded Rialla more than any of the others of the slave she had been. Like Rialla herself, Sora had the advantage of being tall and willowy, allowing her to appear more graceful. She was very good, and driven to be even better. Her competitiveness drove her to conquer more and more difficult moves as she labored diligently to please her masters.

It made Rialla's skin crawl with unwanted memories. She'd tried to forget that she had been like that: driven to exceed the expectations of her master, to be a good slave. It made her almost physically ill to watch Sora strain for the perfect motion of her hand.

She had been careful not to appear to be a challenge to Sora; the girl didn't need any more encouragement in her effort. Rialla used the dancemaster's permission to go easy on her leg to restrict herself to lesser moves.

Rialla knew the dance already, but she stood with the rest while Sora performed it from beginning to end. The younger slave was good, but not quite quick enough on the turns, and she didn't have the experience to bring out the implicit eroticism.

When Sora was finished, the dancemaster nodded at Rialla. She understood his reasoning for having her dance second. Although Rialla knew the dance, Sora had proven herself the better dancer and would give the others something to strive for.

Rialla began her dance, making sure that her gestures were a touch cruder than Sora's, her moves more hesitant. Because she deliberately held herself back, she was far into the dance before she lost herself to the beat of the drums. She didn't see the blow that knocked her off her feet.

"If," said Lord Winterseine, looking down at her coldly, "I had not seen you dance at my nephew's hold, I just might believe you had lost the talent you had in the seven years you were gone. I might have believed that you were as stiff and unpracticed as you appear. Get up."

Impassively Rialla got to her feet, wiping the blood off her cut lip with one hand, ignoring the sweat that dripped down her temple. She had the sick feeling that she wouldn't like what was coming. She instinctively tightened the barriers that she used to keep out of Tris's mind.

Lord Winterseine strode up to the line of watching

slaves and grabbed one of them, pulling her back to Rialla.

"You are valuable," he purred to Rialla. "I won't mar your skin by whipping you—but this one will never be worth much as a dancer." He held out his free hand, and the dancemaster gave Lord Winterseine the staff that he used to keep discipline. The dancemaster's face was as impassive as Rialla's, but she could all but taste his fury. "Just in case you don't believe I'm serious, I think that a little demonstration is in order."

He pushed the girl facedown on the mat and swung the staff. The slave screamed when her ribs collapsed under the blow. Forewarned, Rialla had blocked out most of the girl's pain.

Winterseine turned to the dancemaster. "Take her to the side and wrap her ribs, but I want her here until this one," he patted Rialla gently on her cheek, where the skin was already starting to turn purple, "finishes her dance to my satisfaction. I hope she won't need another demonstration, but it is always better to be certain."

This time there was no question of favoring her bad leg. Rialla knew her master well. She knew that there was a good chance that Winterseine would have the other girl beaten to death no matter how well Rialla danced. So she danced to surpass her best, to keep from living with guilt of the girl's death. If she danced as well as she could and Winterseine still killed the girl, the guilt would be his.

Her spins had the extra snap that separated excellent from merely good. Knowing that what the master wanted from the dance was not just excellence, but arousal, she emphasized the erotic moves—dancing with more fire and less grace. She managed to make the simple practice costume into something much more erotic. The drummer was better than she had thought. He added the last touch of spice that turned the dance from esoteric and airy into something that belonged only in the most private of clubs or bedrooms.

When Rialla stopped dancing, there was silence.

Breathing heavily, she looked at Winterseine, and was reassured by the satisfaction on his face.

"I want her, Father." Terran's rasping voice broke through the silence. Rialla had been so focused on Lord Winterseine, she hadn't seen that his son was with him.

"No," replied Winterseine. "She's been Laeth's slave for who knows how long. You know as well as I do the loyalty that a slave can develop for her owner. I'm not letting her run loose in the keep until I am sure that she is properly retrained."

Terran looked away from Rialla and focused on his father. "I want her," he repeated.

Rialla turned her impassive gaze to Winterseine. A strange expression crossed his face, and it took a moment for her to recognize it as fear. It was such an odd reaction that it distracted her from her distress at having attracted Terran's attention.

Lord Winterseine turned to the dancemaster and said curtly, "See that she is taken to my son's chamber this evening after baths. I'll send a guard to escort her." He turned and left. With a last look at Rialla, Terran did the same.

The dancemaster bowed his head in submission and gestured for Rialla to wait with the others, while he made sure that the injured slave had been properly treated.

Rialla stood where he placed her and closed her shaking hands over her arms, not bothering to wipe off the sweat that crept down her face. There would be more there before the day was done. She had made the dancemaster look bad and hurt one of his students. He was not going to make the rest of the day easy. Rialla tried to forget what would come after that.

WHEN RIALLA EMERGED FROM THE BATHS, IT WAS TAmas, Winterseine's manservant, who waited for her. The thin silk shift that the bath attendants had given her didn't cover much, and what it did cover was clearly visible through the fine fabric. Seven years a slave had left her largely uncaring about her state of dress or undress, but Tamas made her wish for a blanket to cover herself with.

She kept a bland expression on her face when his hand wrapped around her arm, but the emotions that he was forcing on her by his touch made her ill; so did the thought of what was in store for her.

He led her into the keep and up a back staircase. On the third floor, they walked down a long corridor to a locked door that Tamas opened with a gilt-edged key.

The room she was led into was large and open, larger than the suite that she and Laeth had been given at Westhold. The floor was covered with soft woven carpets in dark colors. The stone walls were whitewashed to make the room look even bigger than it was.

"Stay here and wait for his lordship." She heard the key turn in the lock as Tamas left.

With resignation that just barely covered her panic, Rialla walked around the room. It didn't appear to be a bedroom; there was no bed or cot anywhere. Two long, yellow velvet benches provided seating on Rialla's left and right, drawing attention to the wall opposite the door she'd entered.

A stylized cat was scribed from floor to ceiling in blue so dark that it was almost black. It was bracketed by two doors that were the same shade of blue. In front of the cat figure was a raised platform that extended from one door to the other. A small rose-colored marble altar occupied the place of honor on a small rug in the center of the platform. Terran, at least, seemed to be taking the worship of Altis seriously.

Next to the bench on her right was a low table on which was a neat row of books between two black bookends. Rialla knelt in front of the table and slipped one of the thin volumes out and opened it. Script Darranian was almost beyond her power to decipher, but she read enough that she could tell that she held a journal in her hands.

Men's voices echoed from the outer hall.

". . . there are other things more important."

"With the mages behind us, it will be much easier."

"I *told* you. It doesn't matter if the mages bow to our whim or not. There are other things to be done and I will not waste power on trivialities."

She slipped the journal back in place and ran to the door. The distortion from the hall was so great that she couldn't tell who was speaking, but she recognized the touch of Winterseine's mind. Since she couldn't feel anyone else in the hall, she had to assume that the other man was Terran.

When Terran entered the room, Rialla was sitting on the floor with her head properly bowed. He ignored her at first, walking directly to the platform before the altar. He knelt on the rug and bowed his head in apparent prayer. Rialla's neck grew stiff as she waited.

Finished, he got lightly to his feet and walked back to stand before her.

"Stand up," he said.

Rialla stood. Terran walked around her once, stopping directly in front of her.

"I remember you, when Father first brought you here. You were frightened of everything." He reached out and touched her chin.

She shuddered visibly. Even when her empathy had been crippled, she had an awareness of other living creatures that was missing with Terran. Being touched by someone she couldn't feel on more than a physical level made her feel as if she were being caressed by a corpse. She felt a rising desperation, a need to leave that was fast becoming irresistible.

"Easy," he said softly. "I know you've been with Laeth for a long time now, but I will give you time to adjust. Come, there is a better place for this."

THE DEEP BLUE CARPET WAS SOFT UNDER RIALLA'S CALloused feet as she shifted carefully off the bed. Silently she picked up the shift that she'd worn to the room and put it on. Without looking at the man sleeping on the bed,

Rialla left the bedchamber and slipped into the outer room, emerging on one side of the raised platform.

Rialla walked quickly to the table that contained Terran's journals, sparing an uneasy glance at the cat on the wall behind her. If anyone knew what Winterseine's plans were it would be Terran, and he might have written them in his journal. Rialla would rather have had the dagger to prove Winterseine's guilt, but she couldn't go through this again, not even to ensure that slavery in Darran would be ended.

She looked at the books, but knew from her earlier perusal that they were not obviously dated. As she hesitated, she heard a faint rustle in the bedroom.

She snatched the first book on her left, hoping that it would be the most recent one, and strode quickly to the door. To her surprise and relief, it was one of the guardsmen, not Tamas, who waited just outside to take her back to her cell.

With a subtle use of her talent that she'd almost forgotten, Rialla turned the guard's attention from the book she held. Because of her intervention, he saw nothing unusual in a slave taking a book from Terran's room. If no one questioned him about it for a day or so, he probably wouldn't remember he'd ever seen it.

TRIS PACED THE CELL RESTLESSLY. SHE WAS LATE. MUCH later than could be easily explained by normal delays. He'd checked the baths and they were empty. She'd been blocking her thoughts since early in the day and he couldn't break through. He stilled and cocked his head when footsteps sounded in the corridor. He slipped quickly into the shadows when the key was turned into the door.

Mutely, with head bowed, Rialla walked to the center of the cell. The light coming through the window surprised her and left her slightly disgruntled. It felt as if several days had passed since this morning: it could at least be dark.

She knew that Tris was standing in the shadows, but he didn't say anything. She didn't know if it was the guard's presence that kept him back or if something showed in her face. She stood for a while after the door closed, finally exchanging the silk shift for the clean white tunic that had been left for her by the door. She set her discarded clothes carefully over the book; Tris could find something to do with it before morning. With nothing more to keep her busy, she sat on the clean straw.

He didn't come up behind her and begin rubbing her neck as he usually did, and she was grateful. She didn't think that she could stand to be touched for a while, not even by Tris. She wished they'd let her take a bath before bringing her back, though she knew from experience that water wouldn't make her feel clean again.

After a very long while, she curled her legs up against her chest and hid her face against her knees. The healer was very patient; she could hear him breathe and knew that he hadn't moved since she came in. Rialla knew she ought to tell him something, but she was afraid if she spoke she would shatter the fragile shell that guarded her tears.

Instead she lowered the tight barriers that she'd placed around the part of herself that was linked to Tris.

*Tris, I . . .* Even in her thoughts she couldn't form the words, so she pulled him into her memories instead.

Rialla waited numbly for his reaction—though she wasn't sure what that would be. Anger, perhaps, or even disgust; sorrow would not be unthinkable for a healer to feel at rape—even if the victim consented to it.

What he felt was white-hot rage. It was strong enough that Rialla pulled her head away from her knees to look at him. He stood where he had for so long, his face still. Without the link she wouldn't have known that he felt anything.

She didn't know what to say in the face of his fury. It surprised her that she could think of saying anything at all. If it had been Laeth, standing quietly in the darkness of the little cell, she'd have been cowering in the opposite corner.

"I found some journals of Terran's," she said finally, pleased that her voice sounded calm. "I thought he might have known about Karsten's murder and recorded it. I'm not sure if I got his oldest journal or the most recent one; I didn't have time to check."

"You found it in Terran's room?" She felt his rage focus, and realized he must not have picked up who it had been.

*There was too much. I couldn't catch everything.* He told her, apparently catching her thought.

"Yes," she said. "I found it in Terran's room."

"He just let you take it?"

She shook her head. "No. He was asleep in another room. I don't think that anyone will notice that it's gone until Terran tries to write in it again. I . . . umm . . . *suggested* to the guard who escorted me back that there was nothing uncommon in a slave taking one of Terran's journals."

Tris grunted.

"Even if I took the wrong one, he might have written about Winterseine's use of magic," she added.

The shadows in the cell deepened with the lengthy silence, until the only light came from the stars.

Rialla cleared her throat, uneasy because Tris's rage wasn't abating. "What happened is just part of being a slave, and not the worst part either. He was clean and didn't go out of his way to hurt me. I don't think that he was impressed enough with my performance to want another one." She knew that she wouldn't cry now, because slaves don't, and she felt more like a slave right now than a horse trainer or spy.

"Is ending slavery in Darran still so important to you?" he asked, his head turned away from her. "The slaves here don't appear to be fighting nearly as hard for their freedom as you are."

Rialla nodded her head wearily.

"Even after this?"

"Yes."

"Tomorrow," asserted Tris heavily. "Tomorrow we will leave."

Rialla stubbornly shook her head. "The journal isn't going to be enough by itself. We need something—" Her breath caught as the answer came to her. "We need Winterseine's spellbook. All wizards have one . . . I think. Can you find where Winterseine's study is?"

Slowly, Tris nodded. "It's somewhere on the upper floors. I can try to break in tomorrow."

"Then we leave," said Rialla, feeling a wave of relief at the thought of being away from this place.

They talked a while longer, discussing ways of leaving the keep. There were several possibilities, depending on the time of day and how many guards they met. But, eventually, they lapsed into silence.

It was strange how much Terran's demands bothered Rialla. Sex had never been something that she enjoyed, but it was a part of slavery. She hadn't liked it, but she didn't remember the revulsion being so strong it was difficult not to fight back.

The time when Tris usually left for the night came and went. She'd reestablished some of the barrier between them, but it was more difficult to do this time than it had been the last. She found his presence comforting.

Rialla curled up on her side in the straw and closed her eyes. She was exhausted, but couldn't sleep. After her fourth or fifth attempt to find a comfortable position, she heard a polite murmur at the edge of her awareness.

*Sweetheart.*

She hesitated, then, reluctant for any kind of intimate contact, she spoke out loud. "What is it?"

*Come with me*, Tris invited, his mind tugging gently at her.

*Where?* she asked, curious despite herself.

*Here.* He pulled her into his dreams.

She stood on a boulder and looked down at the im-

mense waterfall, its thunder vibrating the very rock she
rested on. The chilly mist that rose from the water settled
on her clothing and darkened the rock under her feet. She
glanced up to see mountain peaks looming on all sides;
the ridges were white with new fallen snow, but the lower
slopes were the rich blue-green of conifers.

The rushing sound of water falling onto the rocks far
below deafened her, and she looked down, but the rising
mist blocked her view of the bottom. She took a deep
breath of the air and felt it again, that disturbance which
had brought her to this place.

A narrow path wove along the damp stone cliff face,
and she found herself striding down it as if it were a broad
highway. As she put her hand on the rough bark of the
cedar tree that clung precipitously to a narrow ledge just
above the one she walked, she was aware of the slow
migration of nutrients from its roots and the nourishing
warmth of the sun from above. She paused for a moment,
recognizing the peaceful triumph of the gnarled cedar. As
she lingered, her insight grew and encompassed the growing things around her.

The broader awareness stayed with her as she continued
her descent. There was something waiting in the mist,
something special; Rialla could feel the tingling currents
of magic in the rocks and air.

The trail she'd been following ended abruptly as the
cliff sloped down into the water a stone's throw from
where she stood. She squinted, but couldn't see anything
through the dense fog of the waterfall. Moving water created powerful magic currents; there was enough magic in
the gorge to have called a thunderstorm over a desert.
With a wave of her hand, Rialla used some of that magic
to dismiss the fog.

In the center of the roiling water, a large black stone
protruded; the strange whisper of inner understanding des-
ignated the rock as a fire-stone, formed deep in the molten
heart of the earth. On this stone something slept. If it
hadn't been for the faint rise and fall of its breathing, she

might not have seen it. As she distinguished first the side and then the back of the creature, she realized that most of the upper surface of the stone was actually a giant black lizard.

It was beautiful. Rialla searched for the inner knowledge that allowed her to know that the tree was cedar and that rivers held magic—but it wasn't there.

*I'd never seen one before,* said Tris unobtrusively. *I'd been out walking when I felt the disturbance in the forest.*

*That's not a wyvern,* stated Rialla, staring at the creature, not wanting to say anything further for fear of being wrong.

*What do you think it is?* replied Tris, with a touch of amusement. *I didn't think that my carving was so far from the real animal.* An image formed of the intricately carved game piece that resembled the sleeping lizard.

Even as Rialla questioned Tris, a jeweled green eye opened warily and the graceful head and neck uncurled and lifted, until the creature had as good a view of Rialla as she had of it. As it moved, the pattern of color on its scales shifted to match the white and blue of the rushing waterfall, then continued through a range of colors.

"Ah," said the dragon, in a voice rich with music and rustling scales, "I had thought that all of the children of the forest were gone."

TRIS WAITED UNTIL HE WAS CERTAIN SHE WAS ASLEEP. He shifted her clothes aside and picked up the book she'd taken. If it were discovered with her, he was sure Winterseine would find an appropriate punishment.

It was harder leaving through the stone than it was coming in, when gravity aided his descent. He emerged outside the keep on his hands and knees in the dirt.

Rising, he shook the dirt off his clothes as best he could. He used his magic to summon the darkness and muffle the sounds of his movements. So concealed, it was a simple matter of stealth for him to arrive unseen at his small hut, nestled in the outer court like one of so many beehives. He'd been offered accommodations in the servants' hall, but he'd chosen a domicile that offered more privacy—even if it was less than impervious to the weather.

Rape in any form had always enraged him. It was a violation of the male's protective role—even among the humans—but this anger went deeper. Rialla was *his,* whether she knew it or not.

Guilt struck him at that thought. Rialla was his because she hadn't understood what the bond between them meant.

Despite the appearance of stolidity that his size and usual manner lent him, Tris had always been impulsive, even rash. He acted on the moment, without thought for the consequences—and he very seldom rued his actions. Even when he had been banished from the enclave, he hadn't regretted helping the girl. But this . . . this was different. This time he wouldn't be the only one to suffer for his impetuousness.

He'd done it on impulse: initiating the link between the fire-haired dancer and himself. He could have figured out a better way to keep in contact if he'd wanted to—but he wanted her . . . a human. He hadn't intended to bind himself to a human at all, though he had more tolerance for them than most of his kind. Even when he realized that she was the one Trenna had meant in her vision, he had no intention of bonding to her; Tris was not one who believed in fate. But he had known she was his. He would have recognized it even without Trenna's vision.

Rialla had intrigued him from the first, and not just because of her appearance, spectacular as it was. He relished her humor, her reluctant courage and her ability to play Dragon and win by fair means or foul. He hadn't known her long before he realized that the only way she was going to trust him enough to let him close to her was if he refused to allow any barriers between them.

There were not many among his people who were so joined anymore. Most had fallen into the simple marriage ceremony the humans used. Too often a perfect mate could not be found and the link waned rather than strengthened with time. But he had known it wouldn't be that way with Rialla, known it before he established the bond between them.

The connection was strong enough now that he couldn't break it. It had been too late once she inadvertently used his magic to find the water when Winterseine had "disciplined" her.

She could still block him out if she tried hard enough, but he didn't think that she could do that indefinitely— then she would find out what he'd done. He wondered if she would prefer slavery. He wondered if she'd see any difference between him and Winterseine. With a sigh, he closed his eyes.

IT WAS THE SOUND OF THE GUARD'S KEY IN THE LOCK that woke Rialla the next morning. Tris was gone, of course, but it would have been nice if he'd told her what he planned to do before he'd left. She glanced casually at yesterday's clothes, but the journal she'd taken was gone too. She hoped Tris had been the one to take it. With a slight shrug, she followed the guard out to the practice floor.

The raised platform that served as a dance floor could also serve as a battleground. Even as Rialla worked to rid herself of the night's stiffness, she could feel the hostility of the other slaves.

Of course they blamed her for the injury Winterseine had inflicted on the other dancer. The slave who had been hurt had been a comrade; Rialla was an outsider. She couldn't expect them to blame Winterseine: they were too well trained to object to their master's actions. Rialla had shirked her duty, something that a good slave never does, and it had hurt of one of their own.

The other dancers' hostility didn't upset Rialla, but it served as an unpleasant reminder that once she would have reacted the same way.

As the first moves of the dance began, the girl next to Rialla waited until the dancemaster was looking away before she extended a foot too far. Rialla took a short step and avoided falling, having read the girl's intention an instant earlier. After that, Rialla used her empathy to avoid most of the mischief, and simply ignored the rest of it.

The dancemaster was good; he saw what was happening and moved Rialla away from the others: too much contention would disturb the training. She smiled grimly and concentrated on her dancing.

At break Tamas was waiting for her. He grabbed her arm with bruising force as she wiped her forehead with a rough piece of cotton towel. Rialla stiffened in surprise, not at Tamas, but at the snarl she felt from Tris; she hadn't noticed how near he was. Turning her head slightly, she saw him sitting in the shade near the keep, rubbing oil onto a smooth piece of wood.

To regain her attention, Tamas shook her lightly. "It seems you caught the young master's attention. He wants you to come with me."

She looked at him for a second in blank horror before she dropped her eyes, letting him drag her across the bailey and into the darkness of the keep.

Rialla trailed Tamas meekly enough through the twists and turns of the halls and up two flights of stairs into the more private area of the keep. When they reached a place that was quiet enough for her purposes, she struck.

Her elbow hit Tamas hard in the center of his chest. While he struggled for breath, she pushed his head violently into the wall.

"Nice," commented Tris from just behind her. He made no move to help as she lowered Tamas carefully to the floor.

"Did you find out where the study is?" Rialla asked from her position on the ground.

"Yes," Tris nodded, "one of the servants told me. Though I thought that we'd be looking for it in the dead of night. Traveling through the keep unseen in the middle of the day is going to be difficult.''

Rialla turned her attention to the unconscious servant and reached reluctantly to touch his face with her hands, wishing that physical contact didn't make mental touch so much easier.

The initial contact with his surface mind wasn't too bad, but when she probed more deeply, she felt as if she were being immersed in filth. Carefully, she ensured that he would sleep for a while longer, and then backed out of his mind. She was sweating when she stood up and tugged him into the shadows underneath the nearby stairs. She shook with the effort that it had taken to keep herself in contact with Tamas's distorted frame of reference. Tris's warm hands on her shoulders brought a measure of peace with them.

''Some people are harder to contact than others,'' commented Rialla hoarsely, wiping perspiration off the back of her neck with the cloth that she'd been using before Tamas took her into the keep. ''I hope I never have to do that with him again.''

''You won't if we make it out of here,'' said Tris. ''Follow me, keep alert and let me know if we are going to run into anyone.''

They walked quietly down the corridor until they reached another, smaller stairway that circled up to an oaken door. From the shape of the walls, Rialla assumed that this was one of the two towers in the keep.

Carved into the door, the stylized cat of Altis eyed them austerely from above. Tris pointed upward, indicating the door. Rialla probed hastily for anything that hinted the room was occupied.

Tris waited until Rialla nodded before he started up the stairway. The door opened inward without a sound. There was a ostentatious gold key on the inside of the door. Rialla turned it, locking them in Winterseine's study.

The heavy drapes blocked most of the light, and as Rialla turned to her right she bumped into a narrow bookcase with her shoulder. It was nearly as tall as Rialla was, and apparently filled with books. It should have been heavy enough that a horse could have bumped into it without knocking it over.

Rialla looked with stunned disbelief as it tipped and started to fall. Tris grabbed at it, and managed to steady it.

"I thought that you were supposed to be graceful," he quipped as she joined him straightening the books that had been disarranged.

"Graceful, yes," she agreed, "but dancers don't need to see in the dark."

As she spoke, Rialla picked a book off the floor where it had fallen from an upper shelf. It was finely bound in leather, with a brass clasp to keep it closed, nothing to distinguish it from any other book—except that it rattled.

"Tris, could you light this room?" asked Rialla, working the clasp.

Light flared, then steadied. She opened the book to reveal that a section in the center had been cut out. In the resultant space was a plain silver ring, its only ornamentation a small blue stone, dislodged from the cloth it had been wrapped in. The ring's stone was polished smooth, and the indigo depths glittered oddly in the magelight. Rialla shivered with the uneasy sensation that the ring was examining them as much as they were inspecting it.

"There's magic in that," said Tris softly. "Old magic." He shut the ring in the book without touching it and slipped the tome back into place on the shelf.

He took down the one next to it and opened it. It was hollow as well, but empty. The dagger, with its distinctive handle, was in the third book. The serpent's ruby eyes twinkled at them for a moment. Tris took it and tucked it into the leather apron that was standard garb for a woodcraftsman.

He put the book that had held the dagger back on its shelf. Hastily they continued to straighten the books, until the bookcase looked as neat as the others in the room.

Rialla shook her head. "Do you know how much those books were worth before he ruined them?"

Tris snorted. "They were never books—there's no sign of ink on the paper. I suspect that he had them bound with blank pages then hollowed them out."

"I hadn't thought of that," admitted Rialla, getting to her feet and looking around the room.

The rug she stood on was only slightly less valuable than that one in Terran's chambers. Tris's light clearly revealed the rich reds and golds of the elaborately woven patterns. The room was small, but it contained two more bookcases and a large desk.

"Over here," said Tris, moving to the desk.

He ignored the ledgers that covered the desktop, and ran his hands over the locked drawers, stopping at the bottom one on the left side.

"There's something powerful in this one," he commented. He slipped a ring of keys out of his belt pouch and inserted a likely one into the lock.

"Are those clan keys? Where did you get those?" asked Rialla.

"I believe so; they were left as payment," answered Tris.

The lock turned over, and he pulled the drawer open. Inside was a thick book with a silver clasp. Embossed on the expensive white leather was a symbol that Rialla knew well.

Tris glanced at her and then back at the book. "That's the design he used for your tattoo."

"It's Winterseine's," agreed Rialla. "But is this a *grimoire*?"

"I'm not going to open it. From the feel of it, that book has enough magic in it to destroy this keep and half the surrounding countryside," replied Tris briskly.

"It's magic and it has Winterseine's personal seal," said Rialla. "That's enough for me."

Tris took the book out, shut the drawer and locked it. He undid his belt and slipped the book under the loose tunic, shifting it until it sat in the hollow under his ribs. Once he had it placed to his satisfaction, he cinched the belt tightly around his waist. Under the heavy woodcrafts-man fabric, Rialla could hardly tell that the book was there.

"Can you tell if there is anyone nearby?"

Rialla relaxed for a moment and concentrated. "No one, as long as Terran isn't there."

"What do you mean?" Tris raised an eyebrow.

"Terran could be listening from the other side of the door and I'd never know. For some reason my empathy can't detect him at all. However," she added, "I suppose that we can chance it."

They made it down the circular stairway without inci-dent. As they approached one of the stairs that would take them farther down, Rialla stopped Tris with a tug on the back of his tunic.

*They've found Tamas,* she told him, *and instituted a search. They'll block the stairways and search the lower levels first before they start up here.* Rialla felt a cold knot of dread form in her stomach. She wanted out.

*Then we need to find a window up here,* said Tris.

*You're enjoying this!* accused Rialla hotly.

He grinned unrepentantly at her and started back up the hall, leaving Rialla to scurry indignantly after him.

The first door that Tris tried opened into a guest bed-room, complete with window casements. Winterseine hadn't bothered with the expense of glazing them in, so when they folded the casement doors back, there were only two barriers to their escape from the keep: guards and gravity.

Rialla looked around cautiously, but no one was watch-ing the back side of the keep. There was a good reason for this. The only windows on this side were on the third floor. Anyone stupid enough to jump out of one of them and onto the hardpacked dirt of the courtyard below would wait for the searchers.

Rialla peered cautiously down the ivy-covered walls. *I don't know, Tris. It looks like a long way to the ground.*

*Don't fret,* advised Tris, reaching out to touch a strand of ivy.

Rialla watched closely, but she couldn't see any difference in the plant after he touched it.

*I want you to follow me. This will only support our weight if we climb straight down.* Without giving her a chance to protest, he climbed out the window, twisting to get his shoulders through the narrow opening.

Looking at the fragile strands, Rialla felt some trepidation—but anything capable of holding Tris was more than capable of holding her. She waited until he was well on his way before starting after him.

The ivy felt unnaturally stiff, providing easy handholds. The edges of the leaves were sharp, as if they had been fabricated out of metal, and she gained a few cuts before she discovered how to reach through the leaves to the vine beneath. When she neared the ground, Tris caught her by the waist and set her aside. He touched the ivy again, returning the plants to their original state.

Rialla turned to look around nervously, but there was still no one observing this corner of the keep. She dropped the protection from her empathy to catch any hint that someone saw them, and hoped fervently that Tamas was far enough away that she wouldn't have any more contact with him.

*Here now,* said Tris, *let me change your hair color to something less distinctive. The gatekeepers are going to be looking for a lone slave with red hair. With the number of slaves around here, they are not going to be suspicious of one walking out with a freeman.*

*Winterseine has been known to reward fine work with an older, less valuable slave,* agreed Rialla. *If you can add some gray to the brown it will look better.*

He touched her hair for a moment then took his hands away. *Done.*

Without further ado, they strode casually around the

keep and toward the gate in the surrounding wall. Tris stopped where he had been working on the door and picked up the heavy tool bag that rested nearby. No one challenged them until they reached the portcullis.

"Hold," called the older of the two men on the wall. "What's your purpose?"

"I'm Jord Woodcraftsman; the hold stores are low on cherry. This slave knows where there are some cherry trees big enough for making furniture after they are seasoned."

The guard frowned down at Rialla. "I don't recognize that one."

Tris nodded. "She's a kitchen slave. She's been sent out after wood for the fires—so she should know the trees nearby. If she doesn't, I daresay I can find them without her and she'll still serve my purposes." He said the last with a leer.

The other men laughed and pulled the portcullis up high enough that Tris and Rialla could duck under it. Rialla led the way down an obviously well-worn trail into the woods.

# NINE

As soon as they entered the shelter of the woods, Tris dropped the heavy leather satchel to the ground and began to sort through its contents with brisk efficiency, setting most of the tools aside.

"Do you have the journal?" asked Rialla hopefully.

"In the bag," he answered, loosening his belt and removing the book.

He took off the leather apron and set the dagger in the bag with the two books.

"Hold a moment." Rialla tore a strip off the bottom of her tunic and retrieved the dagger. She wrapped the blade in the cloth, leaving no edge showing, and replaced it.

Tris quickly gathered the discarded tools together and wrapped the apron around them to protect them from the weather. Someone would find them and put them to good use.

Throwing the satchel's strap around one shoulder, Tris diverged from the trail at a steady lope. Rialla followed, grateful for the long hours of work that would lend her stamina for the run ahead.

Tris ran effortlessly, obviously slowing his pace for her. The path he chose seemed random, but she was content to follow his lead. He gauged her endurance nicely; when her bad leg started to hurt, he slowed to a walk.

"Can you tell if there is anyone following us?"

"Let me stop a bit and I'll see," replied Rialla, coming to a halt.

Breathing deeply, she wiped a trail of sweat off her forehead. Starting with the area nearest to them, she felt carefully outward. It was difficult to tell animal emotions from human, so she looked for a group of creatures; but she couldn't sense anything.

"Nothing," she said, hoping that it were true.

Tris stretched out a hand and caressed the bark of a nearby tree before starting off again at a brisk walk in the direction he'd been taking. "It feels good to be out of that cursed place. It is irksome to be surrounded by nothing but dead stone."

Rialla spoke hesitantly, casual conversation seeming odd after the past few days. "I know what you mean. I grew up traveling from place to place. We only slept in tents when it was raining. Sometimes being hemmed in by stone walls is enough to make me want to scream."

"Why do you live in the city then?" he asked.

"Because Sianim was the first place I found where a woman can work training horses."

"Why didn't you go back to the Trader clans after you got away?"

Rialla shrugged. "There was no one left of my clan. One of the others would have adopted me, I suppose, but . . . I wouldn't have fit in." In truth, she thought, she felt closer to Tris after less than three se'ennights than she did to anyone, including Laeth. Perhaps it was the mental bond: her eyes trailed over to her companion's broad shoulders and she smiled to herself—perhaps it was something else.

"Tris?" asked Rialla.

"Hmm?"

"Where are we going?"

Something caught his attention near a thick growth of cattails along the stream they had been following. He stopped and knelt to gently brush the soil away from the roots of a slender plant with a small white bloom.

"Whitecowl," he explained absently, uprooting the plant and shaking loose the clinging dirt. "Makes a potent sleeping draft. A few of these leaves will make a man sleep for several hours."

He pulled the satchel forward, tucking the plant carefully on top of the books.

He started on again and said, "Sianim."

By that time Rialla had almost forgotten what she'd asked, and it took her a second to realize what he'd said. "How do you know where Sianim is? Have you been there before?"

He shook his head and said, "No, but I can tell where the forest is cut by a great road. According to the cook, the only major road nearby leads east to Sianim or south into the Alliance. The road is about two and a half days' journey from here. I thought we could lose any pursuit in the woods before we get there." He flashed his teeth at her. "There are a number of advantages that we sylvans have over you *humans*."

Rialla bared her teeth in return. "Better to be human than to travel through the forest socializing with the local flora."

He shook his head in mock dismay and said in sad tones, "Always, they disparage what they have never done. Cavorting in the bushes can be an interesting experience with the right person." He leered suggestively at her, but ruined the effect when he caught sight of another plant. "Coralis!" he exclaimed. "I've never heard of one growing this far north."

Rialla had just started to feel uncomfortable with the gentle flirting they'd been doing when the plant distracted Tris from the conversation. She grinned as he bent to inspect the bark of a small tree with remarkably large blood-red flowers. It was *not* flattering to be ignored for a plant.

*Sorry,* he apologized, looking up.

Startled, Rialla met his gaze. "Can you read my mind all the time?" she asked. Abruptly she felt some sympathy with Laeth; it was an unsettling feeling to realize her thoughts weren't private.

He shook his head as he straightened. "No. Only here and there, and then usually just superficial thoughts."

She smiled at him as they took to the trail again. "I'm not used to having anyone read me the way I read everyone else."

He returned her smile and started to say something, but then was distracted by another plant.

They traveled rapidly, in spite of frequent pauses while Tris examined the surrounding flora—which coincidentally allowed Rialla to rest. Mountains lay to the south and west of them, but their route wove through the foothills. After several miles passed without sign of pursuit, Rialla relaxed and enjoyed the feeling of being out of Winterseine's keep. Tris managed to gather quite a few edible plants, and they nibbled as they walked.

Night fell, and they made camp in a small clearing. Rialla found a small area with relatively few rocks and cushioned her head on her arms, while Tris did the same nearby.

The air was summer-warm, but Rialla's slave tunic did little to protect her from the night breeze. After the past few days, however, fatigue more than outweighed the discomfort. She was too tired to do more than shiver once or twice before she fell asleep.

Tris watched as she tossed and turned, but when she drew up her legs in a vain attempt to conserve her warmth he'd had enough. He shifted until he was lying next to her, and reached out to pull her closer.

Before he could do more than touch her shoulder, he felt . . . *Terran's fine-boned hands on naked skin* . . . distaste so strong it amounted to horror . . . humiliation . . . hatred, and a touch of terror . . .

Possessive anger engulfed him, even as he recognized that the bond between them now involved more than mindspeech—at least on his part. For the first time, it was Rialla's emotions that were clearest—a bleeding of her gifts into him. Carefully he damped the edges of his anger. He would get Rialla to Sianim; then perhaps he would provide Terran with an appreciation for the rage of a healer.

Rialla whimpered softly in her sleep. Tris exhaled. When he had the control that he needed, he eased himself back into Rialla's dream.

He caught her gently in his thoughts, luring her from Terran's bedroom to sweeter memories of a northern lake that shimmered silver and gold with the reflected glory of the setting sun.

ALONE AS USUAL, RIALLA WOKE EARLY, IN THE DARK-ness that preceded the sun's rise in the sky. Standing up, she shook out her clothing, though most of the wrinkles and dirt resisted her efforts. She took a deep breath and wondered why she half expected to smell the crispness of snow in the air. Tris's return distracted her from her thoughts, and she bade him good morning.

They left the meadow as dawn's first light broke in the sky. By midmorning Rialla was starting to feel hungry, and when she saw a blackberry patch she stopped to pick some. Tris found several tuberous roots that he cleaned on his pant leg. They had no flavor to speak of, but they were more filling than the berries.

"These are much better roasted over a fire," he commented, taking a second bite of the root.

"If you say so," responded Rialla doubtfully, though she was eating hers with the enthusiasm of hunger. "Any taste would be an improvement, I suppose, even ashes from the fire."

Tris was about to reply when an eerie scream cut

through the woods. After it was through, there was utter silence; not even a bird ventured to chirp.

"Do you know what that was?" asked Tris quietly.

"I'm not sure, but aren't we near the ae'Magi's castle?"

Tris hesitated, as if consulting an inner map. "There's a large castle of some sort a half day's walk to the south," he commented.

Rialla nodded. "That should be it. It must be a Uriah. I've never seen one myself, but there are supposed to be a few left near the Archmage's castle. When the previous ae'Magi died, there was an infestation of Uriah there that spread into the surrounding lands. Sianim mercenaries cleaned them out of the castle, but they couldn't find all the ones in the nearby woods. I've been told that magic doesn't affect them much; the only way to kill them is with fire or sword. I don't even have my knife."

Tris took Rialla's arm and began walking briskly. "Vicious things, or so I've heard. I saw one once, at a distance, and was lucky enough that it didn't see me. That one didn't sound too close, but I suspect that it might be a good idea if we covered some ground all the same."

They walked and then jogged, but the Uriah kept on a path just parallel to theirs, and they heard it call out from time to time.

"Do you think that it's following us?" Rialla glanced worriedly toward the source of the last noise, but the trees grew too close together to allow her to see anything.

A loud scream pierced the stillness, followed by a chorus of the weird noises. Rialla stopped walking, reaching with her talent to see what was causing the commotion. The trees that she'd been looking at rustled with the fury of a battle.

Tris wrapped one hand around her arm and pulled her into a reluctant run, loosing his grip only when she had stopped fighting him. Grimly, Rialla increased her pace, and Tris stayed beside her until the howls were muted enough that they could talk.

Rialla continued several steps before she realized that Tris had stopped completely. She turned to look at him and noticed the anger on his face.

"What were you doing back there?" he snapped.

"I was trying to find out what it had run into. If it was something big, the Uriah will be occupied with it and we won't have to worry about it," Rialla replied steadily, taking a small step back.

He looked at her with an unreadable expression, then took a quick step toward her. "It was a stupid thing to do. Uriah aren't like people; they aren't even like other animals. You could have been hurt, do you understand?"

She set her jaw and took a step forward herself, until she was knee to shin with him. "I understand that it was my choice to make!"

"You could have been caught up in the death throes of the animal it killed," he said, glaring down at her.

"Not likely. I have more control than that. I was far more entwined with the creature in the ballroom at Westhold." Her voice held more than a hint of frost.

Tris turned and took a step away in an obvious effort to control himself. Rialla had started to suspect that it wasn't anger that he was trying to hold in check when she noticed that his shoulders were shaking.

"You were baiting me." If she had had a weapon at hand, she didn't know if she would have had the control not to use it. "You sorry excuse for a snake, you were baiting me."

"Not entirely," denied Tris in a muffled voice. "That thing in the ballroom *hurt* you, Rialla. Uriah are not like other animals—they are driven by hunger and rage; everyone knows that. For an empath to contact one is beyond reckless and well into rashness; the situation didn't require such an act."

Rialla considered what he had said. "You have the right. I apologize for taking an unnecessary risk. You still haven't explained why you are laughing." Her voice didn't warm at all.

Tris turned back to meet her eyes. "I suppose that it was relief, primarily. I was apprehensive that after . . ." His eyes lost their laughter, and Rialla felt the dark rage that had never died down. "I was worried that the past few weeks would affect you more than they have. I remembered that little speech that you gave Laeth in my cottage—the one about once a slave always a slave—while you were yelling at me. It struck me as funny."

"Laugh at me when I'm mad again and I'll see that you don't do it a third time," said Rialla solemnly.

"I'll look forward to it," said Tris courteously.

He stepped toward her and offered his arm. After a brief hesitation, Rialla set her hand in the bend of his elbow. They continued down the path Tris had chosen.

"WHAT DO URIAH LOOK LIKE?" ASKED RIALLA CURIously. "I've never seen one."

They had long since left the Uriah in the distance. Lengthy shadows from the trees around them dappled the ground, and the eastern sky darkened with reds and golds.

Tris shrugged. "They look like a human that has been dead for a month, and then decided to grow fangs and get up and hunt. They smell like it too."

"Not something that I want to run into in the middle of the night," commented Rialla.

"I'd rather not run into them at all, day or night," responded Tris absently as he examined the nearby brush.

"What are you looking for?" asked Rialla.

"I smell thornberry around here somewhere. This time of year the blooms have a strong enough odor to keep the Uriah from catching our scent if they do pass this way." He narrowed his eyes and pointed to the left. "Over there, near that oak. Come on, we'll call it an early night and wait until the Uriah are somewhere else before we go."

Tris led the way to a dense thicket several lengths from a good-sized oak tree. The tops of the bushes were covered with thick yellow blossoms that reeked like the moat of an abandoned castle in the summer. Finger-sized, wickedly sharp thorns covered the bushes from soil to flower.

"If you slide in under the branches you can avoid the thorns," advised Tris, disregarding the incredulous look that Rialla aimed at him as she held her nose. "They all point up, so it's safe to go under them."

He dropped onto his back and slid cautiously under the brush until he disappeared from view. Rialla eyed the thorns dubiously, but followed him in.

To her surprise, the narrow tunnel that Tris had made widened into a sizable hollow big enough for two or three people to occupy. The brush formed a solid ceiling overhead, but there was room enough for them to sit up in it. The ground was soft with old leaves.

Tris grinned at her expression. "It makes a nice enough home, once you get used to the smell. The cover overhead is so tight it lets in very little rain."

Tris opened his pack and began again to sort out the collection of plants. With a mournful expression he set aside several of the more mangled specimens.

Rialla watched, then took out the books that they'd stolen from Winterseine, shaking them to dislodge the leaves. As she set Winterseine's book aside, she noticed that several pages had slid halfway out of the book—in spite of the clasp that held the white leather cover tightly pressed against the inner pages.

"Tris," she said.

He looked up from the last of his plants. "Hmm?"

She held the book up for his inspection and the crumpled pages slid out further. Rialla quickly turned the book upside down to keep them from slipping all of the way out.

"Don't touch those," he advised, setting the plants aside. "There are any number of unhealthy effects a human mage could place in his spellbook."

He took the book from her and tapped it on his leg, but the pages stubbornly refused to slide back where they had been. He tilted it gingerly, until a spot of daylight touched the creamy surface of the obstreperous sheets.

"Hmm," he said as he flattened his hand and made a brief pass over the book. "These pages were never part of this book—they're too old."

Rialla looked again at the neatly folded sheets. "They don't appear old."

"Magic," commented Tris. "There is more magic in those sheets of paper than any single mage could have collected, human or not. It would take a score or more of the strongest of my people to call that much magic—I imagine that it would take at least that many human mages."

"They're just blank sheets of parchment," said Rialla, surprised.

Tris raised his eyebrows at her and looked again at the parchment. "You can't see the symbols?" he asked.

She shook her head and leaned closer for a better look, closing her hand on Tris's shoulder for balance. As soon as she touched him, the exposed surfaces of the formerly vacant pages were littered with markings that were somehow out of focus.

Rialla blinked and swore softly, pulling her hand off Tris. As soon as the contact was broken, the pages were blank again. "Can you tell what the spell is for?" she asked, her voice a little ragged.

Tris shook his head. "I'm not a human magic-user—I don't use spells that could be written down this way."

Rialla smiled at his obvious contempt. "What should we do with them?"

"Take them to Sianim and let the human wizards worry about them," offered Tris, setting the book on the far side of his satchel, where the straying pages would be out of the way.

As Tris shifted to find a comfortable position, his hand fell on Terran's journal. He picked it up and glanced at the pages.

*Do you mind if I look through this?* he asked.

Rialla shrugged. *I have difficulty with Darranian script when there is sufficient light. If you want to decipher it, be welcome. I think I will attempt to rest.*

She felt him focus his attention on her, and notice . . . *Your leg is bothering you. Do you want me to see what I can do for it?*

She hesitated, but shook her head. She wasn't ready to relax under any man's hands just yet.

*Fine,* Tris said. *The offer is open, if you decide otherwise.*

Rialla was curled up in the old dry leaves with her eyes closed when it occurred to her that she hadn't noticed the difference between talking out loud and using mind-speech. She wondered when it had become so easy to speak mind to mind with Tris. The soft sounds of Tris turning the pages of the thin book blended into the rustling leaves, and she drifted into a restful slumber without further thought.

SHE DIDN'T KNOW WHAT TIME IT WAS WHEN HE WOKE her up, but the makeshift cave was shadowed.

"Rialla?"

"Hmm?" she answered sleepily.

"I think that you might be interested in this."

"Yes?" Rialla struggled to full awareness and sat up, brushing off bits of leaf and dirt.

It was dark enough that she couldn't see Tris's face clearly, but she didn't need to. His intensity was strong enough to alert her that he'd found something in Terran's journal.

"What is it?" she asked.

Tris tapped his finger lightly on the book and then set it down and pulled his knees up comfortably. "Let me tell you a story.

"There was once a boy, just on the point of manhood. His father was both a mage and an athlete. When it became obvious that the boy was neither, he felt himself a failure—an evaluation that his father shared.

"Like most children of his age, it was hard for the boy to see past the trials of adolescence to the man he might become. He was clumsy and self-conscious, with a tendency to stammer when he was nervous.

"In addition to being a magician, his father was also a trader in slaves. He traveled upon occasion to the mysterious lands east of the Great Swamp, because slaves from that region were valuable, if difficult to acquire. The boy's only talent was a certain facility for languages, but it was valuable enough that he traveled with his father.

"It happened that one day they were traveling through a small, war-torn country in the East. They stayed overnight in a house that had once, long ago, been a shrine to the god Altis. Though most of it was rebuilt or an outright addition to the original structure, its origin was a matter of some pride to the owner—a rich merchant in his own right.

"That night at dinner, the boy made a fool of himself once again. One of the daughters of their host spoke to him, and he became so nervous that he knocked over his drinking glass and spilled the wine over his lap. With the laughter of his father and their host ringing in his ears, he stormed out of the dining hall and ran to the room he and his father had been assigned.

"The room itself was unusual. Unlike the rest of the rooms that the boy had seen in the house, this one had a floor and walls made of stone rather than wood. The cot that he'd been assigned was crowded against one wall; his father occupied the luxurious, silk-sheeted bed. The long, low marble table that was built into the floor restricted the remaining furniture to smaller pieces.

"The table was very old . . . its surface pitted by generations of rough usage. An altar, the merchant had explained with a shrug. There were several of them in various rooms of the house.

"The boy, seeking the refuge of solitude, entered the room carrying an oil lamp that he'd taken from its place outside the dining chamber. Made clumsy by youth and embarrassment, he stumbled over a small rug and fell. His forehead grazed a corner of the table. Though the wound was minor, it bled copiously, as scalp wounds frequently do.

"Less frantic away from the sounds of the laughter, the boy collected himself. Somehow the lamp had escaped being completely overturned, though the oil splashed. He set the lamp carefully on the white marble, ignoring the mess that the oil and the blood from his head had made on the pristine surface.

"He knew that he was going to have to ask someone to bind the cut on his head, but he couldn't bring himself to suffer the scrutiny of a stranger, far less his father, who was certain to comment on his son's clumsiness.

"He was dizzy, and since he was kneeling in front of the table he rested his arms and then his head on the cold marble. Gradually he slipped into a light doze."

Tris paused, then said, "What happened next might depend on your point of view. I'll tell it to you from the boy's and you can make up your own mind in light of what we've seen.

"In his dream, he found himself walking down a white corridor with rooms on either side of him. Glancing into the first one, he saw a shrouded figure lying on a table similar to the one in his room. He couldn't tell if the figure was alive or dead, and something kept him from entering the room to look more closely. In large relief on the wall above the table was a design of two red dragons intertwined.

"Now, our hero was a learned boy—books were his retreat from his father's scorn—so he recognized what few would. The dragons were an ancient symbol for Temris, the god of war.

"Believing that he was dreaming, the boy didn't fight the odd compulsion that drew him down the corridor. As he walked, he saw more rooms with shrouded bodies and the symbols of the old gods on the walls. Most of them he knew, but there were several he'd not seen before.

"The corridor went on and on, and still the boy walked. At last the compulsion pulled him into one of the rooms and he left the corridor.

"He noticed that a heavy layer of dust lay over everything, as if no one had been in the room for a very long time. On the wall was a symbol that he recognized not only from his own readings, but from its liberal use throughout the merchant's house: the cat of Altis.

"Cautiously, he approached the covered figure on the table. As he did, he noticed that the dust on the shrouds had been disturbed and that the cloths didn't lie as neatly as their counterparts had, as if the figure who slept beneath had been restless not long ago.

"With dream-born courage, the boy touched the fine blue silk with the intention of removing it. But touch it was all that he did, for it dissolved into nothingness under his fingers; the figure it covered disappeared with it, leaving only an empty table behind.

"As he looked down at the unoccupied table, he noticed first a drop of his blood on the table and then a drop of oil that had escaped the container he held in his shaking hand. The drops mingled as they wouldn't in the waking world. He couldn't look away, not even when a deep voice spoke behind him.

" 'Who disturbs the rest of the old ones, boy? Who meddles with forces beyond human ken? There is great magic worked on earth again that disturbs the sleepers, and a dragon rides the currents of the sky once more. This is no safe time to walk the halls of the gods and risk awakening them.'

"The boy felt the voice as much as heard it.

"He knew that he was shaking, though he felt no fear; the speaker seemed kindly, even fatherly. He answered slowly, 'I don't know about dragons or great magic, but I touched the shroud. I am Terran.'

"As he finished speaking, Terran awoke draped over the altar. Worried about what his father would say about the mess, he took off his tunic and wiped the marble surface as best he could.

"There was an ewer of water on the floor near the door, with a clean cloth folded neatly beside it. He scrubbed the blood off his hands, face and neck before he noticed that there was no cut on his forehead. The only evidence that he'd been wounded at all was in the bloodstained tunic and washcloth and the pinkened water in the bowl.

"Terran emptied the ewer out the window and hid his tunic and the stained washcloth among his clothes."

Tris drew a deep breath. "That was Terran's first encounter with the god Altis. In further dream conversations with the night god, Terran was favored with immense power that mimicked the magic used by Winterseine.

"Several months later, Terran—calling himself the Voice of Altis—began to set up an organized religion worshipping Altis with the help of his father."

"Gods," swore Rialla. "It wasn't Winterseine at all." She thought about the odd way that Winterseine had given in to Terran's demands to bed her.

Tris spoke quietly, "The only proof that the dream was real is that Terran's wound disappeared. A small cut in the scalp bleeds freely and heals fast. If the cut was actually above the hairline and very small, it would have been easy to miss it. Moreover, a blow to the head often leads to strange dreams that seem almost real."

Rialla continued the thought. "Of course he would dream of the old gods in such a setting, given his proficiency with the legends. Everyone knows that oil and blood are common components in spell-making; certainly the son of a magician would."

Tris picked up the logical discussion. "I understand that many human mages don't come into full power until after sexual maturity. If he experienced such a phenomenon after his dream, then he would attribute it to the old gods rather than himself—especially someone like Terran, who'd been taught he was useless."

Rialla rested her chin on her hands and gave him a half

smile, though it was too dark for him to see it. "I should be reassured; all that we have said points to the idea that Terran's power is the product of latent magic—something we are familiar with. But . . ."

"But," agreed Tris in a troubled voice, "there is the healing of Tamas's arm on the way to Winterseine's keep. I could feel no magic. I thought that a skilled human mage might use magic in such a way that I couldn't detect it, but I felt the magic in Winterseine's book from the moment we walked into his study."

"I can't feel him with my empathy at all," added Rialla. There was a slight pause, then she said, "I think Winterseine believes Terran is a prophet. When Winterseine touches me, I can read him. There is an undercurrent of fear in him now that he never had before, when I was his slave. I think . . . I think that what he's afraid of is Terran."

"Do you think Terran really is a prophet?" asked Tris.

"Yes."

"So do I."

Rialla was silent for a moment, then she said, "If Terran is really the prophet of Altis, the invasion we are facing is directed by a god. How powerful are the gods anyway?" She was pleased that her voice was steady.

Tris shrugged. "I've never had a close conversation with one. We can wait here and you can ask Terran if you like, but I'd prefer to remain ignorant. I understand the gods weren't strong enough to halt the Wizard Wars."

"Maybe they didn't want to," commented Rialla.

"Now, there's a cheerful thought," replied Tris dryly.

Rialla laughed reluctantly. "We'll get this information to Ren and let him decide what to do with it."

"Will he believe it?" Tris questioned.

Rialla shrugged, flopped back and pillowed her head on her arms with a sigh, saying, "I don't know. I don't think I was ever intended to be a spy. When we get to Sianim, remind me to tell the Spymaster that he ought to stick with the professionals. I seem to have turned a simple information-gathering mission into defying the gods with a man who claims heritage with an obscure, all-but-forgotten race of tree-folk. I'm sure that if I reflect upon it I can explain how it happened, but I really don't want to think about it that much.''

She caught a flash of white in the gloom as Tris smiled. "I haven't heard anything outside, so I think I'll go scout. Let me know if you come to any brilliant conclusions while I'm gone.'' He picked a double handful of grasslike stalks out of the satchel and rolled over on his back to shimmy out of the thornberry cave.

After Tris left, Rialla sat up again. It would be good to have some time to herself again; she wasn't used to being continuously around people. In Sianim sometimes she would go for days without talking to anyone except her horses. The past month had left her little time to herself, and she was beginning to feel suffocated.

Tris negotiated the dark forest as if it were daylight; his eyes were well adapted to the dim light of the moon. He chose to follow their backtrail, checking carefully for signs of being followed. After traveling a respectable distance, he broke the stalks of grass into small pieces and scattered them on the trail he and Rialla had left. Histweed would be even more effective than pepper for irritating the nasal tissues of any animal tracking them. When he had used the last of the herb, he dusted his hands clean and looked around.

He had reacted without thought this afternoon when he realized Rialla had exposed herself to such danger. When she'd backed away from his anger, her fear had tugged at the link that bound them together and triggered an atavistic rage for which he'd been unprepared. Although he'd been told a threat to the bond could cause such a reaction, he'd dismissed the warning when Terran's rape had called forth nothing unusual. Apparently the rape hadn't qualified as a threat to their bond. He'd been able to control the rage this afternoon long enough to continue his attack deliberately, hoping she would fight back. If she had run from him . . . He would rather not know what could have happened. His laughter had been as much relief as amusement. He needed this time away from Rialla to collect himself.

Their backtrail covered, he decided to find the Uriah; it would be helpful to know where it was so they didn't waste time avoiding it unnecessarily. Without Rialla's human presence, he was free to travel by sylvan ways. That would let him find the Uriah and return to Rialla before she started to worry about him.

Humming under his breath, he called to the magic around him, and spun it swiftly to form a tunnel before him. He continued to spin as he walked into the shadowed way that lead straight through the hills and valleys lying in his path. The abundance of yew and oak here heightened the effect of his magic, and it took him minutes to cross the distance it had taken half a day to travel.

When he reached the place where he and Rialla had last seen the Uriah, he closed the tunnel and emerged near the stream they'd followed most of the day. He set off in an easy lope through the trees. It didn't take him long to find the kill: a moose. Its bones were scattered along the path the things had taken—from the tracks it seemed that there had been more than one Uriah.

Tris stumbled over half of one of the heavy leg bones, snapped neatly in two; he marveled briefly over the strength needed to crack the dense bone. He spared a moment to be glad the creatures had happened upon the moose rather than him and Rialla. The Uriah's trail was easy to follow, even in the dark. Broken branches and torn-up sod where several had briefly scuffled over something were as clear to Tris as a chalk arrow drawn on the trees.

Topping a hill, he caught sight of a small fire to his right. He dropped to a walk and left the Uriah's trail to investigate the camp.

As he neared the fire, Tris caught the salt-sweet smell

of horses and was careful to stay downwind as he approached. The animals shifted uneasily at the noise he made climbing a tree, but they calmed down when he made no aggressive moves.

From his vantage point, he could see there was no one in the small clearing, but the wood in the fire hadn't been burning long. Tris assumed that whoever had built it would return, and he settled in for a long wait.

He made out Winterseine's voice first, as the campers returned.

". . . don't understand why you insisted on leaving the guards behind. This is a dangerous place."

"Precisely, Father. The more people that are running around the more likely we are to attract the attention of any brigands or Uriah that are in the area. I can handle thieves or Uriah, but I can't protect a troop of men from them." Terran's voice sounded more decisive than Tris remembered.

Tris crouched where he was and watched as Terran and Winterseine returned to camp with several cleaned fish on a string.

"We can't afford to let her get to Sianim with that dagger. If I am implicated in Karsten's death, it would keep me from controlling Darran. Are you sure that you know where she is? We haven't seen as much as a footprint." From Winterseine's intonation, Tris received the distinct impression that it wasn't the first time that Winterseine had questioned the direction he and Terran were going in.

"I told you, she's stopped a league or two southwest of here." Terran's voice had a bite to it. "We'll catch up with her sometime tomorrow. You haven't seen her tracks because we're not following their trail. This route is more direct than the one they've been taking."

Winterseine asked the question that was foremost on Tris's mind. "What do you mean *their* trail? I thought she was alone."

Terran grunted then said slowly, "No. She's been traveling with someone else. I can't quite see who it is—he may be a magician of sorts." He paused, then commented, "He's not with her now, but he was most of today. I suspect that he might have helped her get out of the hold."

"You mean that she's traveling with a magician?" asked Winterseine in arrested tones.

Terran nodded and began to prepare the fish for the fire.

Winterseine had his back turned so that Tris couldn't see his face, but tension coiled in the human's stance. "She stole my *grimoire*. We need to find them as soon as possible, before the magician realizes what he has."

Terran stopped working with the fish and looked at his father intently. "And just what is it that he has? Your spellbook? The one taken was the one that you wrote as an apprentice; certainly there is nothing there which a magician wouldn't already know."

Tris, watching unseen, thought about the sheets of parchment that had fallen out of Winterseine's spellbook and wondered.

Winterseine hesitated. "There were some spells there my old teacher gave to me that I would rather not pass down . . . and I do not relish the thought of another wizard paging through the book."

Those pages must be important, thought Tris with satisfaction.

Terran turned his attention back to their dinner, and Tris took advantage of the moment to leave the tree. He eased quietly back into the forest and lost himself in the shadows.

Thoughtfully, he resumed his search for the Uriah. The search had more urgency now, as it seemed that he and Rialla would be traveling tonight, and he didn't want to be stumbling into a group of Uriah in the dark.

He smelled them long before he saw them and, remembering tales of their acute senses, used his magic to draw the darkness more tightly around him and cover any sound he might make before he approached more closely.

There were six of them sleeping; Tris was struck by how human they looked at rest. When he'd seen the one before, he hadn't noticed the resemblance; they didn't move like humans any more than a wolf moves like a dog. At rest in the dark, they seemed nothing more than a filthy group of people.

Tris found another tree to climb, one that gave him a clear view of the Uriah. All of them were male, but Tris had expected that. He'd never heard of a female Uriah.

On the far side of the pack, one of them had used the root of an old oak as a pillow. There was a heavy branch above it that looked sturdy. Closing his eyes, Tris felt for the magic that connected all of the trees in the forest, then he looked for the particular tree he wanted. When he found it, he traveled along the flow of magic, reemerging on the branch of the oak, with the Uriah sleeping just below him.

As he looked down, he realized he was closer than he'd ever been to one of them; a shiver ran up his spine. Irritated with himself for his uncharacteristic fear, he craned his neck until there were no leaves between him and the sleeping creature. That was when he noticed something around its waist. A sturdy leather belt hung loosely on the Uriah's hips; the broken strap of a sword or knife sheath was still attached to it, though the sheath was gone.

The thing below him, in spite of everything Tris had ever heard, had once been human. The healer in him stirred. If this were some kind of disease, he might be able to reverse it.

A single Uriah he might have held still with his magic so he could examine it, but there were too many for him to risk coming any closer. The one below him was touching the root of the oak Tris perched in. It would not be as efficient as touch, but the tree could serve as a conduit for his magic.

Tris braced himself more securely on his branch, then

searched for the thread of magic all living things have. He followed the flow of the tree's magic to its roots and reached out for the creature that he knew was there, and touched . . .

BACK IN THE SHELTERING THORNBERRY, RIALLA ROSE TO her hands and knees at Tris's agony. Taken unprepared, she cried out. She sought him, dropping her barriers recklessly in her worry.

*Rialla?* It was faint, but it was clearly his voice that answered her frightened call.

*Are you all right?* she asked urgently, though she could tell that he wasn't hurting now. The revulsion and shock that he felt were still strong, and made it difficult for her to read his thoughts over the din of emotion.

*Yes . . . talk later, when I get back,* he said.

She sent her agreement and withdrew from him, waiting alone for his return.

The Uriah had woken at Tris's involuntary cry. Realizing that food perched just overhead, the one below him began to climb the tree, making an odd mewling sound as it did so.

Tris pressed his face to the rough bark of the oak. It was almost more than he could do to reach for another tree near enough for his purposes. He found another oak on the far side of the clearing and used his magic to pull him there. It took four such jumps before he quit smelling the Uriah.

Tree bark slid past his hands as Tris fell to his knees with bruising force, retching helplessly.

The Uriah that he'd touched was dead, but held to mock life by human magic so twisted that when he touched it and tried to coax it to his use it felt as if he'd touched molten rock with his hand.

Tris took in a shuddering breath and rose to his feet. Seeking out the stream, he threw cold water on his face. The shock of the temperature did much to alleviate his queasiness. Traveling through the trees was hard and draining work; it took him two tries before he was able to form the tunnel that would take him back to where Rialla waited.

RIALLA WAS PACING OUTSIDE THE CAVE OF THORNBERRY when Tris came back with his backpack. On a forked stick near her were two good-sized trout.

"Are you hurt?" she asked, taking a step toward him.

"No, but I'm hungry."

She eyed him narrowly, but the link between them informed her that he was not lying. After catching the fish, she'd gathered enough wood for a small fire, and she nodded at it. "Is it safe to light the fire? I don't know about you, but I prefer my food cooked."

"The Uriah are too far from here to smell the fish cooking. Our other pursuers are doubtless asleep by now." He lit the fire with a bit of magic and sat down near it.

"Other pursuers?" Rialla questioned, filching the knife he carried in his boot.

"Winterseine and son are camped an easy morning's walk from here. Apparently Terran doesn't have any trouble tracking our movements from a distance." He described briefly what he'd overheard.

"Is that where you got hurt?" Rialla questioned with a touch of concern, cleaning the fish. She discarded the entrails behind a nearby bush.

Tris shook his head. "No, that was the Uriah and my own stupidity. After I saw Winterseine and Terran, I hunted for the Uriah—there's a pack of six—so we wouldn't run into them trying to escape Winterseine. When I found them, I thought that I could help them with a touch of healing. That's where I got hurt."

"Stupidity is right," said Rialla with a dawning grin. "You lectured me all day about Uriah. Do I get to return the favor?"

"No," he answered. "I think I learned my lesson the hard way."

She laughed and handed him a fish and a handful of

willow branches. Taking her own fish, she hooked it on a larger forked willow branch and began to weave a crude basket around it. "Tell me how you traveled 'an easy morning's walk' and back in such a short time."

"Magic," he replied easily as he worked on his fish.

They roasted their fish in silence broken only by the spit and hiss of the fire. Watching flames dance, Rialla examined all the possibilities that she could think of, until only one remained.

"How long would it take you to travel to Sianim by yourself?" she asked.

Tris looked up from his fish. After a moment he shrugged. "I can only use the faster ways until I reach the road, so it should take two days, maybe three, assuming the cook was right when she told me how far it was from the crossroads to Sianim."

He turned his gaze back to the fire. "I'll not leave you behind. Getting the dagger and the books to Sianim is not worth your life."

"Nor is it worth yours," she answered. "I agree, but I don't think they'll kill me—I'm a valuable slave, remember? I believe Terran is the Voice of Altis, and it is important that Sianim be made aware of it. You said Terran can track me; then let him. It will give you time to get the journal away. If we wait for him to catch up with us, they may win it all. It would be idiotic to assume your magic could overcome both a magician and a prophet of Altis. In fact, your being with me could put me in worse danger. They still think I am a slave. They want the items we stole, and they'll keep me alive at least until they find out where those things are."

Tris said nothing, so Rialla spoke again. "I might be able to evade them while you take the books to Sianim and return here to help me. Without the necessity of reaching Sianim, I can choose a path that gives me an advantage over a mounted pursuit." She knew that if Terran had some god-given means of tracing her, she would be caught. If she were careful, though, she might be able to stall them until Tris could return and help her escape.

"Your fish is burning" was all the reply Tris made. He pulled his own dinner out of the fire.

Rialla didn't push him. She picked up her fish and began to eat.

Finally Tris threw his fish bones into the fire with a harsh sigh. "I'll be back in four or five days. Don't worry, I can find you. Now, tell me how to locate your Ren."

Rialla hesitated, trying to decide how to describe the ancient maze in which Ren kept his office. At last she said, "I think that it would be easier to tell you how to find Laeth. He should be back by now. Ren is more likely to listen to him then he is to a stranger." She explained where Laeth's apartment was. "If you can't find the apartments, then just ask anyone in the street how to find the Inn of the Lost Pig; the innkeeper is a friend—he'll know where Laeth is."

"I'll find him," he said shortly.

Tris slid under the thornberry branches and returned with the spellbook and its loose pages in one arm and the journal tucked under his belt. Regaining his feet, he walked to the satchel and brought out the dagger. As he bent over, the pages won their freedom at last, sliding out of Winterseine's book to flutter to the ground.

"I don't think that I want to leave those for Winterseine to find," said Tris, giving them a grim look. "Nor am I overanxious to pick them up."

"What about the fire?" asked Rialla.

"It's worth trying," answered Tris.

With the aid of the cooking sticks, Tris lifted the pages and set them into the small camp fire.

For a moment nothing happened, then a hollow boom echoed through the woods, and the flames converged on the parchment sheets, deserting the wood until even the coals were black and cold. Gradually the flames died down and left the pages glowing.

"This could be difficult," commented Tris in an abstract tone.

"Cursed difficult," agreed Rialla, shaken.

Tris turned to grin at her, saying in a theatrical voice, "But I have the most destructive force in nature at my call. Watch and marvel, fair lady."

He hunted diligently under the nearby trees, summoning a magelight to help him. At last he retrieved a wrinkled sacklike ball that he pick up gingerly between two fingers. He carried it back to the dead fire and set it delicately on the still-glowing sheets. In the light emitted by the radiant parchment, Rialla thought the gray ball looked shriveled and harmless.

"What is that?" she asked.

"Spore sack."

Tris used one of the cooking sticks and prodded the leathery sack lightly. Rialla plugged her ears as the ball exploded . . . with an inaudible puff. She could see fireless smoke escape from the ball and leisurely settle in an ashy mist upon the pages.

Rialla snickered.

Tris ignored her and stared intently at the spore-bearing parchment. The pages' glow began to dim then flow outward, fading as the nearby grass lengthened and flowers bloomed from the magic that was released. Rialla could hear a soft sighing sound as the leaves of the nearby bushes brushed against one another, growing with the magic that human mages had used to saturate two thin sheets of lambskin.

Gradually, darkness regained its hold and the light faded. Tris stood over the dead coals of the fire and called a magelight.

As they watched, a soft breeze danced lightly against their skin and dissolved the buff-colored sheets into minute fragments that scattered in the wind's path, leaving a ring of white mushrooms on the ashes of the fire.

Rialla laughed softly. "The most destructive force in nature, huh? Rot."

Tris grinned. "Exactly."

# TEN

"Tris," said Rialla, as she watched Tris double-check to make sure that he had everything. "I don't know if I've ever thanked you for what you've done. If I don't see you again, I wanted you to know that I've," she gave him an odd smile, as she realized the truth of what she was saying, "enjoyed our association."

He gave her an indecipherable look that faded to humor as he stood up. "If I don't see you again then . . ." He moved swiftly for one so large and cupped her chin in his hand.

As his words trailed off, Rialla thought about backing away from his light hold. With a mental shrug she decided to enjoy his kiss instead. When he stepped back, his breathing was as unsteady as hers.

He held her gaze and said firmly, "I'll see you in three or four days."

Rialla watched him run until he was lost in the darkness, before starting off on her own. If Terran and Winterseine were so close, she would need to travel through the night to stay ahead of them.

Rather than continuing in the direction that they'd been traveling, Rialla moved directly away from where Tris had indicated Terran and Winterseine were camped.

The path she took led through the thickest undergrowth she could find. Without a trail Rialla was forced to struggle through the interwoven leaves. Branches grabbed at her hair and tripped her when she least expected it. When she rapped her shins against a fallen limb for the fifth time in as many minutes, she reminded herself that she'd chosen this path because it was much more difficult for a rider to get through, and pressed on.

Tris had told her that the ground in this direction was marshy, and twice she was forced to edge around boggy patches that looked like open meadow. She crossed a rock-strewn stream that left her feet wet and cold. By the time morning light began to filter through the trees, she had covered several miles, and the constant awareness of Tris had faded.

As she journeyed, Rialla used the position of stars, and later the sun, to guide her so she traveled in a straight line Terran could not shorten. She walked until she was stumbling with exhaustion, then climbed up into the shelter of a large old apple tree to rest in the late afternoon.

As the sun was setting, Rialla was up and walking again. She tried to contact Tris, but evidently he was now too far away to reach. Twice she found bear tracks, but no sign of Uriah. She would have been more comfortable in the desert of her childhood rather than the temperate and moist climate of southern Darran, but this had its advantages as well. Because of the high rainfall, there were streams scattered all over the gentle hills and valley bottoms.

Knowing that Terran could track her by whatever mysterious process his god allowed, she didn't try to hide her tracks. Instead she waded through mud and crawled under thickets that the men on horseback would have to ride around.

On the afternoon of the second day they found her.

She was drinking from a stream when she heard their horses, and she sat back on her heels to wait for them.

Winterseine spurred his horse to a gallop and pulled it up rearing in front of Rialla. Blank-faced, she focused on the horse's legs, noting absently that its hooves needed to be trimmed and reshod.

Winterseine jumped to the ground and grabbed her by the hair, pulling Rialla roughly to her feet.

"Bitch!" he spat. "Where is it? Where is the book?"

"She can hardly answer while you are shaking her like that, Father," said Terran in mild rebuke.

Isslic dropped her to her knees and grabbed something from his saddle. "Answer me, bitch. Where is the book you stole? Where is the dagger?"

Keeping in mind the part she had decided to play, Rialla answered dully, "He took them."

The whip whistled when it came down on her back. Terran caught his father's hand before he could hit her again.

"She's telling the truth." There was cold certainty in the younger man's voice. "Why don't you ask her to explain before you damage her beyond reclamation? Your temper could cost you a valuable dancer." Without waiting for his father's response, Terran addressed Rialla. "Who took them?"

Rialla eyed Winterseine warily from under her brows. He was all but shaking with rage at Terran's interference.

She kept her voice submissive as she answered, careful to be truthful—it sounded as if Terran could tell if she weren't. "The man who traveled with me, the one Laeth told me would come here. He told me that it was time to leave the hold and go to Sianim—so we did. After a day or so, he said that you were following me—so he left with the dagger."

"He took the book too?" snapped Winterseine.

Rialla nodded her head.

"How long ago did he leave?" The slave trainer's voice was tight.

"Two days," Rialla said evenly.

"This man you were with," asked Terran, his voice soft, "was he a magician?"

"Yes."

"What was his name?"

"He named himself Sylvan."

"After the forest-folk?" said Terran, sounding momentarily intrigued. "Father, do you know of such a mage?"

Winterseine shook his head. "I doubt he was using his true name."

Terran turned back to Rialla. "How did he find the dagger?"

"He spent several days searching before he accidently bumped the book you hid it in," Rialla replied. "He disguised himself as a woodcraftsman. He'd learned the trade in his youth."

"Why did you escape with him? I would have thought that you knew better than that by now." It was Winterseine's question.

Rialla tilted her head and spoke in the tones of one stating the obvious. "He said it was time to go. Laeth is waiting for me in Sianim."

"Don't you understand, Father? She wasn't escaping. Laeth is still technically her owner. He told her to obey this Sylvan. It isn't up to her to question his orders." Terran petted her cheek with the same affection a man might show a dog. "She's a good girl—aren't you?"

Rialla remained impassive though anxiety coursed through her—was that sarcasm that she heard in Terran's voice? It was hard for her to decipher from his tone alone, but she didn't dare look up at his face.

"Just because you slept with her is no sign that she is telling the truth," snapped Winterseine impatiently.

"Father," said Terran slowly, without the deference that Rialla was used to hearing from him, "just because my magic works differently than yours does not make it weak. I can tell truth from falsehood." His voice took on undercurrents that were meant for Winterseine alone. "If you choose to forget my capabilities, that is *your* problem."

"I don't understand what you mean." Winterseine's voice was full of innocent affront as false as a glass ruby.

"Of course not. Just remember that without me, your chances of become King of Darran are minimal at best. Especially if the dagger should arrive in Sianim." Cold menace laced Terran's speech. Rialla kept her head lowered.

"I think that we understand each other," commented Winterseine coolly, as he slipped the heavy leather collar around Rialla's neck again and tugged her to her feet. When he touched her, Rialla felt his fear . . . and hatred. "Shall we head back?"

THERE WAS NO HORSE FOR RIALLA TO RIDE; THEIR PACK-horse was heavily laden with supplies. Instead, she walked briskly beside Winterseine's mount. The ground was rough, and the horse could travel no faster than she. It picked the easiest path through the brush and left Rialla to fight her way through as best she could.

That evening they stopped beside a stream and ate camp fare from the packs the spare horse carried. The stew was unseasoned, but might have tasted better without the tight knot in Rialla's stomach.

After they'd eaten, Terran filled a small earthenware bowl with water from the stream. He knelt beside the bowl and nicked his thumb with his knife, letting a few drops of blood spill into the bowl. With the bowl in his hands, he sat cross-legged with his eyes closed.

While he meditated or prayed, Rialla finished washing the dishes from dinner and repacked them. Winterseine tied Rialla's arms tightly behind her and attached her leash to a tree. He unrolled his bedroll and closed his eyes.

Rialla was too uncomfortable to sleep, so she laid her cheek against the rough bark of the tree and watched Terran without interest. The setting sun still gave enough light that she could see him clearly.

She shifted awkwardly, trying to ease the discomfort of her arms, and wished that Tris were around to untie her. She was familiar enough with the whip to know that Winterseine's blow had only raised a welt, but it was rubbing painfully against the tree.

A weird cry reverberated eerily through the darkness and was answered almost immediately from the other side of their camp. Rialla jerked reflexively against the ropes that held her helpless as yet a third Uriah sounded from somewhere just behind and to her left.

She stared intently at a moving shadow in the nearby bushes, gradually becoming aware of other forms that surrounded the camp. She realized she'd been smelling them for a while, but had been too tired to realize it. Tris was right; they smelled like rotting corpses.

As she watched, they crept closer, mute now. This was a much larger group than the one she and Tris had found. She could count twenty easily, and suspected that there were more lurking in the shadows.

Winterseine had come to his feet at the first cry. He stood between Rialla and the small camp fire, so she saw him only as a shadowed figure that slowly pivoted until he'd looked all the way around.

Terran set the bowl aside and rose to his full height. He seemed relaxed and unworried. "It's all right," he said. "They have come because they know who I am."

When he spoke, the creatures quit moving. If Rialla hadn't been watching them before, she wouldn't have been able to pick out where the Uriah stood in the darkness.

"Poor things," Terran commented in a conversational tone. "The first Uriah were made before the Wizard Wars, and the black secrets of their making should have died with the last of the Great Ones. But Geoffrey ae'Magi had to play with the twisted magic once again. His perversion of magic was what awakened the old gods." Terran shook his head. "The purpose of having an ae'Magi, an Archmage, was to prevent such forbidden magic; obviously it hasn't worked.''

Terran waved his hand vaguely at the Uriah. "This is the reason, Father, that Altis must conquer the West. Magic is too powerful a force for humans to wield unchecked."

Rialla thought that Winterseine's silhouette stiffened, but she couldn't be certain.

The Uriah began to move again, closing in on the small camp. The horses shifted nervously and began tugging at the ropes that held them—so did Rialla.

"Poor things," said Terran again and held both hands over his head, palms facing outward. "Listen!" His voice became that of the prophet of Altis, echoing oddly in the trees. At his first word the Uriah halted their slow advance. If her hands had been free, Rialla could have reached out and touched the one nearest to her—not that she had any desire to do so.

"Hear me, Altis, Lord of the Night. Release these thy children. Release them, Altis. They suffer for another's sin."

The Uriah began to make a whispering noise, over and over again. The hair on the back of Rialla's neck prickled as she listened closely to the nearest Uriah.

It spoke, but not in Darranian. In the Common tongue, it whispered, "please," over and over again. Rialla looked at it closely, and saw that it wore the remains of the uniform of one of the Sianim guard units. Shock rippled through her as she realized that it must have once been human.

Rialla was no magician, but even she felt the power in Terran's voice as he shouted, "Release them, now!"

Slowly at first, then all at once, the Uriah fell to lie on the ground. Rialla kept her gaze on the Uriah nearest her. As she watched, the thing's body twisted and changed until she was looking at the corpse of a human in a state of advanced decomposition.

It lay still where it fell, without breathing.

Winterseine looked around at the corpses and then said, "We'll have to move camp. I don't know about you, but I can't sleep with this smell."

Rialla stared at the dead body that lay beside her. Uriah were said to be virtually immune to magic, and Terran had just killed at least thirty of the thrice-cursed things.

She didn't know how strong Tris was, but she didn't think that any kind of magic, human or otherwise, was going to be able to defeat Winterseine's son. If she didn't escape before Tris returned, there would be a confrontation that she and her healer would lose.

TRIS COULDN'T USE THE SYLVAN PATH TO TRAVEL THE whole way; the magic was draining and less effective as the yew and oak forest gave way to willow and birch. Still, in less than two days, he reached sight of Sianim—considerably faster than a human would have.

In the center of a large valley rose a steep-sided plateau with a single narrow, walled path leading upward to the city. The path was crowded at this time of the day, and Tris was forced to dawdle slowly behind a train of donkeys.

The noise from the city was deafening after the quiet forest. Tris followed the donkeys to the center of Sianim, where the markets were, then he tried to find someone with whom he could communicate. Living in Darran most of his life, he spoke Sylvan, Darranian and only a smattering of Common: a combination of gesture and slang that merchants had developed and the Sianim mercenaries had made their own. He'd hoped to find someone who could speak Darranian, but he had to make do with his poor Common.

He gave up trying to find Laeth's apartment, but the Lost Pig was easier. When three or four people pointed to one of the winding streets that Sianim was inflicted with, Tris started down it.

After a short walk, Tris found a building with heavy rusting chains attached to all four corners. As the large sign in front of the building had an orange pig rolling its eye slyly, Tris assumed that this was the place he was looking for.

He stepped inside, and almost retreated at the press of noisy people. On the far side of the room, a sultry woman slid through a doorway bearing a tray filled with brimming mugs. Surmising that the innkeeper would also be behind the doorway, Tris began to work his way through the room.

He was only partially through the tavern when someone caught at his sleeve. He spun around to see a man in leather armor pointing mutely to the far end of a long table.

Tris's gaze followed the gesture, to discover Laeth and Marri trying to push their way through the crowded pathway. Laeth was trying to say something, but the noise in the room prevented any sound from carrying even such a short distance.

When the two managed to make it to where Tris waited, he started back to the main door. Only when they were outside did anyone try to talk.

"Tris, what are you doing here?" asked Laeth. "Where's Rialla?"

"Somewhere in a Darranian forest, I hope," replied Tris wearily, rubbing the back of his neck. "I need to deliver these," he slipped the books out of his tunic and pulled the dagger from the sheath he normally used to carry his own knife, "to the Spymaster, Ren, then I need to get back to Rialla. Can you help me find him?"

"Why didn't you bring Rialla with you?" queried Marri.

"Winterseine and his son were following us. Rialla thought that she could evade them until I could bring these here; after all the trouble we went to, it would have been a shame to have to return them." Tris knew that it was overly easy to read his concern for Rialla in his voice, but he was too weary to disguise it.

"I could take the package to Ren," offered Laeth.

"That would leave you free to return. If you can describe where you are, I can get some friends together and ride after you with reinforcements."

Tris was tempted, but shook his head. "No. The journal I brought needs explanation. It would take me as long to explain it to you as him—and *I* can make him believe me. If you can take me to Ren, I'll get this over with."

"Right," said Laeth. "Follow me."

He led the way through the streets to a large building that was probably as old as the city. Centuries of minor additions had made the building look lopsided and disordered. The stone steps inside were worn with the weight of generations of feet. Laeth knocked briskly on a scratched wooden door.

"Go away!" ordered a voice from within firmly. "I filed the report yesterday."

Laeth looked at Tris and shrugged before opening the door and peering in. "It's only me," he said with his head inside the door.

Tris trailed Laeth and Marri into the room. The enclosed space smelled musty, as if it hadn't received fresh air in a long time. Seated behind a desk too large for such a small room, a frail-looking man was running his fingers through his thinning hair.

A second man had been seated comfortably on a padded chair facing the desk, but when he saw a woman enter the room, he came to his feet. Tris knew that his eyes had widened, but he'd never seen a man dressed in such a manner—not even among the more foppish Darranian nobles. The man's expensive leather boots were dyed a hideous shade of orange, contrasting with emerald-green velvet trousers trimmed in orange lace. The man's tunic was also mostly emerald-green, except for the long, flowing orange sleeves. His hair was curled in ringlets that descended to his shoulders in a cascade any woman would have been proud to claim.

"Ah, what a pleasure to be interrupted by such a lovely

visitor," he said, stepping forward to kiss Marri's hand. "Allow me to introduce myself. I am Lord Kisrah."

Before anyone had a chance to respond, the man behind the desk, who Tris assumed was the Spymaster, came to his feet as well. "Laeth, I *told* you that I had someone scouting Winterseine's holdings looking for Rialla. I will tell you when I have news."

"I have news for you, sir," answered Laeth, blithely ignoring the irritation in the Spymaster's voice, even as he deftly pulled Marri behind him and away from Lord Kisrah.

Tris narrowed his eyes at the human peacock. "Lord Kisrah," he said slowly, "the Archmage."

Kisrah bowed formally. "The same."

Ren cleared his throat and took charge. "I am *Ren*," he announced firmly. "This young idiot is Laeth, sometime Darranian lordling and currently mercenary of Sianim." Somehow Ren managed to make the second title the more imposing.

His voice softened as he continued, "With him is Lady Marri, widow of Lord Karsten of Darran, and soon to be Laeth's bride. Lord Kisrah has done us the courtesy of introducing himself, and I am not sure who you are, sir." He directed the last toward Tris.

"I am Tris," replied the healer. "Sometime healer of Tallonwood, currently messenger for one Rialla, slave turned horse trainer turned spy. I have several things to deliver to the Spymaster of Sianim."

Tris handed Ren the books and pulled Laeth's dagger from the boot sheath he normally used to carry his own knife. "The dagger is the one used to kill Karsten. Rialla and I found it in Winterseine's keep."

Lord Kisrah gestured, and Ren gave him the dagger. The Archmage curled his fingers around the hilt and muttered a phrase. "Winterseine held the pommel when it last killed—but I didn't know Lord Karsten. I'll have to have something of his to confirm he was the man who died. I have to confess, however, I am curious how you expect to get a Darranian court to believe the word of a magician.''

"Rialla was confident that Ren was capable of such a feat," replied Tris briskly, "but we found something that might help. The larger book is Winterseine's *grimoire*, conveniently embossed with his seal—complete except for a few pages of vellum that slid out as we escaped.''

Kisrah took the book Tris extended. As soon as he touched it, his casual interest became intense. He held the book for a moment then set it on Ren's desk. "What did you do with those pages?" The indolent manner that had characterized him until that moment was gone. In its place was the powerful presence that belonged to the ae'Magi.

"They were impregnated with magic to the extent that I was not sure they were safe to touch. When they fell out of the book, I destroyed them, rather than leave them for Winterseine's use.''

"Destroyed them? How?" asked Lord Kisrah, his face white and shaken.

"With magic, Lord Kisrah, how else?" Tris's eyebrows rose.

"Ah, well," said Ren, "at least they are not in Winterseine's hands. What is the small book?"

"That," said Tris, "is the most interesting item we retrieved. Rialla says you are concerned about a prophet who is planning to take over our lands.''

"The book implicates my uncle?" said Laeth without surprise.

Tris shook his head. "It's the private journal of the Voice of Altis. You would know him better as Terran.''

Laeth and Marri looked at Tris in astonishment; the others obviously didn't know who Terran was.

"My cousin *Terran*?" asked Laeth incredulously.

"Winterseine's son," said Ren.

Lord Kisrah stiffened. "Winterseine's son is not a mage. I was there at his testing."

"No," agreed Tris blandly, "Terran is not a mage, he is a prophet.''

"Winterseine's using his magic to allow his son to declare himself a prophet." Ren's disbelief was obvious.

"No," said Tris again, "Terran *is* a prophet of Altis—at least Rialla and I think so."

"Gods," swore Laeth in a soft tone.

"Yes," agreed Tris. "I think that you'll find Terran's journal most—" He broke off and flinched as a searing pain touched his back.

Laeth gripped his shoulder. "What's wrong?"

Tris shook his head grimly, reaching for Rialla through the bond between them; but he couldn't touch her mind. All that had reached him over the distance was the brief lash of pain.

"I have to get back," he said. "Read the journal . . . and keep an open mind."

TRIS HAD REQUESTED A HORSE, KNOWING THAT IT WOULD be faster to ride until he reached the forests. Laeth led him to the stable, and produced a sleek gray gelding.

Urgency replaced fatigue for the first hour that Tris rode, the gelding moving smoothly in a ground-eating trot. Sianim grew distant and was gradually replaced by the farmland that surrounded the city, which in turn gave way to rolling hills as Tris fretted about Rialla. As soon as the last of the farmland fences ended, he left the road.

Though the distance was too great for him to contact Rialla mentally, the bond they shared gave him a direction to follow. If he assumed that her pain meant that she was in Winterseine's hands, then it would take speed on his part to catch them before they returned to the slave trader's hold.

Tris wanted to catch them in the forest, where his powers were at their greatest, instead of the cold stone building that housed Terran's shrine to Altis. He suspected that Rialla was correct; Terran and Winterseine were too powerful to attack directly. However, the forest was his domain, and in the forest there were other methods of combat.

He rode on, until the horse hung its head in exhaustion and he was in little better shape. His connection with Rialla might allow him to locate her, but it required concentration; twice he had to correct his course when fatigue distracted him.

Reluctantly Tris decided that he would have to stop or risk losing his mount and his trail. The decision was made slightly easier when he concluded that, even if he managed to find Rialla, he would be too exhausted to do anything other than surrender out of hand.

RIALLA SHIFTED STIFFLY WHEN TERRAN UNTIED HER hands. The discomfort from her bonds had kept her awake for most of the night. Her hands were numb, and her arms ached despite Terran's gentle chafing.

When she could move her hands, Terran handed her a cup of something hot and spicy that she didn't recognize. It must have had some medicinal property, as she felt considerably better by the time she'd finished drinking it.

When the camp was broken and the horses saddled and packed, Winterseine untied her leash from the tree and secured it to a ring on his saddle.

It took a long time for Rialla to work out the awkwardness from having been tied up all night. The long chase, combined with lack of sleep, was wearing her down. Her weak leg protested the punishment that she'd given it; after midday her scar began to burn from the abuse.

They finally worked through the worst of the underbrush and came to a clearing bisected by a shallow stream, and Winterseine pushed his horse into a trot. Rialla managed to follow for several paces, then her leg cramped. As she fought for balance, the leash around her neck snapped tight and she fell to the ground with punishing force.

Winterseine dragged her several lengths before stopping his horse, adding to the mounting number of bruises and scrapes that covered her. She coughed and choked from the force of the collar on her neck as she fought grimly to straighten her leg out, but the large muscle in her thigh kept it firmly pressed against her chest.

Terran dismounted and placed one knee on her shoulder and both hands on her knee. With his greater leverage he was able to straighten her leg, forcing the muscle to elongate. As her leg stretched out, he slid his knee down until it rested on her hip and began kneading the rigid muscle.

Rialla stared at his long-fingered hands working on her bare thigh and thought of another time they had done the same. She shuddered as revulsion swept through her; tired and in pain, she didn't have the strength to control her thoughts. She twisted violently to the right at the same time her abhorrence hit Terran with the force of a blow.

Terran flinched instinctively, loosing his hold on both her leg and shoulder. Rialla rolled away from him, crying out as her leg snapped back and the muscle cramped again. She twisted and fought, but she couldn't straighten her leg and keep the collar from choking her at the same time.

Winterseine's horse was used to leading slaves who might jerk or fight the leash. But this mad thing writhing on the ground was something else. It snorted uneasily, then reared and fought in earnest as Rialla's barriers dropped, and exposed the animal to her frenzy.

Terran drew his knife and sawed at the tough leather that bound Rialla to the frantic horse. Winterseine managed to keep the horse from bolting, but the leash wasn't long enough for safety. Both Rialla and Terran were within easy reach of the flashing hooves.

Terran had cut most of the way through the strap when a particularly violent tug from either Rialla or the horse snapped it the rest of the way. Prudently, Winterseine let the animal get some distance from Rialla before he tried to calm it down.

Half-strangled and blinded by panic and the matted hair in her face, Rialla fought tenaciously against any attempt on Terran's part to get anywhere near her. Coughing, she rolled on the ground, unable to run because she still couldn't extend her leg.

She was aware of a sharp sound, as if someone clapped his hands, and then she didn't hear anything at all.

PANIC AND PAIN WOKE TRIS UP FROM A SOUND SLEEP, and he came to his feet before he was fully awake. When he realized that it was Rialla's emotion he was feeling, he called to her, demanding answers, but it was useless.

He swore, once, then collected himself. He was still too far from the heart of the forest; the sylvan ways would be slower than riding.

He tightened the cinch on the saddle and mounted. She was too far from him for his arrival to make any difference to what had happened. It would take him better than half a day to reach her—if she stayed where she was. He touched his calves to the gray's sides, and the gelding leapt gamely into a run.

FROM SOMEWHERE RIALLA HEARD HER NAME BEING called. Something about the voice made her fight out of the darkness that succored her. Just as she was awake enough to respond, Tris quit calling her.

Her offending leg had subsided to a dull ache that was matched by one in her jaw. She assumed Terran had hit her to calm her down. Her throat ached from the slave collar, making it painful to swallow. Her cheek, shoulder and good leg were abraded from being dragged behind Winterseine's horse, but all things considered, she was in better shape than she deserved for acting like an idiot.

Rialla opened her eyes slowly and sat up, rubbing her sore chin. She couldn't have been out long, because Terran and Winterseine were both still trying to calm down Winterseine's horse. Terran's horse and the pack animal weren't in the clearing.

If she could trust her leg, she could sneak off into the forest and call Terran's mare to her. Mounted, she just might be able to get away. When she started to get to her feet, her thigh muscle cramped warningly, so she subsided. There would be a better time.

When Winterseine's horse stood still at last, foam lathered his flanks and chest, a testimony to the violence of his fight. The gelding held his head low, and his ribs heaved with the effort of breathing.

As soon as he'd gone over the horse to check for injury, Winterseine mounted. "I'll go find your mare and the packhorse; you stay with the slave and see that she doesn't go anywhere."

Terran nodded his head and watched his father ride through the brush. Rialla could have told them that he was riding the wrong way, but she wasn't feeling particularly helpful just now.

When Winterseine was out of sight, Terran walked over to Rialla.

"Are you all right?" he asked, kneeling beside her.

He was too close, and Rialla stiffened slightly, but nodded. Terran started to say something else, but stopped abruptly. He turned her abraded cheek to the sun, where he could see in more clearly.

It occurred to Rialla that she wasn't feeling any pain from the scrapes now, just a warm tingle. She pulled her face out of his hand and looked down at her arm that should have been covered with an abrasion from shoulder to wrist. The wound was still there, but as she watched, it faded rapidly, until the only thing that marred her skin was dirt.

She stared dazedly at her arm, and tried to gather her scattered thoughts.

"How are you doing that?" asked Terran with a touch of excitement in his voice.

Rialla blinked at him stupidly for a moment. "What?"

"This," replied Terran, gripping her wrist and shaking it at her. "How are you healing yourself?"

"I'm not." She shook her head and pulled her arm back out of his grip. It wasn't something that a slave would do, she couldn't tolerate his touch. "I don't know what's going on."

"Father says that you're an empath. What else are you?" Terran asked intensely, leaning forward. "This is magic, but it's nothing I've heard of anyone having the ability to do. What are you?"

Rialla scooted back from him and shook her head, whispering, "I don't know what you're talking about." She decided to take the offensive. After her performance when her leg cramped, Terran was bound to think that she was a few kernels shy of a full measure. So she let her voice become shrill as she continued, "I don't know what you're doing to me."

Rialla needed something to take his attention from her, so she used her gift to find his horse. The mare had stopped at a nearby patch of wheatgrass. Rialla didn't have to work hard to persuade the animal to return, because the little horse adored her rider. With scarcely any reluctance she left her snack and started back, the pack-horse following her lead.

"I'm not doing anything. It's you. I can feel it, the healing magic in you." There was conviction in his voice and a touch of wonder. "I've heard there are creatures that live in the Northern forests that can heal like that. Are you a shapeshifter?"

Rialla looked at him incredulously. She knew quite well she had no magical abilities. Yet she could feel Terran's sincerity; he *knew* that she was healing herself. She knew that she wasn't.

Tris could heal, but she couldn't imagine he was stupid enough to do so without making sure than no one else was around. He wouldn't have lasted in Darran if he weren't careful about things like that.

The gray mare trotted unconcernedly into the clearing, followed by the packhorse. She whickered softly when she saw Terran, and thrust her nose against him, rubbing enthusiastically.

Without taking his eyes from Rialla, Terran reached up

and rubbed the mare's face. "Good girl," he crooned soothingly.

Rialla pulled her legs up to her chin and wrapped her arms around them. She rested her face against her knees and closed her eyes, shutting Terran out. After a moment she felt him move away. He was only biding his time, but she was thankful anyway.

*Tris?* she called.

His reply, when it came, was faint, but steady. In it she could feel relief. *Are you all right? What happened?*

*I'm fine. At least I think so. Tris, did you heal me a few minutes ago?*

*What?* he asked. Before Rialla could tell him what had happened, she felt his sudden comprehension followed by a brief flash of guilt.

*It's all right,* he said. *There's nothing to worry about. Do you remember the bond that I formed between us to allow you to communicate with me?*

*Yes,* she answered.

*The healing is a result of that bonding.*

*What?* She let him feel her exasperation at his inadequate explanation.

*The magic I use is not like that of humans,* he explained. *Sometimes it requires little initiative to work.*

She thought about the implications of what he'd said. *Do you mean that some of your magic decided to heal a few scrapes and bruises in front of Terran, without any action from you—and it could do it again and neither you nor I could do anything about it?*

Some of her feelings must have made it through to Tris, because when he answered her it was with a strong burst of reassurance. *I should have warned you that this would happen, but I didn't expect it quite so soon. I can control the healing; I wasn't aware I needed to.*

*You knew that this would happen? What do you mean? What else should I expect?* Rialla didn't know exactly what she was feeling—some combination of anger and bewilderment.

Again she felt a touch of guilt from Tris. *I should have told you before. I'm sorry. I suspect that now is not the time to go into it, but when we get through with this mess, I'll sit down and explain what's been going on.*

Rialla opened her eyes to see Terran watching her intently. She reburied her face in her knees and said, *This had better be quite an explanation.*

Without looking at Terran again, Rialla sat back and began to work her weak leg. Tris's magic had taken care of her cramping muscle, but she needed to occupy herself with something in the face of Terran's steady regard. She had the uncomfortable feeling that he knew she was communicating with someone.

Winterseine finally returned, looking harried. When he saw that the horses had returned on their own, he didn't look any happier.

"Stupid beasts," he commented sourly, swinging off his horse with athletic grace. "We might as well spend the night here. There's a storm coming in, and we won't make the keep before nightfall."

Rialla hadn't realized that they were so close.

While Terran occupied himself with lighting a fire and starting another traveler's stew from dried meat, Winterseine unpacked the horses and staked them out nearby.

Since no one seemed to be paying particular attention to her, Rialla decided to make use of the creek. She took off her shoes before walking into the stream, clothes and all.

Shuddering at the cold, she sat down in the knee-high water and scrubbed off the dirt and sweat she'd acquired over the days of frantic travel through the forest. By the time she was finished, she was numb with cold, but blessedly clean. It was still warm enough out that her clothes should dry before she had to sleep in them—although judging by the black clouds overhead, it would probably rain tonight anyway.

She got out and began squeezing the water from her tunic as best she could without disrobing. She suspected the fabric was permanently stained, but at least it didn't stink anymore.

"Rialla."

Warily, she turned to look at Terran where he stood near the small camp fire. Winterseine was some distance away, picketing the horses.

"There's some wild onion to your left. Would you pick it for me? If you see anything else that'll add some flavor to the stew, get it as well."

Relieved, Rialla knelt to do as he asked. The onion was easy enough to see, once it had been pointed out to her. She wasn't fond of it, but she harvested it until she had a double handful. She looked around for anything else that looked edible and noticed a familiar plant growing in the shade of a small bush.

Sliding over to it, she examined it carefully. It looked like the plant Tris had called whitecowl. Whitecowl, she remembered, was a sleeping draft. She hesitated, but the thought of arriving at Winterseine's hold tomorrow gave her courage.

Rialla didn't know how much to use, so she gathered all the leaves from the plant. The leaves would be obvious next to the onions, but she found some dandelions nearby. Torn off the plant, the two leaves looked similar enough that Rialla couldn't tell the difference.

She took all of the plants to the stream and washed them off carefully before taking them to the pot of stew and dumping them in. Terran thanked her with a nod and continued stirring.

Rialla moved as far away as she dared before finding a likely stump. She sat down and then finger-combed her hair until she could braid it back out of her face. She didn't have anything to tie it with, but hoped it would be a while before it came undone again.

The dampness of her clothes made it seem colder than it was; the wind was stirring with the oncoming storm. However, the shiver that caused her to wrap her arms around herself was caused by anxiety more than cold. She could only hope that the whitecowl didn't do anything distinctive when it was boiled—like turn red and stink.

The sky was darkening rapidly with evening and signs of the summer storm. By the time Terran called them over to eat, it was nearly dark and the wind had picked up speed.

Rialla examined the stew carefully, but she couldn't see anything wrong with it. She smelled it unobtrusively, but it only smelled like wild onions and salted meat. The deepening shadows and Rialla's distant perch made it easy for her to pretend to eat while surreptitiously dumping the stew to the ground.

When everyone was through eating, Rialla gathered the dishes and the pot and carried them to the stream to wash. She took her time, hoping that the others would fall asleep before Winterseine tied her up for the night.

When she turned back to the fire, the small hope that had been steadily growing in her dissipated. Clearly outlined against the fire, Winterseine sat comfortably on a large rock, tossing his knife hilt over blade into the air, then catching it and sending it spinning again. In the distance Rialla heard a rumble of thunder.

Rialla walked slowly to the packs that Winterseine had removed from the horses and put the bowls and the pot away. Hoping nothing showed in her face, she returned to the fire.

"Slave girl," purred Winterseine softly.

She raised her eyes to him in mute question, distrusting the satisfaction in his voice.

"Magicians use a lot of herbs in their spells. Did you know that?" He smiled at her.

Rialla's stomach knotted, but she kept her face blank as she shook her head.

"Whitecowl has a distinctive taste, almost minty. The onions were a nice touch. I almost didn't catch the flavor of the whitecowl in time. Terran didn't." Winterseine nodded across the fire.

Rialla looked where he'd indicated and saw for the first time that Terran was lying on his side—clearly asleep.

"But then he's not a magician. I need to thank you, slave girl." Winterseine's voice drew her attention back to him. "I have been trying for some time to get Terran in just such a position. My poor Tamas is caught up in this Altis cult my son started; I knew it was useless to ask him to poison Terran as he did my nephew Karsten."

Up went the knife in a glittering twisting motion, then back to rest in the deft hands of the magician. Lightning cracked across the sky as the evening storm grew nearer.

"I am afraid that Terran has forgotten that others have ambitions as well," continued Winterseine. "He is so caught up in his own myth he forgets more mundane issues." He shook his head sadly. "He was angry that I killed Karsten. He hoped I would give up when the swamp beast failed."

"But the diversion worked, and Karsten died," commented Rialla.

Winterseine laughed. "It was supposed to kill Karsten, not act as a diversion. I had a geas laid upon it—but the geas couldn't force it away from an empath. Somehow Terran learned of my plans. I didn't realize why he insisted on bringing a half-trained slave to Karsten's celebration—not until the creature attacked you that night. She was an empath too. After she killed herself, Terran must have remembered that you used to be an empath and decided to use you to break the geas instead." Winterseine's voice had gotten quieter with the force of his rage. "He thought that I would not kill if I had to do it with my own hands. Foolish of him. How does he think that my father died . . . a hunting accident?"

Winterseine was talking more to himself than to Rialla. She hoped that he would get distracted enough for her to run. In the darkness she could hide from him for a long time.

"After Terran dies," continued Winterseine thoughtfully, "I think I shall send Tamas to Sianim to poison my nephew Laeth. Lord Jarroh might also be a problem, but one of his servants has done jobs for me before—another one will be no trouble.'' Winterseine smiled with pleasure, and a chill crept up Rialla's spine. She was too far away to touch the madness she had felt lurking underneath his surface, but she could see it clearly in the eyes of the man who talked so casually about murdering his own son.

''Cerric, our little-boy king, doesn't have any legitimate male heirs. After ten years or so of acting as his regent, I will have accustomed Darran to my rule, and when Cerric dies I will be the logical choice to replace him—after all, my bloodlines are tied with the royal house. But perhaps it would be better if Cerric just goes mad, and needs to be locked up for life; I'll take things as they come.''

Winterseine paused and held the knife still for a moment before sending it spinning into the dirt near Terran's head. It landed with a thump, burying itself halfway up the blade in the dirt. He shifted his gaze from his sleeping son to Rialla. She took an involuntary step back and he smiled again, slipping a pouch off his belt.

''I was worried about killing Terran. I trust that you've heard the stories he tells about the coming of the old gods?'' He paused to give her time to answer, but seemed unconcerned about her lack of response.

''Unfortunately, the stories are true. Terran does seem to have some sort of tie with the god Altis. When it first began, I thought that it would be good to have my son with so much power.'' Winterseine shook his head. ''But I can't let him do as he intends. I spent the most productive years of my life bowing to the ae'Magi. When he died, I stole the key to the Master Spells so that I would not have to do that again—now I have to bow to Terran's control. *Terran's!*'' Winterseine spat the name out with outrage, but regained control of himself and said calmly, ''I have discovered that although Altis grants my son power, he does not always watch over him. This . . .'' Winterseine showed Rialla a silver ring that he wore, the one she and Tris had found in a hollow book while they were searching the study. "This allows me to know when my son is watched by his god. As at this moment he is not.

"If I were to kill Terran myself, as I did Karsten, Altis would destroy me—finding who wielded the knife or potion would be child's play even to a hedgewitch. But I have another way." As he spoke, Winterseine opened the pouch and removed four neat bundles of cloth. These he unfolded. There was something inside each bundle, but the darkness kept Rialla from seeing exactly what it was. Winterseine combined the substances until he held only one cloth square in his hand.

"I will, of course, be devastated at the death of my only son. It seems that we went out chasing a runaway slave and she knifed him while he slept—I warned him that she was subject to such fits. I, his grieving father, destroyed the slave—but vengeance is no substitute for a lost child." His voice was sad, belied by the wide smile on his face. He said something in a language that Rialla didn't understand and then blew the contents of his cloth in her direction.

"Take the knife, and kill him with it." Winterseine's tone was cold and harsh, demanding instant response.

Rialla took a step toward Terran, then stopped. She bit her lip in an effort to resist Winterseine's command.

"Take the knife and kill Terran with it," repeated Winterseine, adding a hand gesture.

Two steps more, and her hand closed firmly on the warm haft of the knife. It felt heavy in her hand, as if it weighed more than any knife should. She tried to drop it, but her fingers merely tightened their grip.

"Kill him." She couldn't see Winterseine now; her gaze was focused on Terran's face, but she felt the demand and raised her knife. Hoping that Tris was near enough to hear, she called out to him silently.

*Rialla?* In the time it took her to kneel beside Terran, Tris was able to grasp what was happening and . . . Rialla felt a surge of strength.

She stumbled to her feet and took a step back from the sleeping prophet. She tossed the knife into the fire and turned to see Winterseine rush to his feet, his face a mask of rage.

"Who are you, slave girl?" Unknowingly, he paraphrased his son's question from early that day.

She gave him a gentle smile. "I am Rialla, horse trainer of Sianim."

# ELEVEN

"A horse trainer?" questioned Winterseine, smiling. "Well, who would have thought it? Leath brought a Sianim spy with him to his brother's castle."

"As you are contemplating the murder of your son, I don't think you have the purity of soul to pass judgment," commented Rialla dryly as the rain began to fall.

"Ah, my dear," Winterseine said, shaking his head sadly as he picked up a nearby stick and used it to knock the knife out of the fire. "Familial elimination is an old Darranian art form. Spying, on the other hand, is a betrayal that is much more difficult to overlook. Ah well, with you dead, there is no way to prove Laeth's espionage activities—and I need you dead." As he spoke, he made a faint motion with his hand and the compulsion to pick up the knife returned.

With Tris to strengthen her, Rialla didn't even sway. Winterseine's lips tightened with annoyance. "When did you become a magician, slave?"

The power that Tris had poured into Rialla to let her escape Winterseine's spell was as effective as a drug—

and as dangerous. Even as she warned herself to be cautious, a smile stretched its way across her face and she heard herself answer, "As I said earlier, though perhaps you did not hear, I am not a slave. I have not been one for a very long time."

She touched her cheek with her hand. With magic-heightened senses she could feel the scar where she'd sliced her cheek, despite Tris's spell. Almost without thought, she strove to dismiss the magic that marked her as Winterseine's possession.

Lightning illuminated the dark forest momentarily, followed soon after by the reverberation of its accompanying thunder.

As soon as Rialla sought his help resisting Winterseine's spell, Tris slid off the horse. He pulled the bridle and saddle off, setting the animal free to go or stay as it would.

He knew he wasn't going to find Rialla in time to help her directly; the bond would have to serve them. He wasn't sure how much he could help her over such a distance, but there was green magic in the storm that had awakened in the night. Tris drew it to him ruthlessly, ignoring the rains that began to pour from the heavens.

He thought only to keep Rialla out of Winterseine's control; he hadn't considered the possibility that she could use the magic that he gave her. When she began to dispel his illusion, Tris stepped in delicately to guide her manipulation.

*This way,* he said. *It doesn't waste so much magic.*

Rialla accepted his help gratefully. The kidskin fell into her hand, the shadow of the tattoo fading away, but Tris's magic, under her control, had chosen to do more than that. Under her fingers her cheek was smooth, without scar or blemish. Her smile widened as she met Winterseine's gaze fully.

"I'm neither slave nor magician." She took a step

closer and gripped his left hand firmly in her right. "Have you forgotten? I am an empath."

The unexpectedness of her move kept Winterseine momentarily motionless, and then it was too late. Rialla caught him in a maelstrom of emotion.

This time there was no room full of people for her to draw upon, only Winterseine himself. She ignored her instinctive revulsion and sought the faint trails of destructive emotion that he kept hidden from himself in the far recesses of his mind. She ignored the rage that had more than a touch of insanity in it: it would merely strengthen him. She found instead all the fears that had been growing since his son had discovered that the god of night still lived.

She took his fear, strengthened it with doubt, and pulled it closer to his conscious mind . . .

Winterseine ripped himself free of her hold. She could see the sweat that stained his shirt in the light of the fire.

"Bitch," he said. His left arm, the one she'd touched, hung limply at his side—a reflex only; she had done him no physical harm.

He motioned sharply with his right hand. This time the hand motion was no arcane move. She saw the flash of silver and dodged to the side.

Rialla had trained almost obsessively at Sianim, struggling to rebuild her confidence. The knife Winterseine had produced from a hidden sheath on his arm merely slipped across the skin of her upper arm before landing in the dirt behind her.

Resting her weight lightly on the balls of her feet, she flexed her knees slightly, looking for the opening that would allow her to touch him again. Not over his clothing—that would diminish the effect; she needed to touch him skin to skin.

Already the terror that she'd pulled to the surface of Winterseine's thoughts was receding as the slave master replaced it with rage. Though she couldn't feel his anger, she could see it in his face.

*Careful,* warned Tris without disturbing her concentration. *He's getting ready for something. Can you feel the magic he's amassing?*

Winterseine smiled and stretched his right hand toward her. He made a grasping motion, and Rialla felt pain explode in her chest. She fell to her knees, gasping for breath that wouldn't come. Tris's warmth spread slowly across her chest, and with it the ability to breathe, though the incapacitating pain remained.

Rain began to fall, pounding the ground with the force of its descent.

Winterseine had stepped closer. Rialla rolled, extending her arm; she touched his boot for an instant before he stepped away. In that moment she took the ache in her chest, and Tris's empathetic pain, and thrust them at Winterseine. Even through the heavy leather, the contact broke his concentration and Rialla's agony faded.

Rialla rolled to her feet, panting with the triple effect of her own pain, Winterseine's and Tris's. The hurt faded rapidly. Without Winterseine's magic to interfere, Tris quickly repaired the slight damage that had been done.

"There *is* magic in you," accused Winterseine. "I felt it."

In the few naked moments she had touched Winterseine, she'd discovered the fear that haunted him. The moment had come to take advantage of it.

Rialla shook her head and then slanted a glance at Terran, ensuring that the slave master saw the adoring expression with which she regarded his son. In a soft voice she said, "No. It is in *him.*"

A touch of fear crept back into Winterseine's face. "You only slept with him. He's slept with many women." There was defensiveness in his voice.

Rialla remembered then that Winterseine had objected to his son's relations with an empath. She smiled slowly, to make him nervous. "They weren't like me."

"If you are so ensorcelled, why did you send him to sleep?"

Rialla noticed that he wasn't paying as much attention to what she was doing, and she inched herself closer to him. She shook her head. "He is not like you. He would have objected to your death." She amplified his fears with words instead of empathy. "He knows it is the best thing to do, but he is too honorable. It is unfortunate that you didn't eat that stew. Your death at my hands would have been much less painful than the one that Altis has planned if I failed my task."

For an instant Winterseine's fears caused him to freeze. In that moment Rialla pounced. With a move she had practiced countless times, she gripped his wrist and twisted, locking his elbow. Stepping to the side, she placed her free hand on his shoulder blade, pushing him forward and down. When she knocked his feet away, she held him pinned face down in the mud with her foot on his shoulder and his arm twisted painfully behind him.

Wearily, she turned her face into her shoulder to wipe away the sweat and rain so she could see.

*Tris,* she said, *you'll have to break the connection that binds us together. If you don't, you'll get caught up in the backlash. I can't protect both of us.*

*Rialla!* he said urgently, but she pushed him away.

Assuming Tris would heed her warning, Rialla turned to Winterseine. He'd quit struggling as soon as it became obvious that the only thing he could accomplish was dislocating his shoulder. Rialla's hand was on his bare wrist.

She began with his fears, the ones that were readily apparent. Winterseine would know what she was trying; his mind was disciplined, orderly. Only the touch of insanity—the rage fueled by the fear that his son was controlling him—gave her the means to defeat him.

She tried to ignore the stray thoughts that crept in; emotions were her weapons. She found his first fears: *his son emerging from his room, white and shaken, glowing with power* . . . *the first time Terran stood up to his father and Winterseine backed down, knowing without a doubt that in a power struggle the son was stronger* . . . and presented those feelings to Winterseine. Her own heartbeat picked up in time with his. These were the fears spawned by his memories; because she used his own emotions, Rialla couldn't step away from them as she had managed to when she'd killed the empathic feeder the night Karsten died.

Rialla took his reaction to the old thoughts and reinforced them, driving him deeper into his own nightmare. She reached further, for older hurts and uncertainties. She reached the boy he had been, vulnerable to taunts and shame, and presented those voices to him again.

Only when she heard him cry out did she fan the flames of his rage. Earlier his anger had been a focused flame, protecting him from the fear; with Rialla's intervention it became an overwhelming wave, drowning out coherent thought.

It wasn't enough.

She added her own terror, the memory of the battle with the swamp creature, the horror of becoming a slave again. She reached deeper and found the terror of being helpless at the mercy of ruthless captors, the sick fear of being beaten, knowing just how much it was going to hurt . . . *deep, soul-eating sorrow of living alone among strangers with no family bonds, and no chance of it changing . . .* Some part of Rialla knew that the last thought wasn't hers or Winterseine's, but she was too preoccupied with what she was doing to search out where it came from. Even as she worked to project her emotions, she felt Winterseine fighting for control.

If she didn't take Winterseine out now, he would kill her, but it wouldn't stop there. Tris would hunt Winterseine down, and she was afraid that the healer wouldn't stand a chance against Winterseine's magic.

Shuddering, she reached into herself for the small place she kept hidden for fear of her sanity. It was here that the emotions and last thoughts of her family dwelt with the death of Jarroh's child-slave and a hundred others. She drew the veil of shadow aside, pulling a thread of the tangled horror and thrusting it at him viciously. She struggled to keep aloof; knowing what was to come allowed her to deal with the pain and fear faster than Winterseine could.

She fed her horrors to him one by one, and slowly she could feel Winterseine weakening. She had to break him and get away from the campsite before Terran woke up.

Momentarily distracted by her fears, she reached for one last memory, searching deep.

This time she lost the small thread of calm that allowed her to maintain the distance from the pain, and became tangled in the morass of emotion. It wasn't until she fought her way through that she realized why it had been so hard to maintain her distance.

*Alone, even among his own kind. Set apart both by his refusal to let fear dominate his actions and by the kind of ability that had been dying from his race for a long time. Another man might not have been banished for saving the human child, but he was different, with no one to speak for him.*

Rialla was caught up in Tris's memory.

Frantically, she fought to free herself of it and the others that were beginning to seep in through the breach of her defenses; she needed to be detached or she would be swallowed in the tempest she'd created in Winterseine's mind. To do that she had to find Tris and get him out.

At that instant, when the last of her bastions against pain and fear were failing, Winterseine lost his battle. The growing miasma of terror and anguish that he'd been holding back hit Rialla with the force of a blow.

Almost without thought, she abandoned her efforts to rebuild her shields and tried to protect Tris long enough so that he could leave her. Apparently he knew what she was doing, because just before she lost herself in the storm of emotion, his words echoed to her.

*Sorry, love.* His mental voice was ragged with the same pain that was ripping through her. *I tried to tell you earlier; I* can't *leave you anymore.*

†    †    †

ON THE EDGE OF THE FOREST, TRIS FELL QUIETLY TO
rest on time-faded leaves from autumns past. The gelding,
too well trained to leave its rider, nudged gently at Tris's
cheek, then began to graze as the rains poured down and
lightning flashed in the sky.

RIALLA CRIED OUT AS SHE LOST HERSELF IN THE STORM
of emotion. Something hit her hard on the shoulder,
throwing her away from Winterseine's jerking body. She
hit the ground and collapsed into a fetal curl, whimpering
with the pain in her head. She was too close to uncon-
sciousness to appreciate the difference between a bad
headache and the much more harmful torment that had
been tearing her apart.

Lying on the ground, Rialla listened to Winterseine's
hoarse moans and started to shake as her body responded
to the stress of the battle. Some part of her recognized
what must have happened: Terran had knocked her away
from Winterseine in the moment before she would have
joined him in perpetual madness.

The emotional torment she'd just been through pre-
cluded any sort of emotion at all. She couldn't even manage to be worried about Tris. There would be time enough
for that, she supposed, if Terran allowed her to live long
enough to discover how Tris had fared.

She could hear Terran mutter over his father, but she
didn't think that even the power of the gods could restore
Winterseine's reason. It would have been kinder to kill
him, but she'd failed.

Winterseine's noises quieted, and Rialla heard Terran
get up and move to the supply packs. He came back and
picked her up with a grunt. If it had been anyone else
touching her, he would have fallen to the ground screaming; she hadn't even begun to restructure the shields to
keep her emotions from others—but she still couldn't
touch Terran with her mind.

Air hissed involuntarily between her teeth from the pain

in her head when Terran set her down on one of the blankets. He wrapped it securely around her and braced her in a sitting position. With one arm around her chest, he pressed a cup against her lips and half-forced several swallows of spicy alcohol down her throat.

She choked and gasped, but the alcohol did its job, and her tremors slowly subsided.

"Better?" asked Terran in a neutral tone, giving her the half-full cup.

Rialla nodded warily, and he backed away until she was supporting herself. He got to his feet and fed the dying camp fire until it was dancing merrily. She couldn't read anything on his face.

From nearby darkness came a choked-off cry, and she saw Terran momentarily tense, but he didn't look toward his father. Instead he turned to face Rialla fully. The fire was behind him, allowing night to shadow his face, while he could see her clearly. She didn't know if she showed anything beyond the distant numbness that protected her.

"The damage to him is permanent?" Again his voice was detached.

Rialla nodded. She paused and said in a voice that matched Terran's, "He hasn't been totally sane for some time. He would have reached this point eventually regardless."

Terran nodded. "I know." He studied his foot as if it had some sudden significance. "I owe you my life, Rialla. Thank you."

She hadn't expected gratitude. Rialla eyed him warily and inclined her head.

Terran sighed. "He would have killed me. Tamas warned me that my father had approached him. I took Father aside and explained what would happen to anyone who attempted to harm me—I thought it would be enough to stop him.

"It started when I caught him using Altis's name to gain willing slaves. Altis isn't opposed to the natural order, but he has no need of slaves, and dislikes having his name used frivolously for personal gain. When I explained this to Father, he reacted badly.

"I think he made his decision to kill me after I tried to save Karsten. I liked Karsten, and his death wasn't necessary for Altis's purposes—just Father's. I thought I could take care of the spirit-eater, the swamp beast Father intended to kill Karsten. He thought that such a creature would fan Darran's fear of mages and stop any alliance with Reth. But once it touched you, killing it would have killed you as well, so I gave you the chance to defeat it. Father was right: it didn't occur to me that he would kill Karsten himself."

Rialla sat mutely through his speech, nursing the remaining drink and gradually recovering from her efforts as her headache eased. When Terran stopped speaking, she thought of something that bothered her.

"How is it that you recovered from the sleeping draft that fast?" she asked.

Terran shrugged and said, "Poisons and drugs affect me only as much as Altis sees fit to allow. I was never really asleep, but I couldn't move. Altis wanted Father rendered harmless and he chose you to do it, because I would not."

Rialla jerked her head back at his last statement, her anger outweighing her fatigue. "No," she said firmly. "I chose to attack Winterseine on my own. Altis may rule your life, but he does not rule mine."

He smiled then, a tired and sad smile. "Doesn't he?"

Rialla set aside the blanket and stood, turning away from Terran.

"Where are you going?" There was no threat in Terran's voice, but Rialla stopped, turning back to face him.

"Where I belong," she replied.

"To Sianim?" he asked. "You could stay here, with me. Altis appreciates beautiful things, as do I. He will rule this world, you know; it will be a wondrous place. He will allow no violence, no wars or hatred; people will worship him and have no need for power or gold. They will hold to Altis's purposes and be at peace."

Rialla met his gaze steadily. "Your utopia cannot exist when humans are given the right to make their own decisions. People can always find something to disagree about."

Terran shook his head. "In Altis's kingdom, people will be granted the wisdom through Altis, to make correct choices."

"I understand now why Altis does not object to slavery," commented Rialla quietly, "as that is what he is proposing for everyone. A slave is still a slave, even if she is well treated. I will never willingly be a slave again, Terran. I would die first." There was peace in that knowledge, a peace she hadn't known before.

"So be it." Terran nodded, stirring the fire with a convenient stick.

Rialla waited. Terran watched her a moment and then smiled again. "Go back to Sianim, Rialla. You have served Altis's purposes this night."

Rialla wasted no time escaping the clearing where Terran sat with his father. As soon as she could no longer see the light of the camp fire, she stopped and searched with her weary empathic talent for any hint of Tris's presence.

*Rialla?*

She could tell that he was exhausted and in pain, but she was so happy to find him alive she didn't care.

*I'm coming,* she told him. *Wait there.*

*No,* he replied shortly. *I'm fine, and I can come to you faster than you can travel here.*

Rialla found a comfortable place to sit, under the shelter of a large tree where the rain didn't fall as hard. She waited.

IT TOOK TRIS LESS THAN A THIRD OF THE TIME IT WOULD have taken a human to find Rialla where she slept on the wet ground.

She stirred briefly when he wrapped the saddle blanket around her, but she didn't really open her eyes until he started cooking over the fire—it smelled good.

"I had to leave the horse when I came," he said, stirring the small pot suspended over the fire, "but I brought the saddlebags with me." Without pausing in his speech, or looking away from his cooking, he continued, "I believe I owe you an explanation."

Rialla sat up and rubbed her eyes. Though the rain had stopped, it was still dark; she hadn't slept long. She felt surprisingly good for the brief rest—but that was one of the benefits of traveling with a healer.

"I believe you do."

He set the long-handled spoon on a rock and left his stew. He crouched on his heels in front of her. He called a magelight to him, giving Rialla a clear view of his face. "Among the sylvan, the bonding I set between us is used to mate pairs for life," he said baldly.

She stared at him. "You mean we're married, and you didn't tell me?"

She surprised a laugh out of him. "I suppose you could look upon it so, yes."

"Why did you do it?" she asked.

"Before I met you, the woman who called me to Tallonwood gave me a seeing. Such things are unclear by their nature, but from what she said I knew that I would meet the one with whom I could bond."

"You mean that you could not bond with anyone you pleased?" Rialla asked.

"No. I have never met anyone with whom a bonding would work. There are so few sylvan now, fewer still ever find a bond mate."

Rialla thought about what he had said. "You formed the bond between us because a seer told you it could work?"

"No," he said. "I did it because I finally found someone with whom I could belong." He stood then, going back to the food, but he didn't pick up the spoon.

Instead he bowed his head and said softly, "I'm sorry."

Deep in her own thoughts, Rialla only dimly heard him continue. "I thought at first that I could break the link, if you didn't want it. It isn't supposed to strengthen as fast as it did. In the old days, when my people were many, the initial ceremony lasted for three months. If the couple were unwilling to continue so bound, the link was removed. Trenna told me we could bond. She didn't say that you'd be willing."

Rialla remembered the things she'd learned about him last night, remembered the soul-eating loneliness and found its echo in herself. If she'd known of such a bond, she would have moved mountains to achieve it. When she considered it, the bond didn't frighten her—not at all. She hugged her reply to herself for a moment, then said softly, "I'm not."

"I know," said Tris, misunderstanding. "But there's nothing that I can do about it. It's been too late since Winterseine put you on the water wheel."

"No," said Rialla, lifting her face so he could see her smile. "I meant that I'm not sorry, not that I'm not willing."

Tris whirled to face her, and gave her the autocratically displeased look that she'd seen him turn on Winterseine. Rialla bit her lip, knowing that he'd be offended if she laughed. Half her euphoria was caused by fatigue, so she fought to keep properly sedate.

"You let me grovel," Tris growled.

Rialla buried her face in her knees and lost the battle, giggling helplessly.

Tris's magelight faded into darkness.

"THEFT," PURRED TRIS, SOMETIME LATER.

"Thief," acknowledged Rialla with sleepy laughter.

# FINIS

Lord Jarroh looked up in some irritation when a light knock sounded on his study door. He had left clear instructions that he did not want to be disturbed. Glancing out the window, he saw that night had fallen while he was working on his books.

With a sigh, he set his accounting aside and walked around his desk to open the door.

"Yes?"

The hallway was dark, so he couldn't clearly see the person who had disrupted his work.

"Your pardon, honored sir. I have information for you, of a private nature."

Lord Jarroh received many such private messages—one of the reasons that he always wore a fine mail shirt under his clothes. He stepped away from the entrance and waved the messenger in, shutting the door softly behind him.

"Your business?"

"Lord Karsten's murder," said Rialla, lowering the hood of her cloak so he could see her face clearly. "I told you to consider the logic of designating Lord Laeth as Karsten's killer. Have you?"

Lord Jarroh's hand went instinctively to his knife, closing on the haft, but his face lost none of its calm aloofness. "Yes. Disregarding what I saw when Karsten died, Lord Winterseine would be the most logical candidate. I have known both him and Lord Laeth almost as long as I knew Karsten; if I had not seen Laeth stab Karsten myself, I would never have believed it. Unfortunately, Lord Winterseine has recently been struck with an illness that makes it impossible to question him."

Rialla slipped the messenger bag off her shoulder and brought out a thick book, Laeth's dagger and two sheets of parchment. "I have, sir, for your perusal, several items of interest.

"The first is Lord Winterseine's *grimoire*. It has been rendered harmless by the ae'Magi, Lord Kisrah. You will notice Lord Kisrah removed several pages and destroyed the lock.

"The second is the dagger used to kill Lord Karsten. We discovered it in a small keep where Lord Winterseine trains slaves.

"The third item is a letter from Lord Kisrah detailing his reading of the dagger. Furthermore, he is willing to swear that Lord Winterseine is a mage powerful enough to have served on the wizard's council. Certainly he could have created an illusion so you would believe it was Laeth's hands on the dagger."

Lord Jarroh shook his head. "That does not matter. Do you think that a Darranian court will take the word of the Archmage on a matter of state?"

"No," replied Rialla. "We had hoped, though, that you would be willing to consider the evidence."

"To what purpose?"

"My lord," said Rialla, "we would like you to insure that Winterseine and his son Terran do not inherit Lord Karsten's estates. If you are not convinced of Laeth's innocence, then let the estates go to the crown.

"The fourth item that I brought for your consideration, my lord, is a letter from Ren, Spymaster of Sianim. He feels it should answer any questions that you might have about Sianim's interest in this matter."

Rialla took a step forward into the light. "Lord Jarroh, Lord Karsten was killed because he believed in an end to the feuding that has cost both Darran and Reth so much. He foresaw a day when peace would rule. Winterseine was not alone in planning Karsten's death; do not allow the killers to triumph. Giving them the power and prestige of Karsten's estates will destroy his dream."

Lord Jarroh reached out to tilt her face until the light of a nearby oil lamp illuminated her clearly.

"You are Laeth's slave."

She shook her head and took a step back. "No, I am Laeth's friend."

He dropped his hand and pursed his lips in thought. Finally, he met Rialla's steady gaze. "Tell Laeth I will do my best to clear his name. For his brother's sake, I will see to it that the marriage between our princess and King Myr of Reth takes place as planned." He paused, looking at Rialla's flawless face, then continued softly, "Even if it means an end to slavery."

# THE ULTIMATE IN FANTASY!

From magical tales of distant worlds to stories of those with abilities beyond the ordinary, Ace and Roc have everything you need to stretch your imagination to its limits.

**Marion Zimmer Bradley/Diana L. Paxson**

**Guy Gavriel Kay**

**Dennis L. McKiernan**

**Patricia A. McKillip**

**Robin McKinley**

**Sharon Shinn**

**Katherine Kurtz**

**Barb and J. C. Hendee**

**Elizabeth Bear**

**T. A. Barron**

**Brian Jacques**

**Robert Asprin**

penguin.com

M12G1107